Love Under Fire

Randall Parrish

Contents

LOVE UNDER FIRE

BY

Randall Parrish

CHAPTER I
BETWEEN THE LINES

I had drifted slowly across the river, clinging with one arm thrown over a log, expecting each moment the musket of some startled picket would spit red through the dark, and scarcely daring to guide my unwieldy support by the slightest movement of hand in the water. The splash of motion might mean death in an instant, for keen eyes, sharpened by long night vigils, were on the stream, and those who had ventured the deed before me had failed utterly. Yet the southern bank remained silent, so black I could scarcely discern its vaguest outlines, while, by good fortune, the sweep of the current served me almost as well as a pair of oars. Thus, trusting to luck, and without exerting a muscle, I finally came to a full stop on a narrow spit of sand, so far out in the stream I could scarcely touch bottom, until the sweep of the current drifted my log inward, and thus left me flat on the wet sand facing the bank, the wood-covered crest, as revealed dimly against the slightly lighter sky, appearing almost to overhang the water.

This shadow served me well, yet did not invite to recklessness. There were surely pickets posted along here, because the gleam of camp-fires had been plainly visible during the early evening from the bluffs opposite, but there was nothing observable from where I lay, my head cautiously uplifted, peering across the log. It was several minutes before I even ventured to creep up the sand-spit into the denser blackness of the over-hanging bank, but, once there safely, I discovered the drift had landed me at the mouth of a narrow gully, apparently a mere crevice in the rocky shore-line. It was the occasional downpour of water after rain which had caused the accumulation of debris on which my log had grounded. At times the dry gulch would hold a roaring torrent, although now it was no more than a gash in the bank.

I was not altogether certain within half a mile of where I was, but this made small difference, so far as my present purpose was concerned. The lines of the enemy were extended from the upper ford east as far as Sailor Springs, and I was certainly well within those limits, probably somewhat to the right of the centre. However, that was a minor detail, as it made little difference where I succeeded in penetrating the cordon of pickets, so long as I returned with the information sought. If I had, through mere chance, discovered a weak spot, then God was good.

My heart beat rapidly as I stared blindly up into the black recess of that narrow defile, listening intently for the slightest unusual sound which would indicate the near presence of anything human. It was caution, not fear, however, which caused me to breathe quickly--my sole, overpowering dread being that I might have to return, and face Sheridan with a report of failure. I preferred anything rather than that. I thought of his stern eyes as he looked me over in the late sunlight of the evening before; the sharp rasp in his voice, as he said, "Geer, this is no boy's work," and the quiet, confident reply of my captain, "Galesworth will do it for you, General, if any one can." The memory of that scene seemed to stiffen my nerves; I had to make good here in the dark, alone, and so, on hands and knees, I began creeping slowly up underneath the tangle of bushes. The path was steep and stony, so densely overhung with branches as to appear like a tunnel. There were loose stones which I had to guard against dislodging, and the drier leaves rustled as I pressed them, aside. This endeavor to avoid noise made progress slow.

I must have been fully ten minutes, thus endeavoring to break through, seeing and hearing nothing alarming, yet constantly feeling an odd premonition of danger, when I finally attained the top of the bank, perhaps twenty feet back from the river, and looked out through a slight fringe of bushes. The first thing noticeable was the dull red glow of a fire, nearly extinguished, some few yards in advance. The little gleam of light thrown out as the wind stirred the smouldering embers served to reveal the dirty flap of a tent set up at the edge of a grove of saplings, and a horse, standing with lowered head, sharply outlined against the canvas. I could even perceive the deep-seated cavalry saddle, and catch the shine of accoutrements. All these details came to me in a sudden flash of observation, for, almost simultaneously with my rising above the edge of the bank, my ears distinguished voices conversing, and so closely at hand as to almost unnerve me. I gripped a root between my fingers to keep from falling, and held on motionless, striving to locate the speakers. They were to my left, scarcely four yards distant, yet so dimly revealed against the background of leaves I could tell nothing of their rank--merely that one was short, and heavily built, while the other, a much taller, and seemingly more nervous man, was wrapped in a long cavalry cape. It was his voice speaking, a rather peculiar voice, as though he possessed some slight impediment of speech.

"Do not look at it in that way, General," he protested earnestly. "I am not opposing your plan, but merely urging the extreme peril of the undertaking--"

"Human life cannot be considered at such a time, Hardy," broke in the other warmly. "The cause for which we battle, the duty confronting us, outweighs all else. A life may be sacrificed, but that single life may save thousands."

"True; very true. I am sufficiently a soldier to realize that. Yet what you propose seems an impossibility. Two aides have endeavored this service already, and failed, their lives forfeited. Others stand ready to go the moment the word is spoken, but what possibility is there of success, that any volunteer could get through alive?"

"Practically none," admitted the other, his deep voice more grave. "There is only one in whom I feel the slightest hope, Hardy; that is why I have sent for you. I naturally hesitate to say so, but I believe the moment has now come which demands this sacrifice. You recall the offer of service made us last night, Major?"

The man addressed took a single step backward, one hand flung up, as though warding off a blow.

"You--" he stammered, "can you mean Billie?"

"Yes; the South can have no more urgent need than now. These despatches must reach Beauregard, and I must have the report from Carroll. If the latter is not already in Beauregard's possession, then it must be sought even in the enemy's camp. Every hour of delay adds to our danger. If Carroll is dead I must know it; if he has gained the information he was sent after, then I must have it. I can stand this waiting no longer--there is too much at stake. As you say two men have already fallen endeavoring to pierce the lines, and I doubt if there is a soldier in my command who could succeed. Billie might have a chance, and I know no one else who would--do you? I sent for you to gain your consent, and I ask it, Major, in the name of the South."

The taller man remained silent, his hands clasped, and head sunk on his breast.

Finally he glanced up into the face of the other, with shoulders thrown back.

"No Hardy ever yet failed in duty," he said sternly, "nor will one now. Where are the papers?"

"In my tent, but the bearer will be safer not to come here for them. Even my orderly may be a spy. An aide shall deliver them at Three Corners in an hour--will that be too early?"

"No; which aide? There should be no mistake."

"There will be none. I will send Lieutenant West, and he shall act as escort as far as the outer pickets; beyond that--"

"Wit and good luck, of course. What is the word?"

"'Cumberland'; now listen, and repeat exactly what I say to Billie." His voice fell into lower, more confidential tones, and, listen as I would, I could catch only now and then a word, or detached sentence. "The upper road"; "yes, the wide detour"; "coming in by the rear will be safer"; "that isn't a bad story"; "he's a tartar to lie too"; "just the thing, Major, just the thing"; then, "But that's enough for the outlines; details must take care of themselves. Let's waste no more time; there are only four more hours of darkness."

The two men separated hurriedly with a warm hand-clasp, the stocky general entering the tent, and brusquely addressing some one within, while the major swung into the saddle of the waiting horse, and driving in the spurs rode swiftly away, instantly disappearing.

There was no doubt as to my own duty. By the merest accident I had already become possessed of most important information. What it was all about was still only guess-work, yet it was evidently enough a most serious matter. I could better serve the cause of the Union by intercepting these despatches, and running down this spy, than by carrying out Sheridan's original instructions. And it seemed to me I could do it; that I already knew a way in which this might be accomplished. Our army had held all this ground only a few months before, and I recalled clearly to mind the exact spot where the aide was to meet the despatch-bearer. The "Three Corners"; surely that must be where the roads met at the creek ford, with the log meeting house perched on the hill above. It would be to the west of where I was, and not more than two miles distant.

CHAPTER II
AFTER THE DESPATCH-BEARER

I was cool-headed, and accustomed to this species of adventure, or I should never have been there. Yet, I confess my nerves tingled as I crept cautiously forward through the fringe of bushes, seeking the exact spot where the major had disappeared down what must have been some species of road. There were sentinels posted about the tent; I saw the silhouette of one, and heard several voices conversing gruffly as I slunk past, yet could not definitely locate these last in the gloom. There was a little row of tents--three or four--back of the larger one occupied by the general; but these were unlighted and silent. I crept past them unobserved, emerging into a more open space, where my groping hands encountered wheel-tracks, and the beaten earth of a road.

This apparently ran nearly east and west, as I recalled direction, and I turned to the right, bending low in the shadows, and advancing at a crouching run. Seemingly there was nothing to obstruct progress. The noise of stomping and restless horses reached me from the left, evidence of a nearby cavalry or artillery camp; yet I saw no one, perceived no light even, until after advancing at least a quarter of a mile. Then a sudden slight turn in the road brought me upon a rude shack, showing a blacksmith's fire glowing within, and the smith himself pounding busily away at an anvil. The gleam of the forge shot out redly across the road. As I crept closer I could perceive the figures of others lounging about inside--soldiers, no doubt, although I could not be certain. There was a ragged Confederate cavalry jacket hanging over a rain-barrel just outside the window, and, getting hold of it, I slipped it on over my woollen shirt. The night air was chill, my clothes still damp from the river, and besides it might help later on. As I did this a rider came flying up the road, bending low over his pommel. He went past at a slashing gallop, his face showing an instant in the red glare of the flame. That, no doubt, would be the aide with the despatches, yet, in spite of his haste, he would have to wait to the end of the hour for Billie. One or two of the men came lazily to the front of the shop to watch him go by, and I crouched down behind the rain-barrel until they went back again. Then I skirted the bar of flame, and ran on down the road, a bit recklessly, fearing the horseman might get too far ahead.

It was intensely dark, one of those dense nights when the blackness appears to press down upon one, and there were noises on either side to make me aware that I was in the midst of a great encampment. Fires shone dimly through the trees, and I could hear voices and hammering. I supposed the road I was travelling ran directly through the main camp, with troops on either side, and, for that reason, was not patrolled by pickets. Anyhow I passed without challenge, although I met a few fellows slinking along about as I was--soldiers out of bounds most likely, as afraid of me as I was of them. At least whenever I bumped into one, he got out of the way fast enough. And I never paused to explain--all I wanted to do was to arrive at those cross-roads in advance of Billie.

However I failed in this ambition, but merely because the road I was following did not keep on directly west, but drifted off toward the river. I only became aware of this change in direction when we intersected a cross-road, and then I ran squarely up against a picket-post, the men having a fire burning to keep them warm. The light of the flames revealed everything within a radius of a hundred feet, and I could distinguish a dozen infantrymen sitting and lying about, while a couple of others marched back and forth across the road. I wanted to get farther south, but had only wriggled through the bushes a few yards in that direction before sinking to my knees in mud and water, and being compelled to crawl back. There was nothing left except to circle the fire in the opposite direction, and come out on the road below. I must have used up a good quarter of an hour getting through. Twice I made missteps, and some racket, but there was no challenge. I emerged at the opening of a small ravine, where I could lie down flat behind a low rock, and look back up the road, which ran down hill. I felt reasonably certain Billie would have to come this way if he intended to cross the river at Carter's Ford, and I knew of no other place he could cross this side the big bridge. The aide would be riding with him, of course, and that would make me certain of my man when he came, although how I was ever going to manage was more than I had as yet figured out.

I must have been there some twenty minutes, maybe more, burrowing down into the mud under the lee of the stone, staring straight up the hill at the fire. The post was relieved while I lay there, the fellows going off duty tramping past so close I could have touched them. I could still hear the tread of their feet when one of the new guard yelled out "Halt!" and I saw two or three men spring up from around the fire, while the corporal in command ran out into the middle of the road. Some sort of a rig was coming down the hill, with a cavalry officer--judging from his cape--riding along close beside it. I was not able to see very plainly the way the light fell, but the contrivance looked to me like one of those old-fashioned, two-wheeled carryalls, with a low top over it, and drawn by a horse not much bigger than a pony. The officer dug in his spurs and got ahead, leaning over to whisper to the corporal, who stepped back saluting. The carryall never stopped at all, the pony trotting along unconcernedly, and it was so dark beneath the top I could not see sign of anybody. It was a queer-looking outfit, but I had no doubt this would be Billie, and the despatches.

The officer was still riding ahead when they passed me, his cape blown up over his hat, and his head bent forward to make out the road, as though his eyes still remained blinded by the firelight. Without definite plan, yet firmly determined not to be left behind, I squirmed across the road, ran up close to the carryall, and caught hold at the rear. The soldiers back in the glare saw nothing, while the mingled noise of hoofs and wheels left me unheard. I discovered my fingers grasping some narrow wooden slats, held up firmly against the back of the vehicle by a chain at each end. For a moment, running and hanging on as I was in total darkness, I was unable to figure out what sort of an arrangement this could possibly be. Then I managed to feel it out with one hand--it was simply a shelf, capable of being lowered the length of the supporting chains, on which packages, or baggage, might be carried, while above was a roll of canvas, to be used as protection from rain. Here was opportunity, and I went at it with eagerness. It proved a hard job, running over that rough road in the dark, while the pony trotted tirelessly, but I got those chains unfastened, one at a time, and then the shelf settled naturally down into position. It was narrow, and I felt some question as to the strength of the supports, but risking all this, managed to work my way up until I half lay, half crouched, along the slats, holding on grimly as the two wheels bounced briskly from side to side, threatening to send me sprawling out into the road. By this time the officer had reined back his horse, but was still out of sight, and I succeeded in unbuckling the straps, and lowering the strip of canvas over me, stuffing the edges beneath my body so as to keep them from flapping. I was tired and sore, but now reasonably safe, with my eyes at an opening through which I could gaze out. I began to feel happy, too, thinking of the surprise which was about to come to Billie.

We clattered on down a long slope, apparently making no effort to avoid noise. It seemed we must be drawing near the river, yet the night was so dark, and our passage so rapid, I could make out no familiar landmarks through my peep-hole. Indeed I had about all I could do to hold on. We were halted twice, but a word from the officer passed us along safely. One picket-post had a fire glowing in close against the rocks, and the sergeant stood within a foot of me. I caught the word "Cumberland," but whatever else of explanation may have been uttered failed to reach my ears, muffled as they were beneath the canvas. A few hundred yards beyond this point, at the end of a deep cut, the officer drew up his horse sharply, leaned over the wheel, and shook hands with the person inside.

"I have attained my limit," he said. "That was our last picket-post back yonder, and my orders were strict. You know the road, of course."

"Perfectly, Lieutenant," responded a low voice, muffled under the hood. "I have travelled it often before. I thank you so much, and think it will all come out right this time."

"I have no doubt of that," he replied, with a little laugh. "Hope I may renew the acquaintance under more pleasant circumstances. Meanwhile, good luck and good-bye."

He sat erect upon his horse, watching as we clattered past, appearing scarcely more than a dim shadow, yet I thought he held his hat in his hand. Billie laid on the gad, however, as if to make up for lost time, and the pony trotted off at such a burst of speed as to keep me busy clinging to my perch. It was an exceedingly rough road, rutty and stony, up hill and down, while the pony condescended to walk on the steepest grades only, and occasionally took the declines at a gallop, the carryall bounding from side to side as though mad. Apparently no fear of possible disaster disturbed Billie, however, for I could hear every few moments the slash of a whip on the animal's flank. I knew that, by this time, we must certainly be well between the lines, but, for the life of me, could not determine where. I thought I knew the surrounding country as I had scouted over it for months, tracing roads and bridle-paths, yet I was puzzled now. If this road continued to run north and south, as it had back yonder, then we should have forded the river long before this, yet we had splashed through no water, nor did I recall our making any turn.

One fact alone seemed certain: as I knew neither where we were, nor whither bound, and as we were already assuredly beyond the last Confederate outpost, it behooved me to act as quickly as possible. Billie was headed somewhere, and the sooner I stopped him the better--besides, my position was neither comfortable nor safe. I rolled off from the edge of the canvas, and, gripping the chains tightly, managed to sit up, in spite of the vicious pitching of the vehicle. Billie's evident eagerness to arrive at his unknown destination only added to my own recklessness, and I hung on desperately, swearing a little, I fear, under my breath.

CHAPTER III
A FRIEND RATHER THAN AN ENEMY

There was only one way in which I could hope to get in--through the back. That was an exceedingly ticklish job, yet I had tackled many a ticklish job before during the two years of my scouting service, and the knowledge of danger was merely the prick of a spur. The rusty buckles holding the flap in place resisted the grip of my fingers, and, opening a knife with my teeth, I cut the leather, severing enough of the straps so the entire flap could be thrown back, yet holding it down closely to its place until I was ready for action. Through a narrow opening I could perceive a dim outline of the driver. He was at the right of the seat, leaning forward, so as to peer out from under the hood, loosened reins in one hand, a whip in the other. The darkness of the night enabled me to perceive little except a vague sense of shape, a head crowned by a soft hat, and an apparently slender figure.

Whatever slight noise I made was lost in the rattle of the wheels, while the driver, utterly thoughtless as to any danger menacing him from behind, concentrated his entire attention upon the road, and his efforts to accelerate the speed of the pony. The present opportunity was as good as I could ever hope for. I grasped the back of the seat with one hand, a revolver in the other, pressed back the flap with my shoulder, and inserted my head within. Not until my voice sounded at his very ear did the fellow realize my presence.

"Pull up!" I said sternly. "Not a movement now; this is a gun at your ear."

There was a sharp catch of the breath, a half turning of the head in the surprise of the shock, but his hands held to reins and whip. Tossed about as I was the fellow's coolness angered me.

"Pull up," I said; "do you think I'm playing with you?"

He drew in on the reins, letting the whip drop between his feet, and the pony slowed down to a walk, and finally stopped. I could catch merely a glimpse of the man's profile beneath the broad brim of the hat, but his coolness and silence aroused my suspicions.

"No tricks now," I threatened. "If you value your life do exactly as I say."

"Who are you?" It was a rich contralto voice, that of a boy rather than a man, the slight blur of the South distinguishable even in those few words.

"Only a Yankee, son," I replied, satisfied I held the upper hand, and clambering in over the back of the seat. He shrank back from contact with me farther into the corner, but there was nothing in the slight movement to cause alarm. I laughed softly.

"Don't exactly admire my color of uniform, do you?" I asked easily. "Well, I can't help that, and you'll not find me such a bad fellow if you act right. Where were you going in such a hurry?"

There was no answer. I could hear his rapid breathing, and catch a glimpse of a beardless cheek.

"Don't you intend to tell me?"

Still silence, the shapeless figure motionless.

"Come, Billie," I urged, "what is the use of keeping up this game?"

He straightened up in surprise, startled into speech.

"You--you call me what? Why do you say 'Billie'?"

"Because I'm on. I haven't been hanging to the back of this outfit for the last eight miles just for fun, or exercise either. I'm after those despatches you're taking to Beauregard."

"Oh!"

"That's the state of affairs, and the sooner you hand over those particular papers, Billie, the quicker this revolver play ends. Where are they?"

"I haven't any," the slightly tremulous note had gone out of the voice. It was firm with purpose now, even a bit sarcastic. "You've merely got on the wrong trail, Yank. I reckon you mistook me for Billie Hardy."

"I reckon I did," I returned, mocking him, "and I'm still satisfied I've got the right party. You don't get out that easy, son; come now, produce."

"Suppose I don't."

"Then there won't be much argument," I returned sharply, beginning to lose patience. "I'll simply take them, if I have to shoot you first. Come now, which shall it be?"

He straightened up, convinced apparently of my intentions.

"Neither, Mr. Yankee," indignantly. "I told you once you were mistaken. Now I'll prove it--see here!" The soft hat was whipped off the head, and the slender figure leaned forward to where the slight gleam of the stars rendered the face visible. "Do you make war on women?"

I was too astounded for reply; dumfounded, dazed by this evidence of my stupidity. This was a woman beyond all doubt--her hair, released by the sudden removal of the hat, swept in a dark wave over her shoulders, and she flung it back with a movement of the hand. The gleam of the stars gave me the contour of her face, and the sparkle of her eyes. A woman, young, pretty--and actually laughing at me, her white teeth clearly visible. Whatever of conceit or audacity may be part of my nature, deserted me in a flash, and I could only stare in helpless amazement.

"My God! I believe you are!" I ejaculated at last, the words bursting forth unconsciously. "How could I have made--who are you anyhow?"

The restrained laughter rippled forth, as though the expression of my face appealed to her sense of humor. Evidently the lady was no longer afraid of me, nor greatly distressed over the situation.

"Isn't it too funny," she exclaimed cheerfully, "and won't Billie laugh about this when I tell him!"

"Maybe he will," I acknowledged rather regretfully, "but it doesn't make me laugh." Then a vague suspicion gripped me. "Why did you think I took you for Billie?"

"Why, that was what you called me, wasn't it? The officer who escorted me past the pickets said Billie Hardy was going to try to run the lines to-night. So it was easy enough to guess who you were after, Mr. Yankee. It was lucky for Billie you got me instead--or for you," she added doubtfully.

"Oh, I guess I would have pulled through."

"Maybe," the tone decidedly provoking, "but I reckon you don't know Billie."

She began to gather up her hair, coiling the strands about her head carelessly, and I watched the simple operation, all the life gone out of me, unable to decide what to do. It was useless to go back; almost equally useless to go forward. I had no information to take into our lines of any value, and had failed utterly in my efforts to intercept the important despatches for Beauregard. The knowledge of my mistake stung me bitterly, yet I could blame no one for the failure except myself. The apparent carelessness of the girl puzzled me--why should she be so completely at her ease in this adventure? Only at the first had she exhibited the slightest excitement. This seemed hardly natural--alone, thus suddenly attacked by a stranger, an enemy, and openly threatened.

"You seem perfectly contented," I said. "Are you not frightened?"

"Frightened!" and she paused in her hair-dressing to bend slightly forward so as to look into my shadowed face. "Why, of course not; why should I be?"

"But I am a stranger to you--a Yank. You are on the other side, are you not?"

"Oh, of course," her lips revealing again the white teeth. "But I don't think all Yankees are demons. I don't believe you are. I like your voice. You see, I was educated in the North, and so am not prejudiced. Please won't you take off your hat, just for a minute?"

I did so, almost mechanically, not even realizing why she asked, until she bent forward, her eyes on my face.

"No, I am not frightened with you. I was just a little, at first, of course, but not now. You look as though you would fight too, but not with a woman." She stopped with an odd little shrug of the shoulders. "What do you expect me to do--sit here all night?"

I looked about into the darkness, suddenly recalled to the absurdity of our situation by this question. The stars were glittering overhead, yielding a dim light, yet nothing around us afforded any guess as to where we were. The pony stood with drooping head, his flanks still heaving from his late run. To the right the ground appeared open and level, a cultivated field, while upon the other side was a sharp rise of land covered with brush. It was a lonely, silent spot, and my eyes turned back inquiringly to my companion.

"Why, no," I replied rather foolishly. "But I confess I am all at sea just now; where are we?"

It seemed very easy for her to laugh, and evidently my confession was amusing.

"You must pardon me," she excused herself, "but I thought you were a scout."

"I am," vexed at her propensity to poke fun. "I have been detailed for that service for more than two years. Moreover, I was a good enough scout to pass within the lines of your army to-night, and to travel the whole length of your camp--"

"And then get lost an hour later," she interrupted archly. "Tell me, do you know the points of the compass?"

"Certainly; that is north, and this road runs west, but I have no recollection of it. What puzzled me was our failure to cross the river."

"Oh," with a quick glance toward me. "That is easily explained; we turned the corner of the bluff instead. This is the old road to Jonesboro, and has been used very little since the new road was opened. I chose it because I thought I would be less likely to meet with any chance travellers."

I began to comprehend more clearly where we were. The extreme right of the position held by our army would be, at least, ten miles east, and the Confederate left scarcely nearer. Beauregard was off in here somewhere,--at Bird's Ferry according to our camp reports the evening previous. This knowledge prompted me to ask,

"Which way is the river?"

"To the right about three miles."

"And Bird's Ferry?"

I could not be certain she smiled, yet I thought so.

"Yonder," pointing. "The river curves to the south, and this road comes down to it at Jonesboro; there is a bridge there. The ferry is fifteen miles farther up."

The apparent innocence of her answer completely disarmed me. Indeed these facts were exactly as I remembered them now that I had our present position in mind. The peculiar winding course of the river would leave me nearer our lines at Jonesboro than where we then were. Indeed foraging parties were covering much of the territory between, and it was the nearest point where I could cross the stream otherwise than by swimming.

"Are you going to Jonesboro?" I asked.

She nodded silently.

"Then may I ride that far with you?" I asked, rather doubtful of what she would say to such a request. "Of course you will be aiding the enemy, for I expect to discover some of our troops in that neighborhood."

"How can I help myself?" banteringly. "You are a man, and armed. Practically I am your prisoner."

"Oh, I don't want you to feel that way toward me. I have acted as a gentleman, have I not, ever since I understood?"

"You certainly have, and I am not ungrateful. Then you do not order me to take you; you merely ask if I will?"

"That is all."

"And that sounds so much better, I think. I don't mind your being a Yankee if you continue to act that way. Shall I drive?"

"If you will; you know the road, and the tricks of the pony."

She laughed again, gathering up the reins, and reaching down after the whip. At the first movement the little animal broke into a brisk trot as though he understood his driver.

CHAPTER IV
THE COMING OF DAWN

The road was rough, apparently little travelled, and our lively passage over it not greatly conducive to conversation. Besides I hardly knew what to say. The consciousness of total failure in all my plans, and the knowledge that I would be received at headquarters in anything but honor, weighed heavily upon me, yet this depression did not seal my lips half as much as the personality of the young woman at my side. Pleasant and free as her manner had been, yet I was clearly made to realize there was a distinct limit to any familiarity. I could not define the feeling, but it had taken possession of me, and I knew the slightest overstepping of the boundaries would result in trouble. We were neither enemies nor friends; merely acquaintances under a temporary flag of truce. No doubt, trusting me as an honorable soldier, even though wearing an enemy's uniform, she was almost glad to have my protection along this lonely road, but, when the time came to part, she would be equally relieved to have me go. I was nothing to her; if ever remembered again it would be merely to laugh over my discomfiture in mistaking her for another. It hurt my pride to think this, to thus realize her complete indifference. She was a young woman, and I a young man, and nothing in my nature made surrender easy. I desired, at least, to leave behind me some different impression of my own personality. I was not a fool, nor a failure, and I could not bear to have her conceive me as a mere blundering block-head, a subject for subsequent laughter. The silence in which she drove stirred me to revolt. Apparently she felt no overwhelming curiosity as to whom I was, no special desire to exchange further speech. The flapping of the loosened curtain was annoying, and I leaned over and fastened it down securely into place. She merely glanced aside to observe what I was doing, without even opening her lips.

"This is a miserably gloomy road," I ventured desperately. "I wonder you dared to travel it alone at night."

"Its very loneliness makes it safe," was the response, rather indifferently uttered. "Meeting others was the very thing I was most anxious to avoid."

"Indeed! You are tantalizing; you cannot expect me to be devoid of curiosity."

"Of course not," turning her face toward me, "neither can you expect me to gratify it."

"You mean you could not trust me?"

"Rather that you would not believe me, if I did. The reason for this trip is so simple and commonplace that if I were to confess its purpose to you, you would suppose I were attempting deceit. Oh, yes, you would, so I might just as well remain still. Besides it can make no difference anyway. When we reach Jonesboro this morning you will go back to your army, and I shall meet friends. There is scarcely one chance in a thousand we shall ever see each other again. We are the merest strangers--enemies, indeed, for I am a Rebel clear through. We don't even know each others' names."

"Do you care to know mine?"

She hesitated, and I thought her eyes dropped.

"I--I hardly know," doubtfully. "Yet you have been very kind, and, perhaps, sometime I might serve you. Yes, you may tell me."

"Robert Galesworth."

"Of what rank?"

"Lieutenant, Ninth Illinois Cavalry, but detailed for special service."

"Thank you. I--I am rather glad you told me."

"And you," I insisted, determined this confidence should be mutual. "May I not, in return, be told your name?"

"I am Willifred Gray," she said quietly. "That is all--just Willifred Gray."

There was something about the manner in which she said this which held me silent. I should have liked to ask more, a second question trembling on my lips, but the words would not come. It was altogether new to me, this fear of offending a woman, so new it almost angered, and yet something about her positively held me as though in bonds. To this day I do not know the secret of it, but I sat there silently staring out into the night.

I could see a little now, becoming aware that dawn was approaching, the sky shading to a dull gray in the east, and casting a weird light over the landscape. It was a gloomy scene of desolation, the road a mere ribbon, overgrown with grass and weeds, a soggy marsh on one side, and a line of sand-hills on the other, sparsely covered by some stunted growth. Far away, across the level, my eyes caught a glimmer of water, locating the river, but in no direction was there any sign of a house, or curl of smoke. The unproductive land--barren and swampy--sufficiently accounted for lack of inhabitants, and told why it had been avoided by the foragers of both armies. Seeking safety the girl had chosen her course wisely--here was desolation so complete as to mock even at the ravages of war. The gray in the east changed to pink, delicately tinting the whole upper sky, objects taking clearer form, a light breeze rustling the long grass. Tirelessly the pony trotted, his head down, the lines lying loose. I turned to gaze at my companion, and our eyes met. Hers were either gray or blue; I could not be certain which, so quickly were they lowered, and so shadowed by long lashes. And they were merry eyes, smiling, and deep with secrets no man could hope to solve. Perhaps she deemed it only fair that I should look at her as she had been observing me; perhaps it was but the coquetry of the "eternal feminine" conscious of her own attraction, but she sat there silent, the lashes shading her eyes, the clear light of the dawn upon her face. I cannot describe what I saw, only it was a young face, the skin clear and glowing with health, the nose beautifully moulded, the throat white and round, the red lips arched like a bow, and a broad forehead shadowed by dark hair. She had a trooper's hat on, worn jauntily on one side, crossed sabres in front, and her shoulders were concealed by a gray cavalry cape. Suddenly she flashed a glance at me, her eyes full of laughter.

"Well, Mr. Lieutenant Galesworth, have you looked long enough?"

The swift question confused me, but I found answer.

"No; but as long as I dare. You were observing me also."

"Naturally--womanly curiosity is my excuse. Would you like to know what conclusion I came to?"

"From your eyes it may not prove altogether flattering."

"Oh, my eyes are not to be trusted. I warn you frankly of that at the very start. All I shall say is you appear better than I had expected--only, really, you need a shave."

"Better how? In what way?"

"Well, younger for one thing; somehow your statement that you were a lieutenant made me suspect your age--or possibly it was your voice."

"I am twenty-four."

"And look to be scarcely twenty. How did you ever gain a commission? Were you in battle?"

The question decidedly hurt my pride, yet I managed to control my tongue.

"I have met colonels in both armies no older than I," I returned swiftly. "Of course I have been in battle, wounded for the matter of that, and three months a prisoner."

"Oh, I did not mean to question your right to the shoulder straps. War makes men fast; I know that for my home has been in the track of both armies."

"You live in this neighborhood?"

"Yes, about twenty miles south of where we are now. Shall I tell you what I am doing here?"

I bowed, eager to learn although I had not been brash enough to inquire.

"You have been wondering all night," carelessly. "If you had asked I should have refused to answer, but will now reward your remarkable patience with a full confession. I am going to take quinine back to our hospitals. I won't tell you where I am going to get it," a bit defiantly, "although I am not afraid you would try to stop me."

"Certainly not; why should I?"

"There are plenty of Yanks who do; the last messenger was shot by your raiders, and the whole consignment lost. He was my cousin; that is why I am trying what I can do--the boys need it so badly. If you are an honorable soldier you will not interfere with a work of mercy."

"An honorable soldier!" I exclaimed, stung by the words. "Do you question that?"

"Not until after daylight came, and I noticed how you were clothed," and her eyes lost all gleam of humor. "I respect a scout, but despise a spy."

My cheeks flamed, as I realized what she meant--the tattered gray jacket, buttoned tightly, and concealing my blue blouse. In swift disgust I wrenched it open, and flung the garment into the road.

"I had entirely forgotten I had the thing on," I explained hastily. "Don't condemn until you hear my story. You will listen, will you not?"

She sat silent, looking intently into my face, with merely the slightest inclination of the head.

"I came into your lines dressed just as I am now, drifting across the river behind a log. It was my third attempt to get through your pickets, and this time I succeeded. I found myself in thick brush near a cluster of tents, and overheard two officers talking. One was a major by the name of Hardy--do you know him?"

"Yes," a swift little catch in her voice.

"The other was a shorter, heavier-set man, out-ranking Hardy."

"Speaking with short, crisp sentences," she interrupted, "and wearing a heavy beard?"

"He spoke that way--yes; but as to the beard I could not say owing to the darkness."

"It must have been General Johnston."

"I thought as much. The two were discussing the getting of despatches through to Beauregard, and decided no one could succeed but a fellow they called Billie, some relative or friend of Hardy's. It was all arranged he should try it, and the major started off to complete arrangements. An aide, with the despatches, was to meet the messenger at the 'Three Corners,' where the little log church is, and then accompany him through the pickets. It was plainly enough my duty to intercept these if I could, but in order to do so I must pass through two miles of the Confederate camp, meeting soldiers almost every step of the way. That was when I stole the jacket, and slipped it on, and never thought of it again until you spoke."

She was leaning forward now, intensely interested, her lips parted, the quick breath revealed by the pulsing of her breast.

"And--and you got to the 'Three Corners'?"

"To a point just below. I ran most of the way, and then had to crawl through the bushes to get around a picket-post, but I believed I was there in plenty of time. Then you came rattling down the hill, with an officer riding along beside you, and, of course, I mistook you for Billie. I jumped your outfit in the hollow."

She flung up her hands in expressive gesture.

"Were you hanging there all that time--even before the lieutenant left?"

"I certainly was; hanging on for dear life too. My limbs are black and blue. I never saw a pony travel like that little devil."

She burst into an unrestrained ripple of laughter, scarcely able to speak, as the full humor of the situation appealed to her. No doubt the expression of my face did its part, but she certainly found it most amusing. In spite of myself I had to smile in sympathy.

"Oh, that was too good; I shall have to tell the general. Well, I helped Billie Hardy out that time, didn't I? I reckon you don't see much fun in it though."

"No, I don't," frankly, "yet I cannot say I am entirely sorry."

"Indeed," sobering instantly because of my earnestness. "I cannot understand that--the despatches have gone through."

"Without doubt. From a military standpoint I surely regret my failure. But if I had intercepted Billie I should never have met you."

"Oh!"

"Nor come to know you."

Again the girl laughed, and I noticed the dimple in her cheek, the gray-blue eyes glancing up at me mockingly.

"Don't flatter yourself that you do," she retorted pleasantly, "for you might be mistaken altogether."

CHAPTER V
ACQUAINTANCES, NOT FRIENDS

The manner in which this was uttered made me feel that she was in earnest. Indeed I was already beginning to realize that this young woman was an enigma, her moods changing so rapidly as to keep me in a state of constant bewilderment--one moment frank, outspoken, friendly; the next hiding her real self behind a barrier of cold reserve which I seemed helpless to penetrate. Yet this very changeableness was attractive, keeping my mind constantly on the alert, and yielding her a peculiar charm. As she spoke these words her eyes encountered mine, almost in challenge, which I met instantly.

"Perhaps not--but I shall."

"Oh, indeed! Is this conceit, or determination?"

"The latter assuredly. Why is it not possible for one to know you?"

"Really I cannot tell," not altogether displeased at my decision, "yet it would border upon a miracle, for I do not even know myself. Besides I doubt your having the opportunity for sufficient study--that is Jonesboro yonder."

The road rounded the crest of a sharp hill, and, from off the summit, we could look directly down into the river valley. Except for little groves of scrub oak it was open country, the broad stream showing clearly between green banks, with few cultivated fields in sight. We had turned toward the north, and the straggling town lay directly in front two miles away, so hidden behind trees the houses were scarcely distinguishable; a quarter of a mile below was the bridge. I stood up, thrusting my head beyond the carriage cover, so as to see better. To the west the woods concealed everything. It was somewhere in that direction Beauregard's troops were encamped, yet, even if they were already advancing to unite with Johnston, they would hardly cross the country so far to the north. Knowing the situation as I did I felt little fear of any encounter with Confederates. Our cavalry were patrolling all the roads across the river, and, as late as the previous day, were guarding the Jonesboro bridge. I could see no signs of any such guard now, however, yet the trees were thick and obscured the view, and that heavy dust cloud to the right was probably caused by the passing of a troop of horse. Convinced that this would prove to be either a cavalry vidette, or a Federal foraging party, it made me more anxious to get quickly down into the town, hopeful they might have a spare horse with them, and I pointed out the dust spirals to my companion.

"If you have friends in Jonesboro," I said, "I've also got some coming."

"Who are they?" her eyes on the distant dust. "Yankees?"

"Certainly; there are none of your people on that side of the river. Beauregard is out yonder in those hills. Let's drive on, the town looks quiet."

She leaned forward, holding to the edge of the carriage cover to keep her balance, her glance turning toward the southwest.

"If those are your people they mustn't see me," she said quietly, a little accent of pleading in her voice. "You promise that first?"

"Of course," although surprised at her asking. "I know it is our orders to intercept everything which can aid the enemy, but I don't feel inclined to prevent your taking quinine to the poor fellows in the hospital. War hasn't made me as inhuman as that. We can easily reach the town ahead of that squad of cavalry, and if you have some safe place there to go, and will only keep indoors, there is no danger of discovery."

"I have," eagerly, "Judge Moran's house; you can see its gable there among the trees. He is so old he has not even been conscripted." She laughed, flashing a look aside at me as she shook the reins and applied the whip. "I wonder what he will think when he sees me driving up alongside a Yankee. It will be like the end of the world. No, don't talk to me any more; I've got to conjure up a nice, respectable story to tell him."

She remained very quiet as we rattled down the hill, her forehead puckered, her gaze straight ahead. Suddenly she asked,

"Do you sometimes tell falsehoods?"

"Guilty."

"Are they ever justified?"

"Well, really I don't know; from the standpoint of the strict moralist I presume not; but it is my judgment the strict moralist wouldn't last long in time of war."

I was amused at the earnestness with which she looked at me, apparently weighing my words as soberly as though they had important meaning.

"What's the trouble? If there is any prevaricating to be done, turn it over to me--I have become an expert."

"No doubt," her face brightening, "but I must attend to this case myself. Judge Moran will have to suppose you a Confederate spy. No, not a word of protest will I listen to. If you go along with me, it must be exactly as I say; there is no other way, for otherwise he would never receive you into the house."

"Oh, very well," I replied indifferently, my eyes marking the swift approach of that distant squad of cavalry. "The masquerade will be short, and well worth while if it only earns me a breakfast with you."

The toss of her head was hardly complimentary. We were in the tree-lined streets by this time, and suddenly she wheeled the pony in through an open gateway. The house was large, painted white, of distinctly Southern architecture, the broad stone steps surmounted by rounded pillars. On the porch a man sat smoking. He arose instantly, hat in hand, and came down to meet us. His was a tall, slender, slightly stooped figure, a finely chiselled face, the hair and beard white. His eyes, apparently as keen as ever, instantly recognized the girl, his stern features relaxing into a smile of welcome.

"I am surprised and pleased to greet you, Miss Willifred," cordially bowing over her extended hand. "'Tis a long while since we have seen you here."

"Not from any doubt of your hospitality, Judge, but the armies have made travelling unsafe."

"True; we live in constant peril. The Yankees have driven off my negroes, and also robbed me of every horse on the place. Your father, the major, is well?"

"In most excellent health, thank you. He was wounded at Chattanooga, but soon recovered. We had him at home with us for a month."

"So I heard. A young Louisiana officer, a Captain Le Gaire, gave me news of your family. He was through Jonesboro with a scouting party two days ago. He seemed very glad to talk about you, my dear."

The girl's face flushed, as she withdrew her hand, attempting a laugh.

"We are excellent friends, yet really it does not require any deep interest to induce Captain Le Gaire to talk. That is one of his specialties."

"I suspected as much, yet I found his conversation highly interesting. He is intelligent, and has travelled widely. But come, my dear, let me help you down. I am such an early bird I have breakfasted already, yet there will be something ready for you, and your companion."

His gaze surveyed me for the first time, and he stepped back, his eyes darkening suspiciously.

"But what have you here--a Yankee?"

"So far as uniform goes, yes," she answered lightly, descending over the wheel, and adroitly dodging a direct reply. "But all things are not as they seem, outwardly. Surely, Judge, you do not suppose I would ever harbor one of the enemy? If I vouch for the gentleman it should be sufficient."

He took my hand cordially enough, yet with a question still in his keen old eyes.

"I am glad to know you, sir. Any friend of Miss Willifred's is a friend of mine, but I'm damned if I like that color."

"The nature of my mission makes it necessary," I explained.

"Exactly, sir, exactly; I understand perfectly. Alight, and come in, but you wear the first Yankee uniform ever welcomed to my house. Come right along, both of you. I've got one servant left, who will attend the pony."

Twenty minutes later we were breakfasting together in a cool, spacious room the windows of which opened upon the porch. The judge, after satisfying himself that we were being well served, had disappeared, leaving us alone. It was a beautiful morning, the birds singing outside, the sunlight sifting through the branches of the great oaks shading the windows. Not a sound, other than the rustling of leaves, broke the silence. My companion appeared disinclined to talk, her eyes turned away from me. The constraint became so marked I endeavored to start conversation, but with poor result.

"Our meeting has been an odd one," I began, "romantic enough to form a basis for fiction."

Her glance shifted to my face.

"Do you think so? I merely find it extremely embarrassing."

"Then I will withdraw at once," I insisted, hurt by the indifference of her voice. "I had supposed you wished me to remain until now--surely your words implied this."

"Oh, yes! I did, and you are in no way to blame. It was an impulse, and I failed to realize that it would involve deceit to an old friend. Perhaps I am too easily hurt, but I am afraid Judge Moran half suspects the truth. Anyway you must go immediately."

"We shall part as friends?"

She hesitated, as though considering the full intent of my request.

"Hardly that, Lieutenant Galesworth. The word 'friend' should mean much, and we are merely chance acquaintances--politically enemies."

"I had hoped that difference--merely the accident of war--might have been swept aside. It has no personal weight with me, and I supposed you were of broader mind."

"I am," she responded earnestly. "Some of my best friends are Northerners, wearing that uniform, but, as it chances, we have met in war, playing at cross-purposes. You are a Federal scout whom I have unwittingly helped through the Confederate lines. Surely I have done enough already to help you--perhaps to injure the cause I love--without being asked for more. Under other conditions we might continue friends, but not as matters stand."

"Yet later--when the war ends?"

"It is useless to discuss what may occur then. There is little likelihood we shall ever meet after to-day. Indeed, I have no wish that we should."

It was a dismissal so clearly expressed I could only bow, wondering what it was I saw in the depths of her eyes which seemed almost to contradict the utterance of the lips.

"You leave me no choice."

"There is none. I have no desire to be considered an enemy, and there is no possibility for us to become friends. We are but the acquaintances of a chance meeting." She held out her hand across the table, the impulsive movement robbing her words of their sting. "You understand this is not indifference, but necessity."

I clasped closely the white fingers extended toward me, my heart throbbing, but my lips held prisoners by her eyes.

"Yes, I understand perfectly, but I make no promise."

"No promise! What do you mean?"

"Only that to my mind this is no mere chance acquaintance, nor is it destined to end here. Sometime I am going to know you, and we are going to be friends."

"Indeed!" her eyes dropped, the shadow of lashes on her cheeks. "You are very audacious to say that."

"Yet you are not altogether sorry to hear me say it."

"Oh, I do not take your words seriously at all. They are mere Yankee boasting--"

She stopped suddenly, the slight flush fading from her cheeks as she arose to her feet, staring out through the open window. It was the sound of horses' hoofs on the gravel roadway, and I sprang up also, endeavoring to see. A squad of troopers was without, dusty, hard-riding fellows, uniformed in Confederate gray.

CHAPTER VI
A BOLD FRONT

It was but a glimpse through the leaf-draped window of dust-caked horses, the bronzed faces of their riders, and the gray hair of Judge Moran, as he hastened down the steps to greet them. I saw one man swing down from his saddle, and advance toward the house, then a sharp catching of the girl's breath drew my attention toward her, and our eyes met.

"You--you must not suppose I expected this," she faltered, "--that I have betrayed you."

There was no doubting her earnestness, nor her disgust at such treachery.

"Not for a moment. But I must get away. Are you acquainted with the house?"

"Yes; but two of the men rode around to the well. It would be impossible now to slip out the back way without discovery." She ran across the room, and flung open a door. "Go in there and lie down; pretend to be asleep. If the judge does not inform them of your presence here it may never be suspected. If he does I must cling to the old story."

I caught her hands, and in the excitement she seemed scarcely aware of the act.

"You are willing to do this for me?"

"I don't know what I do it for," a little nervous laugh in her voice. "When one once gets started into deceit there seems to be no end--but go quick! the officer is coming now."

The room into which I was thrust was darkened by lowered shades, but the bookcases lining the walls proclaimed it a library. A comfortable leather couch occupied the space between the two windows. The door remained half an inch ajar, and, before I could close it, some one entered the dining-room. The first words uttered held me silent, listening. There was a heavy step on the uncarpeted floor, the jingle of spurs, and a startled exclamation from the girl.

"You! Why, I had no thought of meeting you here."

"Yet I trust you are not sorry," the voice deep, yet so low I lost an occasional word. "Judge Moran says you bear--"

"Hush," she interrupted quickly. "Yes, and they must go on at once. What brings you here, Gerald? A scouting party?"

"We are Beauregard's advance scouts; he is moving eastward."

"Then these papers must reach him at once. Don't stop to ask questions, Gerald, but send some man; have him kill his horse if necessary. Oh, don't stand there looking at me, but go! I'll explain later."

I heard the rustle of papers, the rapid movement of the man as he left the room, the quick breathing of the excited woman. Then she crossed the room to the window, and the next moment a horse galloped past. My head whirled--then it was not quinine for the hospitals which had brought her through the lines; she had deliberately lied to me, and instead, was a bearer of despatches. Sudden anger at the trick banished every other feeling; yet what could I do? My hand gripped the knob of the door, every nerve throbbing, when I heard the officer's voice again in the breakfast room.

"He's off; now let's have the straight of all this, Billie."

Billie! I grasped the full truth of it in an instant. Lord! I had been a fool. The woman had played with me as though I were a mere child; had been laughing at me all night; and doubtless intended now to hand me over prisoner to this squad of gray-jackets. Billie! The very person I was seeking; the only one who could hope to get through after all others had failed. And I had supposed "Billie" was a man, never once thinking of the name as a pet feminine one of the South. The realization of all this confused me so that I missed a part of what was being said, and only aroused as the man spoke more sharply.

"That's all right, of course; I understand what brought you here, but where is that fellow you had with you?"

"Who?" it was an indignant voice.

"Oh, you understand, Miss Innocence," a slight sneer in the utterance. "There was a man in your company when you arrived, dressed as a Yank. Moran told me so. You were breakfasting together--the table proves that."

"Well, what of it? I explained his presence to the judge. Am I obliged to account for all my actions to every one I meet?"

The officer, evidently acquainted with the lady's disposition, and aware that driving would never do, changed his tone, crossing the room toward her, and lowering his voice.

"No, not to every one, Billie, but surely you cannot deny I have some right to this information. Would you wish me to be riding the country at night with a strange woman?"

"If it became part of your duty--yes. I have no remembrance of ever interfering with your freedom, Captain Le Gaire."

I could hear the man's teeth click, as though in an effort to restrain an oath.

"By God, but you are irritating!" he burst forth impetuously. "One would think I were no more to you than a stranger. This is no light affair to be laughed away. Have you forgotten our engagement already?"

"That is scarcely probable. You remind me of it often enough. Don't crush my hand so."

Her provoking coldness was all that was needed to overcome the slight restraint the captain still exercised. Instantly his real nature came to the fore.

"Then I'll make him do the explaining," he threatened fiercely. "I know how to deal with men. Where is the fellow? In that room?"

There was a brief silence. I could distinguish his rapid breathing, and the slight rustle of her skirts as she sank back into a chair.

"Well, are you going to tell me? Or must I hunt for myself?"

"Captain Le Gaire," she began quietly, without even a tremor in the soft voice, "possibly you forget whom I am. The gentlemen of my acquaintance have never been accustomed to question the motives actuating my conduct. You imagine yourself talking to some darky on your Louisiana plantation. Is this the manner in which you propose treating me after marriage?"

He laughed uneasily.

"Why, I meant nothing, Billie. Don't take it in that way. Surely you understand I have a right to be curious as to your companion."

"Yes; but not to carry your curiosity to the point of discourtesy. I have not the slightest objection to answering your questions, if you only ask with some respect."

"You always hold me at arm's length."

"Do I? Well, this is hardly the best time to discuss that. What was it you wished to know?"

"Who is the fellow travelling with you?"

"Didn't the judge tell you?"

"He said he was a Confederate spy dressed in the uniform of a Yankee lieutenant whom you had brought through the lines."

"Well, isn't that information sufficient?"

The gallant captain again smothered an oath, evidently tried to the limit by the girl's cool indifference.

"Of course it isn't. That might answer for Moran, for he has no personal interest in the affair. But it's altogether different with me. It's merely accident that I rode in here this morning, and I immediately discover the woman I am engaged to marry was out all night riding around with a stranger, eating breakfast with him when I arrive. Do you suppose that is pleasant?"

"No; yet my explanation ought to be sufficient."

"Explanation! You have made none."

"Oh, yes; Judge Moran told you the circumstances."

I heard him stomp roughly across the floor, his spurs clanking.

"Explanation, nothing! Who is the fellow?"

"Really I don't know."

"Don't know? Do you mean to say you rode with him alone all night, and took breakfast with him this morning, without even learning his name?"

"He said his name was Galesworth, but I don't know that he told the truth."

"You pretend indifference well," the man sneered.

"It is no pretence; I am indifferent. Why should I be otherwise? I am not interested in spies. I may assist one through the lines to serve the Confederacy, but that is no evidence that I feel any personal interest in the man. Anyhow that is the extent of my knowledge in this case, and I haven't the slightest desire to increase it. When are you going to ride on?"

"Not until I know more than I do now," he retorted savagely. "There is something hidden here. You are pretending all this indifference so as to give that fellow sufficient time to get away. I'm damned if I put up with it."

"Captain Le Gaire," and she was upon her feet, "do you venture to address such language to me? Do you dare--"

"I am no dupe of yours or of any other woman," he broke in, too angry now to restrain his words. "There is something wrong here, and I mean to know what it is. If you won't tell, I'll find out myself." He strode across to the window and called to some one below. "Slade, come in here."

There was a moment of waiting, during which neither stirred, nor spoke. Then the trooper entered, his heels clicking together as he saluted just within the door-way.

"Sergeant," said Le Gaire shortly. "I have reason to suspect there is a man hidden in that room yonder. I'll keep an eye on this young lady, while you find out."

Slade took a step forward, and the girl's dress rustled.

"Wait just a minute, Sergeant," she said briefly. "Am I to understand from this, Captain Le Gaire, that you are not only a bully, but also a coward?"

"A coward!--"

"Yes, a coward. You order the sergeant to open that door--why do you not open it yourself?"

He laughed rather unpleasantly.

"So that's the trouble? Well, it's merely a way we have in the army, but if it will greatly oblige you I'll do the job."

It was useless waiting longer; the room offered me no possible hiding-place, the two windows looked down on the waiting cavalrymen. Beyond doubt boldness was the best card to play. Before the rather reluctant captain could take a second step I flung open the concealing door, and came forth into the breakfast room.

CHAPTER VII
A WOMAN'S PRISONER

The scene before me, the expression on the three faces, caused me to smile. I came forth with no definite plan of action, trusting, as one must at such times, wholly to luck. There was no means of escape apparent, yet my mind was cool, and I was prepared to take advantage of any opportunity. I saw the flash of the sergeant's revolver, the captain's sudden recoil, his hand tugging at his sword-hilt, and glimpsed something in the depths of Billie's eyes that puzzled me.

"Good-morning, gentlemen," I said easily.

So far as Slade was concerned it was evident that all he saw was the uniform, his revolver instantly covering me, held in a hand steady as rock; he even grinned amiably across the barrel. But the expression on Le Gaire's face changed from startled surprise to relief. He was a tall man, with dark hair and eyes, a black moustache shading his lip, and his hand fell from the hilt of the sword as he took an uncertain step toward me.

"Drop that gun-play, Sergeant," he exclaimed sharply. "This man *is* all right; I know him."

Too astounded myself for speech, I could only stare back into the captain's face, seeking vainly to recall ever having seen the fellow before. Not the slightest recollection came to me, but Le Gaire blundered on, blinded by his discovery.

"Didn't know you had gone into this sort of thing," he exclaimed cordially, holding out his hand. "Last I heard your regiment was in New Orleans. Don't remember me, do you?"

I shook my head, so completely puzzled by this unexpected turn of affairs that speech became dangerous. Perhaps he would give me some clue to my new identity, which would enable me to carry out the masquerade.

"Your face is familiar," I ventured, "but--"

"Oh, no excuses," he broke in cordially. "I was a guest at your mess one night when we were garrisoning Memphis. I am Le Gaire, of the Third Louisiana. I sang you fellows some French songs, you may remember."

"Oh, yes!" and my face visibly brightened, as I grasped his fingers, wondering who the devil I might be, yet exceedingly overjoyed at this sudden change of fortune. "We had a gay night of it. I wonder you recognize me in these rags."

"Well, I don't suppose I should," he exclaimed, "only you happened to be pointed out to me specially that evening. It was just after your duel with Major Gillette of ours. Between us, I don't mind admitting I was glad you punctured that fellow--it saved me the trouble."

"Perhaps if you gentlemen are through with reminiscences," broke in the girl quietly, "Captain Le Gaire might present me to his new friend."

"But I thought you knew him already!"

She laughed lightly, her eyes aglow with merriment.

"Oh, no, indeed! It is all a most wonderful mix-up."

"Then it will be a pleasure for me to bring order out of confusion--Miss Hardy, Major Atherton of General Pemberton's staff."

"Atherton!" she gasped. "I--I thought your name was Galesworth."

"Hardy!" I retorted, simulating equal surprise, "and I supposed your name to be Gray."

Le Gaire looked at us, vastly amused, all his former jealousy and suspicion instantly dissipated by this evidence of misunderstanding.

"You certainly must have had a merry night of it, you two--trying to outlie each other, and with honors about even. However, the tangle is straightened out now, and we must be on our way. What are you trying to do, Atherton,--get to the rear of the Yanks?"

"Yes," I answered, with some hesitation, and glancing aside at the girl. I could not determine how much of all this she actually believed, or how far I might venture to carry forward the deceit. Her eyes were upon me, but their shaded depths revealed nothing. I determined to take the chance. "Johnston requires more exact information as to the Yankee artillery, and thought I might get in around the right flank. I saw a dust cloud across the river as we came into town."

"A foraging party; they went west; we have the bridge guarded."

"Beauregard's advance may hurry Johnston," I continued, eager to draw out of him some information of value. "How came he to move without orders?"

"He concluded so wide a gap was dangerous, and that Johnston's despatch-carriers must have been unable to get through, so he began feeling his way east. The orders Billie brought will undoubtedly hurry the advance."

"They have gone forward then?"

"Certainly--I sent a man with them at once."

I shot an inquiring glance toward her, but she had found a seat at the table, and was toying idly with a spoon, her eyes cast down.

"And Beauregard is marching along this road, I presume?"

"No; back behind the hills where he runs no risk of being seen by any prowling Yankee scouts. We are in advance on the left flank."

I understood the movement clearly enough now, and realized the importance of getting this news to our headquarters. A swift advance of troops would throw a column between these two forces of Confederates, and hold them apart for separate battle. But there was no time for delay. Le Gaire failed to comprehend my anxious glance out the open window.

"We all better be at it," he said quickly. "By the way, with that cavalry uniform you ought to have a horse. We're leading one with Yankee accoutrements you can use. Come on, Slade. Miss Hardy, I hope to see you at your own home in a few days."

He bowed, hat in hand, the girl rising to her feet, as the sergeant left the room. She did not smile, her eyes flashing from his face to mine.

"I may remain here until the armies leave this section," she replied quietly. "There is too much risk in travelling alone."

"You might ride with us," he suggested gallantly. She shook her head, her lips smiling.

"I think I better not."

"Does that mean you are still angry?"

"I didn't know I had been, Captain. Perhaps I spoke rather hastily, but you must forgive that."

Her hand was extended, and he came a step back from the door to grasp it, and lift the fingers to his lips. With a fierce throbbing of the heart I turned my back to them, staring out the window. There was a low murmur of voices, and then the door clicked. I never moved, watching Le Gaire go down the steps, his men swing into their saddles, at a sharp order, and ride away in column of fours. When they had all disappeared a single horse remained, tied to the railing of the veranda. I turned about, and picked up my hat from the floor. Miss Hardy was seated again at the table, her head resting upon one hand. I could see the round, white arm where the sleeve fell away, and her cheeks were flushed. She did not lift her eyes at my movement, and, half angry at her studied indifference, I advanced straight toward the door. But there I hesitated, unable to part without at least another word. She was looking at me now.

"May I hope ever to meet you again?" I asked.

"I can promise nothing as to the future," she returned soberly. "But I wish to speak to you now, before you go. Sit down here, just a moment."

I hesitated, keen as to the value of time, yet curious as to what she would say, and swayed strongly by her influence.

"You surely must understand how anxious I am to get away--" I began, but she broke in impulsively.

"Of course I do, but you must listen to me first." She had risen, and was leaning forward, speaking earnestly. "It is true we shall probably never meet again, yet I am not willing you should think me altogether a despicable character. I wish you to know whom I am, and why deceit was necessary."

"My dear girl," I exclaimed, hastily crossing the room, "there is nothing to explain. I understand the circumstances."

"No, not entirely," she insisted, "but it is my desire you should. I--I hardly know why, but--but I would rather have you think well of me. Listen, please; I will be very brief. I am Willifred Gray Hardy, and it was my father whom you overheard talking with General Johnston. Our home is south on the pike road, and was used as headquarters until a few days ago. I have known General Johnston ever since I was a little girl, and everybody--all my friends--call me Billie. Of course you thought the courier was a man--it was only natural you should--and it was, therefore, easy for me to keep up the deceit--they trusted me, and I had to get those papers through."

"Of course you did," heartily. "Surely you do not suppose I would think less of you for your loyalty?"

"I hoped not; nor did I mean to let you go away thinking me a fool."

"A fool!" thrown entirely from my guard. "How could I think that?"

"By imagining that I believe you Major Atherton of Pemberton's staff," with a little, nervous laugh, and quick uplifting of the eyes. "I was glad Captain Le Gaire made the mistake, for I had no wish to see you a prisoner, but your quick pretending did not in the least deceive me, Lieutenant Galesworth." She paused, evidently amused at the surprise expressed in my face, yet with the lines of her lips setting firmly. "Your questions regarding the movements of Beauregard were most ingenuous, but I was able to comprehend your purpose."

"You mean--"

"That you propose bearing the news direct to Federal headquarters. That is why you are in such a desperate hurry to get away."

I took a step backward, reading the meaning of her eyes.

"And you intend to prevent--"

"Exactly," her voice as quiet as ever. "I am a Confederate still."

She had changed her position, standing now between me and the closed door, the expression upon her face sufficient evidence of her determination. Hers was no idle threat--this daughter of a soldier was ready for the struggle and the sacrifice. I recognized all this at a glance, bewildered by the swift change in attitude, unable to decide my own course of action. Argument was useless, a resort to force repugnant. Above all else the one overpowering feeling was admiration for the girl. She must have read all this in my eyes, yet her own never wavered, nor changed expression.

"Please do not make the mistake, Lieutenant Galesworth, of thinking me not sufficiently in earnest," she said firmly, "or that I am unprepared."

"I do not; if you were only a man I should know exactly what to do."

"Your courtesy is misplaced; at least I do not ask it. This is war, and you are upon one side, I on the other. You will remain in this room until I say you may go."

"What will hold me?--your eyes?--the mere threat of your lips?"

"Something rather more to the purpose than either," she answered coldly. Her right hand, concealed by the folds of her skirt, was uplifted, the fingers grasping the black butt of a Colt. Her lips smiled. "I suppose you know the efficacy of this weapon, Lieutenant, and that it is loaded."

My hand dropped instinctively to my belt--the revolver holster was empty! It was my own weapon the girl held.

CHAPTER VIII
THE COMING OF THE ENEMY

No matter how charming she may be, a man can never enjoy being out-played at his own game by a woman. The piquant face fronting me swam in a mist as a sudden rush of anger swept from me all admiration. I had been played with, outwitted from the start, every movement checkmat-ed--even now she was actually laughing at my helplessness. My first wild impulse was to spring forward, and wrest the revolver from her hand; yet there was that in her attitude, in the expression of her eyes, which made me hesitate. Would she shoot? Would the sense of duty to her cause actually induce her to fire at me? A moment before, I should not have deemed it possible, but now, it seemed to me, she was desperate enough to do even this. And that was a hair-trigger she fingered so recklessly! Instead of leaping forward, I stood motionless, outwardly cool, yet with every nerve throbbing. She read all this in my face, no doubt, for her lips half smiled, her manner exhibited confidence.

"Oh, I can shoot," she said pleasantly enough, "so I wouldn't try that if I were you. Now will you do exactly as I say?"

I remained silent, my hands clinched. So this was the gentle creature I had been riding with, had even been falling in love with! This woman, now threaten-ing me with death, was the same happy-hearted, laughing girl whose hand I had held, and to whom I had talked in words of friendship. I could scarcely realize the change, or comprehend this new development of character.

The unpleasant situation was broken by the sound of steps in the hall. The door opened, and Judge Moran entered. Miss Hardy stepped instantly aside, concealing the revolver within the folds of her skirt, yet with watchful eyes on my face. Moran glanced at us both without suspicion, and approached me with outstretched hand.

"Captain Le Gaire explained to me who you are, Major," he said with new cordiality, "and I am very glad to receive you as my guest. Are you one of the Mobile Athertons?"

"No," I answered, flushing, and avoiding her amused eyes, yet not daring to blurt out the truth, "I come from farther north."

"Exactly; I recall now there are Athertons in Memphis and Nashville, delightful people, the real, old Southern stock. I regret greatly to learn from Le Gaire that duty compels you to leave at once."

"Major Atherton has changed his plans," broke in the girl, before I could respond. "The advance of Beauregard's forces makes it safer for him to remain quiet for a few hours,--until night comes. I was just suggesting that he go up to the red room and lie down--he is nearly dead from fatigue."

"The red room!" in surprise. "Surely you jest, Miss Willifred! That is hardly considered a guest chamber."

"No; but the safest place in the house, if, by any chance, it is searched by a scouting party."

The old gentleman nodded, as if in approval.

"Possibly it would be safer, although I hardly anticipate any such calls from the enemy with our own people so near. You will not be the first Confederate to lie hidden there, sir," with a bow to me, and a quick glance toward the smiling girl. "Would you mind showing him the way, my dear?--it is becoming difficult for me to mount the stairs."

"With pleasure; indeed, I was about to propose doing so. Major, you will go first, please."

However cheerily these words were spoken I understood their quiet threat, and the full meaning of that motionless hand held securely hidden behind the fold of her skirt. She opened the door into the hall, and, with one questioning glance into her eyes, I murmured a word of thanks to the unsuspecting judge, and passed slowly through. Miss Hardy followed, closing the door behind her, the revolver now held in plain view.

"Up the stairs, and turn to the left," she commanded briefly.

The short, stern, business-like tone in which this order was uttered might have been amusing under other conditions, but scarcely so then when I was smarting under defeat. I glanced back, half tempted to endeavor a sudden leap; yet she was fully prepared, and I hesitated. Would she actually shoot me down? Could it be possible the girl would take my life? I could scarcely conceive of such a probability, she seemed so womanly in every way, so light-hearted, and yet there was no laugh now in her eyes, no lack of determination in the firm setting of her lips.

"Suppose I refuse!"

"I sincerely hope you will not, Lieutenant. This is hard enough for me; don't make it any harder."

There could be no doubting what she meant, nor what she had nerved herself to accomplish. Feeling like a whipped cur I went slowly up the broad stairs, my hand on the banister rail, and she followed, keeping even pace with me, the cocked Colt pointing sternly upward at my back.

"The last door--yes, beyond the chimney. Step inside, Lieutenant Galesworth. Now close the door."

I stood, with fingers still grasping the knob, listening. There was a click, as though a heavy key was being turned in the lock, and then withdrawn. Following I heard her quick breath of relief, and a half-suppressed sob. The sound made her seem all woman again.

"Miss Hardy!" I called, my lips at the crack of the door.

"What is it?" the answering voice tremulous.

"I want to tell you that you are a brave girl, and that I do not in the least blame you."

There was a moment's hesitating silence, as though my unexpected words had left her speechless. Her breathing told me her lips were also close to the door.

"I--I am so glad you said that," she returned at last. "This--this has been so difficult to do. But you know I mean to do it, to hold you here; you realize I am terribly in earnest?"

"Yes--but for how long?"

"Until late to-night; then you can do us no deep injury." Her voice became firmer. "I shall remain on guard here."

I heard her move away from the direct neighborhood of the door, her steps sounding distinctly on the polished floor. Then something heavy, probably a chair or bench, was drawn forward, following which all was silence. Although I could see nothing the situation in the hall was clear. Confident escape was impossible in any other direction the determined girl had taken up her position opposite the door, prepared for a long vigil. All feeling of anger, even of irritation, had by this time left me. The slight falter, the womanly softness of her voice, had robbed me of all resentment, and I was conscious merely of admiration for her courage and loyalty. But I desired intently to stand equally high in her memory, and in order to do so must exhibit my own wit, my own resources in emergency. I felt the door--it was of solid oak, with no spot of weakness evident, even the key-hole being concealed by a metal flap on the outside. The room itself was small, the walls tinted red, and contained no furniture except a narrow bed and one straight-backed chair. Light was admitted through a small window, placed so high in the wall I was compelled to stand on the chair to look out, a mere round opening through which it would be impossible to squeeze my rather stalwart body. It was almost a typical prison cell, apparently affording not the slightest opportunity for escape. I had a pipe in my pocket, and matches, so I lit up, and lay back on the bed, reviewing the situation.

I am not of the disposition which surrenders easily, and my long experience as a scout had inured me to difficult ventures. Almost invariably there are means of escape, if one is fortunate enough to discover the point of weakness and possesses sufficient time in which to work. Yet as I lay there, my eyes anxiously scanning those bare, solid walls, my brain working coolly, the problem appeared unsolvable. The door, of hard-wood, fitting tightly into the jambs, was hopeless,--particularly with Billie outside, loaded revolver in hand, nerved to the shooting point. I climbed again to the window, but the casing was solidly spiked into position, and I could barely press my head through the aperture into the open air. It was a thirty-foot sheer drop to the hard gravel of the road beneath, the nearest tree limb a dozen feet distant, with the roof edge far beyond reach of the hand. I sat down in the chair, the blue smoke curling overhead, floating out the window, my eyes studying the red-tinted side walls, as I endeavored to recall each detail of the house's architecture, and the exact location of this particular room.

I had turned to the left at the head of the stairway, passing by at least three doors. Then there had occurred a slight jog in the hall, making room for a large chimney, while just beyond opened this door. It was not even visible from the front of the house, and would probably be the rearmost apartment--no, that was wrong;

the hallway, much contracted in width, continued on into the ell. This was quite likely the first of the servants' quarters, and that east wall must abut directly against the chimney. With a new degree of hopefulness, I pushed aside the bed, and began testing the wall space with my knuckles. If any chimney was there, the stones were protected by wooden casing, which, covered by the red paper, was effectively concealed. I was about to abandon the search when a finger penetrated the paper, revealing a round opening--a pipe hole, left uncovered except for the wallpaper. I wrenched out the tin protector, and felt within. The chimney had apparently never been used, the interior being clear of soot, and was built of a single layer of stone, Southern fashion, the irregular fragments mortared together, and plastered smoothly on the inside. Without was a thin, narrow planking, dove-tailed, but secured by nails only at the four corners. This could be easily pried away, leaving the chimney itself open to attack. I could not reach far enough within to touch the opposite wall, but was convinced the space would prove sufficiently large to admit my body. With a knife I tested the resistance of the mortar, breaking the point of the blade, yet detaching quite a chunk, and wrenching out one small stone. Beyond doubt the task might be accomplished--but what was below? How was I to get down those smoothly plastered walls--and back again, if necessary?

I glanced at my watch; it was already nearing noon, and at any moment food might be brought me. I must wait until after that; then I should probably remain undisturbed for several hours. I shoved back the bed in such position its head-board completely concealed the slight excavation, and sat down upon it, planning anew how best to proceed. The time passed with no unusual sound reaching me from the hall without. Billie evidently felt no desire to acquaint Judge Moran with my real identity, and perhaps would thus experience some difficulty in procuring me food,--possibly would make no effort even until night. I succeeded in pushing aside the flap over the key-hole, without making any alarming noise, and applied one eye to the aperture. There was little to be seen--merely the end of a bench, and a pair of bare, black feet. The judge's sole remaining servitor doubtless, doing a turn at guard duty. As I gazed, some outside noise aroused him, and he went softly pattering down the hall.

The same sound startled me also, and I dropped the flap, clambering upon the chair so as to see without. It was a hundred feet to the main road, mostly velvety turf between, with a few trees partially obscuring the view. Yet I could see clearly enough, and up the pike leading through the village, half hidden by a cloud of dust, was advancing a regiment of cavalry, their flags draped, their horses walking in double column. As these swung into the straight road, a battery of artillery followed, gray-jacketed fellows, Confederates--Beauregard's advance.

CHAPTER IX
IMPORTANT NEWS

In spite of the recognized fact that these men were enemies, my heart throbbed, almost in pride, as I watched them pass. They were Americans, and magnificent fighting men. I had seen them, or their fellows, in the ruck and toil of battle, playing with death, smiling in the face of defeat. Now they were marching grimly forward to another clash of arms, through the blinding dust, heedless of all else but duty. This was what stirred me. No proud review, with glittering uniforms and waving flags, would have choked my throat, or dimmed my eyes, as did the sight of that plodding, silent column, half hidden under the dust cloud, uniforms almost indistinguishable, officers and men mingled, the drums still, the only sounds the steady tread, the occasional hoarse shout of command. Here was no pomp and circumstance, but grim purpose personified in self-sacrifice and endurance. With heads bowed, and limbs moving wearily, guns held at will, they swept by in unbroken column--cavalry, artillery, infantry--scarcely a face lifted to glance toward the house, with here and there a straggler limping to the roadside, or an aide spurring past--just a stream of armed men, who had been plodding on since daylight, footsore, hungry, unseeing, yet ready to die in battle at their commander's word. It was war; it was magnificent.

Yet suddenly there recurred to me my own small part in this great tragedy. Here was opportunity. Down below, on the front steps, stood the old judge, and beside him Miss Hardy, forgetful for the time of all else save those passing troops. I sprang from the chair, drew the bed back to the centre of the room, and began my assault on the wall. There was no necessity now for silence, and I dug recklessly into the mortar with my broken knife blade, wrenching forth the loosened stones, until I had thus successfully opened a space amply sufficient for my purpose. A glance down the chimney was not reassuring, no gleam of light being visible, yet I was desperate enough to take the chance of discovering some opening below. There remained but this one means of attaining the lower floor, and no time for hesitation. I tore both sheets from the bed, binding them securely together, and twisting them into a rope strong enough to sustain my weight. The bed-post served to secure one end; the other I dropped down the interior of the chimney. A glance from the window exhibited a double line of canvas-covered wagons creaking past, mules toiling wearily in the traces, under close guard of a squad of infantry. The judge and the girl were still outside. I was back instantly, and clambered recklessly into the hole.

I went down slowly, clinging desperately to the twisted sheets, unable to gain the slightest purchase on the smoothly plastered side walls. My fingers slipped, but I managed to hang on until I reached the very end of my improvised rope, my feet dangling, my arms aching from the weight. To hold on longer was seemingly impossible, yet I could neither see nor feel bottom. I let go, confident the distance could not be great, and came down without much shock a half-dozen feet below. I was in a large fire-place, apparently never utilized, the opening entirely covered by a screen of cast-iron. This fitted closely, but was unfastened, and, after feeling about cautiously in the darkness, I pushed it slightly to one side, and peered forth.

A large, rather handsomely furnished room was revealed, evidently a back-parlor, closed folding doors being conspicuous in the front wall. Three windows faced the north, their curtains partially drawn, and I could perceive through them the lattice work of a porch, covered with the green and red of a rambler rose. I recognized instantly the situation; this room was opposite, directly across the hall from where we had eaten breakfast, its windows also commanding a view of the road. Impelled by a desire to see what was continuing to take place without, I stole silently across the soft carpet, and peered forth. The last of the wagon train was lumbering past, and back of these, just wheeling around the corner, approached another column of horsemen. It would be madness for me to emerge from concealment yet, for even if I remained unnoticed by those marching troops, still there would surely be some stragglers about the premises seeking water. I sat down, staring out, endeavoring to decide about how large this Confederate force was--surely it composed all of Beauregard's corps, and, once united with Johnston, would render the Federal position extremely dangerous, perhaps untenable. Yet even now my warning of the sudden movement would be of comparatively small value, as the gap was too nearly closed for any swift advance to separate the two armies. All I could hope to accomplish was to prevent a surprise attack on our own exposed lines. And this could never be attempted before the next morning, even if Johnston swung his columns to the left in anticipation of Beauregard's approach. The troops were too thoroughly exhausted by the forced march to be hurled immediately into battle--they must be fed and rested first. Convinced as to this I remained quiet, glancing idly about the room, until sounds outside attracted attention.

A company--or possibly two--of cavalry was drawn up on the road directly fronting the house, their centre opposite the open gate, but I was compelled to lean out in order to discover just what was occurring on the driveway. A squad of a dozen horsemen, powdered with dust, yet excellently mounted, were riding slowly toward the veranda. The man slightly in advance was slender, with dark moustache and goatee, sitting straight in his saddle, and on the collar of his gray coat were the stars of a general officer. Even the hasty glance gained told me his identity--Beauregard. As this cavalcade turned at the corner of the house, I drew back, shadowed by the curtain, able thus both to see and hear. At the bottom of the steps the Confederate chieftain halted, and bowed, hat in hand.

"Judge Moran, I presume. While we have never previously met, yet your name has long been familiar. Probably I need not introduce myself."

The judge, his face beaming hospitality, grasped the outstretched hand, but Beauregard's dark, appreciative eyes were upon the girl standing at Moran's side.

"Your daughter, sir?" he asked quickly.

"Not so fortunate, General. This is Miss Willifred Hardy, of the 'Gables.'"

"Ah, yes!" the stern face instantly brightened by a rare smile. "The same fair heroine who brought the despatches from Johnston. I hoped I might reach here in time, my dear, to tell you in person how greatly I appreciate your service. May I ask if you are Major Hardy's daughter?"

Her cheeks burning, she murmured "Yes," curtsying to his rather stately bow.

"I knew your mother rather well in the old days,--a sweet girl, a Du Verne, of Baton Rouge. You have her eyes and hair." He turned toward Moran. "A courier but just arrived has brought me orders to halt my men, as Johnston is marching westward, and it is imperative that we protect the bridge yonder with sufficient force.

Would it inconvenience you, Judge, if I made your house my headquarters for the night?"

"Everything I possess is freely at your service."

"Thank you. From all I have heard I could never question the loyalty of Judge Moran." He spoke a few short orders, swung down from the saddle, and, followed by a half-dozen others, began climbing the steps, talking with Miss Willifred. I heard the party enter the hall, and pause for a moment, the sound of voices mingling but indistinguishable. Then a door opened, and the men trooped into the front parlor. There was a rattle as accoutrements were laid aside; then a table was drawn forth, and Beauregard's voice spoke:

"The portfolio, Sternes; now, Captain, let me read over that last despatch again. Ah, yes, I see. Is Colonel O'Neil waiting? Tell him to post Williams' brigade at the bridge, with Ozark's battery. Pickets should be advanced at least two miles. Lieutenant Greer, ride to the Three Corners, and have the regimental commanders close all gaps in the line; in case of attack we must be able to exhibit a solid front. A moment, Major Mason,--you are to bear my report to Johnston." There followed the rapid scratching of a pen, and a subdued murmur of voices. Then the deep bass of the general again broke in: "You may as well clearly understand the proposed plans, gentlemen, so you can execute my orders with intelligence. They are extremely simple; our main attack will be directed against the enemy's left flank; the troops selected for this service will cross at the lower ford early to-morrow night. Our own movements will depend altogether upon the success of Johnston's advance. Chambers will be up sometime to-night, and will hold a position at rear of the centre in reserve. Is this sufficiently clear?"

"Do we cross the bridge?"

"Not until Johnston informs us his assaulting column is in touch with the enemy."

"There is no absolute hour set?"

"No; that will depend upon the arrival of Chambers. And now, gentlemen, we will adjourn to the dining-room."

They passed out, evidently in the best of humor, and I could hear them chatting and laughing in the hall. But my thoughts were now concentrated upon my own work. This was important news I had overheard, and must be in the possession of the Federal commander without delay. No personal danger could be considered. But how was it possible to get away unobserved? I was in full uniform, and unarmed; the house--now Beauregard's headquarters--under close guard; the surrounding roads lined with troops. It would be simply madness to attempt crossing the river before nightfall, and yet I could not hope to remain where I was all the afternoon without discovery. As soon as the duties of hospitality were over Miss Willifred would certainly recall her prisoner, and it could not be long before my escape from the room above would be known. I must be safely out of the house before this occurred. It seemed to me the stables offered the best hiding-place, or else the deserted negro cabins.

I could examine the greater part of the front yard from the windows, the squad of troopers camped near the gate, and the sentinel pacing before the steps, but was compelled to lean far out to gain any glimpse of the rear. I could perceive no soldiers in this direction, however, and was encouraged to note a long grape arbor, thickly overgrown with vines, extending from the house to the other extremity of the garden. Once safely within its shadow I might get through unseen. And there was but one means of attaining the grape arbor--through the back hall, **via** either the kitchen or the cellar. I opened the door with all possible caution, and took silent survey of the hall. The front door stood open and a guard was stationed without, but with his back toward me. I could hear voices in the dining-room, but the hall itself appeared deserted, and, feeling that it was either now or never, I slipped forth, and started toward the rear. There were two doors, one at the very extremity of the hall, the other upon the right, both closed. Uncertain which to choose I tried the first I came to, but, even as I cautiously turned the knob, the second was opened from without, and a man entered hurriedly. We stared into each others' faces, both too completely surprised for speech. He was a cavalry sergeant, a gray-beard, and, with my first movement, was tugging at a weapon.

"Hold on there, my buck!" he said gruffly. "None o' that, now. By God! it's a Yank. Bill, come here."

The guard at the front door ran down the hall toward us, his gun thrown forward.

CHAPTER X
MISS WILLIFRED INTERVENES

Any effort at escape was clearly useless; the noise and shouting had already attracted the attention of those within, and a half-dozen officers streamed out through the dining-room door, eager to learn what had occurred.

"What's the trouble out here, Sims?" demanded the first to appear, striding forward. "Well, by all the gods, a Yank, and in full regalia! Where did you discover this fellow?"

"I'd been back fer a drink, sir," explained the sergeant, still eying me, "an' was just comin' in through ther door yer, when I run inter him, sneakin' 'long ther wall--thet's ther whole bloomin' story."

The officer, a smooth-faced lad, turned abruptly to me.

"Well, what have you got to say?"

"Nothing," I answered quietly, "you are perfectly welcome to draw your own conclusions."

"Oh, indeed," sarcastically. "We'll see what more civil answer you'll make to the general. Sims, bring the fellow along."

The two soldiers grabbed me roughly by the arms, but I made no resistance, cool enough by this time, although realizing fully the peril of my position. I was marched in through the open door, and stood up in the centre of the dining-room, Sims posted on one side of me, the guard on the other, the officers forming a picturesque background. Beauregard was on his feet, and Miss Hardy stood between the windows, her hands clasped, her cheeks red.

"What is all this, gentlemen? A Federal officer in full uniform? How comes he here?"

I made no attempt to answer, unable to formulate an excuse, and the young fellow broke in swiftly,

"Sims caught him in the hall, General. He is unarmed, but refuses to explain."

The general's stern dark eyes were upon my face.

"Hardly a spy, I think," he said quietly. "What is the explanation, sir? Are you the bearer of a message?"

I started to speak, but before the first uncertain word came to my lips, the girl swept forward, and stood between us.

"Let me explain," she cried swiftly. "This gentleman is a friend of Captain Le Gaire's, and was presented to me as Major Atherton, formerly on General Pemberton's staff--perhaps there may be some here who know him?"

She glanced inquiringly about on the faces of the group, and a stockily built infantry captain struck his open hand on the table.

"By Jove, that's it! Thought I recognized the face. How are you, Atherton?-- met you at Big Shanty."

Still puzzled, although evidently relieved, Beauregard remained motionless.

"But the uniform?" he questioned. "And how did you reach the hallway without being seen?"

Her eyes met mine in a rapid flash of understanding, a little nervous laugh drawing the general's attention.

"It is almost ridiculous," she exclaimed. "Major Atherton came through the lines with me last night. He was detailed on special service, for which purpose he donned that uniform. On meeting Captain Le Gaire here, and learning of your advance, it was no longer necessary for him to proceed at once, and, as he was very tired, he was persuaded to lie down in a room upstairs. Waking, he naturally came down into the hall, knowing nothing of your arrival. Have I correctly presented the case, Major Atherton?"

Her eyes challenged me, and I bowed.

"A perfectly clear statement."

"And a most charming advocate," added Beauregard. "We must find you some more appropriate garments, Major, but meanwhile there is room here at the table. Captain Bell, would you kindly move a little to the right. Now, Hughes, serve Major Atherton."

I do not recall ever feeling more awkwardly embarrassed than during the next few minutes. Not that the assembled officers lacked in courtesy, or failed to interest in light conversation. Led by the general they all endeavored to make me forget my strange position, and the unpleasant episode of arrest. Indeed, but for the presence of Miss Willifred in the room I imagine I should have been very much at ease, perfectly capable of doing my full share of entertaining. But with the girl standing silently in the shadow of the curtains, her eyes occasionally meeting mine, I felt a constant restraint which impelled me to answer almost in mono-syllables. She had openly defended me, saved me from arrest; without telling a direct falsehood she had, nevertheless, led these men into a grievous misunderstanding. Why had she done this? Through personal interest in me? Through some wild impulse of the moment? I could not even guess; only, I was assured of one thing: her secret motive involved no lack of loyalty to the cause of the South. Realizing this I dare not presume on her continued friendliness, dare not sit there and lie calmly, filling these men with false information, and permitting imagination to run rampant. Her eyes condemned that, and I felt the slightest indiscretion on my part would result in betrayal. Perhaps even then she regretted her hasty action, and sought some excuse for blurting out the truth. Fortunately conversation drifted into safe channels. Bell was full of reminiscences of Big Shanty, requiring on my part but brief acquiescence, and, after a very few personal questions by the others, sufficiently direct to demand reply, Beauregard asked me about the disposition of Johnston's forces, to which I was fortunately able to respond intelligently, giving him many details, sufficiently interesting, although of no great value. To his desire for information relative to Chambers' advance from the south, and the number of his troops, I was obliged to guess rather vaguely, but finally got away with a vivid description of Miss Hardy's night ride, which caused even the girl herself to laugh, and chime in with a word or two. With the officers the meal was nearly completed when I joined them, and it was therefore not long until the general, noting the others had finished, pushed back his own chair.

"We will adjourn to the parlor, gentlemen," he said genially, "I shall have other orders to despatch presently. When you finish, Major, I shall be glad to talk with you more at length; until then we leave you to the care of Miss Hardy."

They passed out, and as the door closed behind the last straggler, she came slowly across the room, and sat down in a chair opposite me, resting her flushed cheek on one hand.

"What made you do it?" I asked, impelled by a curiosity which could no longer be restrained.

"Oh, I don't know," and her lashes lifted, giving me one swift glimpse into the depths of her eyes. "A mere impulse when I first realized the danger of your position."

"Then it was for me?--because you cared?"

"Perhaps I would have done the same for any one--I am a woman."

"I can comprehend that, yes," I insisted, "but am not willing to believe mere sympathy would carry you so far. Was there not, back of all, a feeling almost of friendship?"

"I make no such acknowledgment. I spoke before I thought; before I even realized what my words meant. And you?--how came you there?"

I told her briefly, answering her questions without reserve, rejoicing in the interest she exhibited in my narrative, and eager to know at once how far I could still presume on her assistance. I wanted to get away, to escape from the web about me, but I could not understand this girl, or comprehend how far I dare venture on her good nature. Already I knew that some feeling--either of friendship or sympathy--had impelled her to save me from immediate betrayal, but would she go even further? Everything between us conspired to bewilder me as to her real purpose. Even as I concluded, it seemed to me her eyes hardened, and the expression of her face changed.

"That was extremely clever, Lieutenant Galesworth," she commented quietly. "I never knew the chimney touched that wall. Now what do you propose doing?"

"You must understand my only interest is in getting away as soon as possible. I am in constant danger here."

"Of course," nodding, her cheeks flushed. "And you also possess very important information. Because I have aided you to escape capture, do you conclude I am a fool?"

"Most assuredly not."

"Or a traitress to the South?"

"I could not think that."

"Then let us clearly understand each other once for all. I have saved you from capture, perhaps death. The reason I have done this need not be discussed; indeed I could not satisfactorily explain my action even to myself. But if the truth ever becomes known I shall be placed in a most embarrassing position. Surely you understand this, and you are a gentleman; I am sure of that. You are not going to carry that news to your camp. Before I should permit that to happen I would denounce you openly, and permit those men yonder to think evil of me. But I do not believe that course necessary. Instead, I am going to trust you as a gentleman--am going to accept your word of honor."

"My word? You mean my parole?"

"You may call it that--your pledge to remain in this house until I say you may go."

"But--"

"Stop! Lieutenant Galesworth, do you not owe this to me?"

I hesitated, fronting this direct question, looking straight across the table into her serious face, as she leaned toward me. What was my most important duty--that which I owed the Federal army, or that I owed to this girl? And then again--did I really have a choice? There was never a doubt in my mind as to what she would do if the occasion arose. I had tested her quality already, and fully comprehended the promise to turn me over to the Confederate guard was no idle threat. She would trust my word, but, failing that, would certainly do the other thing. There was no spirit of play in those eyes watching me.

"Apparently I possess no real choice," I answered, at last. "Either way I am a prisoner."

She smiled, evidently relieved at my tone.

"Yes--but have you no preference as to captors?"

"Put thus, hesitation ends; I accept the terms of parole."

"You mean it?"

"Yes."

She extended her hand across the table, and I as instantly grasped it, both almost unconscious of the actions.

"I ought to thank you," I began, but she broke in as quickly:

"No; please don't. I know I am not doing what I should. It is all so strange that

I am actually dazed; I have lost all understanding of myself. It is painful enough to realize that I yield to these impulses, without being constantly reminded that I fail in duty. I do not want your gratitude."

She had withdrawn her hand, and was upon her feet. I thought her whole form was trembling, her lips seeking to frame words.

"I certainly had no intention of hurting you."

"Oh, I know--I know that. You cannot understand. Only I am sorry you came--came into my life, for ever since it has been trouble. Now you must simply wait until I say go, and then you will go; won't you?"

"Yes--but not to forget."

She turned back toward me.

"You had better," coldly. "It will be useless to remember."

It was my turn to smile, for she could not play the part, her eyes veiling themselves behind the long lashes.

"Nevertheless I shall," I insisted warmly. "I find it not altogether unpleasant--being your prisoner."

CHAPTER XI
THE RETURN OF LE GAIRE

I shall endeavor to make it as little unpleasant as I can," she rejoined, "but will demand obedience. Right wheel; forward march. Yes, through the door; the surroundings are not unfamiliar."

It was the judge's library, where I had hidden before at the coming of Captain Le Gaire, and she paused in the doorway, glancing curiously about.

"Remember now, you are on parole, but restricted to this room."

"For how long?" She made an exceedingly pretty picture in that frame, and I was in no hurry to be deprived of it.

"Until--well, until I am pleased to release you. Don't scowl; I'm sure I'm trying to be nice, and I never was so polite to a Yankee before. Really this is the pleasantest room in the house; I have passed hours in here myself."

"Perhaps this afternoon--"

She shook her head violently, her eyes dancing with laughter.

"Certainly not; with all these Confederate officers here. Sometimes I think you are very conceited--I wonder if you are." And then before I could answer,--"What a handsome man Captain Bell is; and so delightful of him to remember having met you."

The witch was plainly enough laughing at me, but she chose a poor subject in Bell.

"And my sentence, then, is solitary confinement?"

"That is far better than you deserve. Those windows open on the porch, and there is a sentry there; the door leads to the rear of the house. I shall not even lock it, nor this. I leave you here upon your word of honor, Lieutenant Galesworth."

She was gone like the flutter of a bird, and I sank back upon the soft cushion of a library chair, still smiling, my eyes wandering curiously about the room. Then I got up, examined the windows and the rear door, and returned. Escape was dangerous, but possible, yet no serious thought of making such an attempt even occurred to me. For whatever unknown reason, the girl's quick wit had saved me from capture; I owed her every loyalty, and I had pledged her my word. That was enough. The more I turned the circumstances over in my mind the less I seemed to comprehend her motives, yet there could be no doubt she sought to serve me. A word from her to Le Gaire, or to Beauregard, would have ended my career instantly. Instead of speaking this word of betrayal she had deliberately placed herself in my defence, deceiving her own people. Why? Was there more than a mere impulse behind the action? Was she doing for me more than she would have done for another under similar circumstances? Was this act merely the result of womanly sympathy? For the life of me I could not determine. She was like two individuals, so swiftly did her moods change--one moment impressing me as a laughing girl, the next leaving me convinced she was a serious-minded woman. Just as I thought I knew, believed I understood, she would change into another personality, leaving me more bewildered than ever. Suddenly I thought again of Le Gaire, remembering his dark, handsome face, his manner of distinction, and there came to me mistily the words overheard during their unexpected meeting. She had called him "Gerald," and there had been other words exchanged--aye! he had even taunted her with their engagement, objecting to her being alone with me, and she had denied nothing. Somehow this suddenly recurring memory left me hot and angry. I disliked Le Gaire; from the very first moment of gazing into his dark, sneering eyes I had felt antagonism, a disposition to quarrel; but now something more potent rose between us--the girl. I was not blind to the man's attractions; I could easily understand how he could find way to a girl's heart. But a man can judge a man best, and every instinct of my nature warned me against this fellow. The very first sound of his voice had prejudiced me, and when I saw him I knew I was right--with him manliness was but veneer. And Billie! The name sounded soft, sweet, womanly now and I longed to speak it in her presence. Billie! I said it over and over again reverently, her face floating before me in memory, and then my lips closed in sudden determination: not without a fight, a hard fight, was this gray-jacket going to retain her, going to keep her from me.

It was a mad resolve; yet it was there, in my heart and upon my lips. I had come upon the field late, come in the wrong uniform, but I was sufficiently in earnest now. The girl liked me, served me, and she interested me as no other ever had. Her very moods, piquant, reserved, aroused my ambition, stimulated my purpose, and Le Gaire--the very thought of him was a thorn in the flesh. I have wondered since if I really loved her then; I do not know, but I dreamed of her, idealized her, my heart throbbing at every unusual sound without, hoping she might come again. I could hear the noise of the cavalry camp on the lawn, and the tramp of feet in the hall. Occasionally some voice sounded clear enough so I could distinguish the words. I opened the door leading into the dining-room, but that apartment was deserted. There was evidently nothing to do but wait, and I lay down on the couch between the windows, looking up at the green leaves shaking in the breeze. Fatigued with the labors of the previous night, before I realized the possibility I was fast asleep.

I must have remained there some hours, totally unconscious, for when I finally awoke it was nearly dark, the dusk so pronounced I could scarcely see across the room. Some noise without had aroused me, and I knew instantly what it was--the pounding of a horse's hoofs on gravel, the animal being furiously ridden. As I sat up, the horse was jerked to its haunches, and the rider swung from the saddle.

"Here, orderly, take the rein; quick now, damn you!" The words reached me clearly, but as I glanced out I saw only a dark form springing up the steps. Something familiar about the voice caused me to leap for the door, holding it sufficiently ajar so I could overhear what passed in the hall. There was a muttered word or two to the sentry, the newcomer insisting angrily on seeing Beauregard; then a woman's voice suddenly broke in with an exclamation of surprise.

"You back again! I am afraid you will have to wait to see the general unless your mission is of the utmost importance. He is lying down, and left orders he was not to be disturbed before nine o'clock."

"My mission is important enough," was the reply, "but perhaps, it can be attended to without him. Where can, we be alone, Billie?"

"Right in here," stepping through the doorway into the deeper dusk of the dining-room. "If you are hungry I can order a lunch."

"No," impatiently, "I have eaten twice to-day--what I want to know is what has become of that fellow who was here this morning?"

"Major Ather--"

"Oh, hell!" forgetting every pretence to gentility. "He was not Atherton at all, but a damned Yankee spy. Do you mean to say you didn't know it?"

I could see her straighten up, turning swiftly to face him. Whatever the shock of discovery may have been, indignation conquered, and her voice was cool, stinging.

"Captain Le Gaire, I am not in the habit of being sworn at, and will leave you to gain your information elsewhere."

She swept by him to the door, but, gasping with surprise, the man managed to call after her,

"Billie, don't go like that! I didn't mean to swear. It was jolted out of me, and I beg your pardon."

She halted on the threshold, glancing back evidently in hesitation.

"This is not the first time you have let your temper loose in my presence," she said slowly, "but it is the last. If you feel so little respect for me now, the future is not very encouraging."

"But, Billie, you don't understand!"

"I understand enough. However we will not discuss this matter any further at present. What was it you desired to know?"

"Where that fellow has gone!" instantly flaming up again. "He wasn't Atherton at all, but I'll swear he was the very picture of him; he would have fooled the devil."

"No doubt," almost indifferently. "How did you discover the deception?"

"By merest accident. Happened to mention meeting him to old Trevor, and he was up in arms in a minute. Seems Atherton married his niece, and the fellow here couldn't be the major, for he was shot in a skirmish three weeks ago, and has been in the hospital at Athens ever since. He's there now; rode over to Pemberton's headquarters to make sure, and met Gregory, Chief-of-Staff. He saw Atherton Saturday, and he wasn't able to sit up yet. The fellow here was a Yank--and you didn't know it?"

"I very naturally supposed he was what he represented himself to be," she replied, coming back into the room. "And when you recognized him as an old acquaintance I never gave the matter another thought."

"But he came through the lines with you," bewildered and doubtful.

"The best of reasons why I should never have suspected him of being a Yankee. He was very pleasant and gentlemanly."

"Oh, indeed! all a man has to do is smile and say nice things to get you women on his side."

"Then why don't you try it? You are certainly disagreeable enough to-day."

"Perhaps I am," endeavoring to laugh. "But if I could get my hands on that Yank I'd be in far better humor. Where is he?"

"The last time I saw him," with provoking coolness, "he was at dinner with General Beauregard and staff."

"At dinner! Here! Good God! he must have nerve. How did it happen?"

"Through my introduction originally, and then later he was recognized by Captain Bell."

Le Gaire sank down into a chair, glaring at the girl's dim, white-robed figure, his teeth savagely clicking in an effort to keep from swearing. As though to exasperate him yet more she laughed.

"I fail to see the fun," he snarled impatiently. "This is no joke, let me tell you, and we'll both find it out if Beauregard ever learns the truth. What did they talk about?"

"Army matters mostly. The general wished information regarding the movement of Johnston's and Chambers' forces, and Major Atherton--"

"Don't call the fellow that!"

"Then what shall I call him?"

He struck his fist on the table, almost devoid of the power of speech.

"I don't care, only not that. I tell you he's not Atherton, but a sneaking Yankee spy."

"Why, he was in full uniform!"

"He'll hang, just the same, if we get him. Now see here--did Beauregard let out any facts?"

She drew a quick breath, one hand on her breast, and it seemed to me her voice trembled.

"He talked as he would to one of his own officers. They discussed the plans of operation quite freely among themselves."

Le Gaire groaned, his elbows on the table, his head in his hands. She remained motionless, looking at him. Suddenly he glanced up.

"I'll be hanged if I understand you, Billie," he exclaimed. "Don't you care, or don't you realize what this means? That fellow has got all our plans, and he's got safely away with them too, I suppose."

She nodded, as he paused an instant.

"Before morning they'll be over there," with a wave of the hand, "and our move checkmated. Whose fault is it? Yours and mine. It's enough to drive a man crazy, and you stand there and laugh."

"I am not laughing."

"Well, you were a minute ago. Do you even suspect who the fellow is?"

"You said he was Major Ath--"

"Oh, hell!" springing to his feet, with sword rattling, and hands clinched. "I won't stand this, not even from you. You're hiding something; what is it? Is this Yank anything to you?"

"Absolutely nothing, Captain Le Gaire. Take your hand from my arm, please. Now I will trouble you to stop this controversy. I am not indifferent, but I refuse to be bullied, and sworn at. If you are so wild to capture this spy why don't you make the rounds of the pickets instead of remaining here and quarrelling with me? The man is not hiding behind my skirts. I will bid you good-night."

She was gone before he could even fling out a hand to stop her. A moment he raged between table and wall; then flung out the door and down the steps, calling for his horse.

CHAPTER XII
AN ATTEMPT AT ESCAPE

The seriousness of my situation was clearly apparent, yet what could I do in order to save myself? My word was pledged, and it was evident the girl had no intention of betraying my presence. But would she come to me? Would she give me the opportunity of escape? It must be accomplished now if at all, before Le Gaire returned, or had time to complete his round of the pickets. Every instant of delay robbed me of a chance--and my life hung in the balance. There was little doubt as to that; I could advance no military reason for being treated other than as a spy, and my fate would be the short shift meted out to such over the drum-head. All this swept through my brain as I listened to the hoofs of Le Gaire's horse pound the gravel outside, the sound dying away in the distance. The sentinel marched slowly past the window, his figure silhouetted against the red glow of a camp-fire inside the gate. Then, without a warning sound, the door was pushed ajar, and the girl slipped silently through. The distant reflection of the fire barely served to reveal her face, and outline her figure. She was breathing heavily and trembling with excitement, her voice barely audible.

"You--you heard what was said in there?" she asked, eager to gain time. "You know Captain Le Gaire has returned?"

"Yes," thinking to calm her by an appearance of coolness. "He seems to be a most blood-thirsty individual."

"He was angry at being deceived. No one can blame him, but I simply had to tantalize him in order to get him away."

"Was that it? Do you mean so you might come here to me?"

"Why, of course. I had promised you. Do you think I would demean myself by lying--to a Yank? Besides," her voice faltered, "you would have kept your parole, and--and--"

"Waited here to be hung, probably," I broke in, "as that ceremony appears to be part of the programme. My only hope was that you might possibly object to this item of entertainment."

"Don't laugh," soberly. "There is no fun in it for me."

"Then you would show mercy even to a Yankee spy?"

"I am not sure of that. I am a Rebel, but that has no serious weight now. You are not a spy; if you have acted as one, it has been more through my fault than your own. Besides you are my prisoner, and if I should permit you to fall into the hands of those men, to be condemned to death, the memory would haunt me forever. I am not that kind, Lieutenant Galesworth. I don't want your gratitude; I would rather fight you than help you. I want you to understand this first of all."

"I do, Miss Hardy; you simply perform a duty."

"Yes; I--I keep my word."

"But, after all, isn't it a little easier because--you like me?"

She drew in her breath so quickly it was almost a sob, the swift, unexpected question disarming her in an instant. It was no longer the tiger cat, but the woman who gasped out a surprised response.

"No; oh, no! that is what makes it harder."

"Harder to aid me?"

"To see you unjustly condemned, and--and to realize that perhaps I am disloyal to my country."

Something about these simple words of confession, wrung from her lips by my insistence, held me silent. I failed to realize then the full significance of this acknowledgment, and she gave me no opportunity.

"This is ungenerous," she broke in quickly. "I do feel friendly toward you; surely I need not be ashamed of this, even though our interests are unlike, our causes opposed. Everything has conspired to make us friends. But you must not presume, or take advantage of my position. Now listen--I am here for one purpose: to give you an opportunity of escape. After that we are strangers; do you accept my terms?"

"You offer no others?"

"None."

"Then I accept--until Fate intervenes."

"You believe in Fate?"

"When aided by human persistence, yes; I intend to represent that goddess."

She drew back a step, her hand on the door.

"You almost make me regret my effort," reproachfully. "However I warn you the goddess this time shall play you false. But we waste moments in talk. Here is your revolver, Lieutenant; now come with me."

She thrust the butt into my hand, and crossed the room to the door opening out into the back yard. An instant she peered forth into the night; then turned her face back toward me.

"Take my place here," she whispered. "See that line of shadow yonder--it is the grape arbor. I am going to steal along to the end of the house where I can watch the sentinel. The instant I signal make for that arbor, and lie quiet until I come."

I watched the dim outline of her form. She was actually doing all this for me-- for me! She was running this great risk, smothering her own conscience--for me! I could not doubt this as a truth; I had probed deeply enough to be assured there was personal interest, friendliness, inspiring the sacrifice. She would never have lifted a hand to save a Yankee spy; all her sympathy was with the Confederacy. Yet she was risking all--her reputation, her life--to save me! The knowledge seemed to send fire through my veins, my heart throbbed fiercely. Oh, she could dissemble, could pretend all this was merely duty, could rage against herself and me, but nevertheless I understood--she was doing it for me! I knew, and she should know--yes, this very night, out yonder in the shadows, when we were alone together I would make her realize what it all meant. Le Gaire? What cared I for Le Gaire! This was Love and War combined, and all is fair in either. Besides, it was the girl who counted, who must say the final word--why should I hesitate for the sake of Le Gaire? Let him fight for himself; surely the prize was worth the battle.

Her hand waved; I could catch the glimmer of the white sleeve, and recognized it as a signal. With a dozen steps I was at the entrance to the arbor, crouching down low in the shadows. As noiseless as a ghost she sped across the open space, and joined me. I could feel her form tremble as I touched her, and she caught my arm with both hands, her face turned backward.

"They are relieving guard," she faltered, "and will come past here next, for there is a sentry on the opposite side. We must get farther down under the vines."

I drew her forward, for she clung to me strangely, as though all the courage and strength had suddenly deserted her.

"There are no guards down here?"

"No."

"Nor at the stables?"

"I cannot tell; I was afraid to ask."

The arbor ended some thirty feet from the stables, with a low, vine-covered fence between. There have been darker nights, yet I could distinguish merely the dim outlines. Still feeling her clasp on my arm I came to a halt, startled into absolute silence by the approach of the relief guard. The sturdy tramp of feet, and the slight tinkle of bayonets against canteens, told plainly the fellows had turned our way, although, crouched where we were, we could at first see nothing. I drew my revolver, my other hand clasping hers, and waited breathlessly. The little squad came trudging down the opposite side of the fence, only the upper part of their bodies dimly visible against the slightly lighter background of the sky. I made out the officer in command, and four men, then they wheeled into the shadow of the stables, and the sentinel stationed there challenged. There was a reply, the sound of a musket brought sharply to the shoulder, a gruff, indistinguishable order, and then again the tramp of feet, dying away in the distance. Every movement, and word, told the story, revealed the situation. I turned my eyes back to the girl's face, questioningly, barely able to perceive its whiteness.

"They have a guard there," I whispered, my lips close to her ear. "Is there no other way out?"

"Yes, on foot, but I supposed you would need a horse."

"And there are horses there?"

"I do not know about any others; I understand the judge has lost all his, but the one Captain Le Gaire left for you this morning was taken there."

"You know the situation,"--the cavalryman's eagerness for a mount overcoming all thought of danger,--"how best to get in."

"Yes; I went out there with Tom when the judge told him to put up the horse,--I wanted to see how my pony was getting along. The door is on that side to the east, just around the corner. It is closed by a wooden button. The pony is in the first stall, and the horse in the second; the saddle and bridle were hung on a peg behind," she said this clearly, anxious to make me understand, but then, as the other thought came to her, her voice broke. "But, Lieutenant Galesworth, you--you cannot get the horse with the guard there!"

My clasp closed more tightly on her fingers, my resolve hardening.

"He's only a man, perhaps sleepy and careless, while I am wide awake. One must be willing to assume risk in war. With the horse under me I have a chance, while on foot I should probably be caught before daylight. Don't worry; this is not my first attempt."

"You--you mean to try?"

"Certainly; I should be a poor specimen if I did not. But I am going to say good-bye to you first, and then lie here quietly until you are safely in the house."

She drew in a quick breath, her face lifting.

"The house! I am going to remain here."

"But the risk you run, and you can be of no help."

"Oh, don't argue!" impatiently. "There is no more risk of my discovery here than there. I want to know what happens; I would rather face anything than suspense. Lieutenant Galesworth, I have always had my way, and I shall now."

Down in my heart I rejoiced at her decision, but all I said was:

"Very well, Miss Willifred, it makes me feel like a knight going forth to battle under the eyes of his lady." The slight flutter of a ribbon at her throat caught my eye, and I touched it with my finger. "May I wear this in token of your good wishes?"

"You--you are not going to kill any one?"

"Not if it can possibly be avoided."

She was silent a moment, so still I could hear her breathing; then her hands undid the ribbon knot, and she held it toward me.

"I--I do wish you well," she said softly. "I--don't know why, but I do."

CHAPTER XIII
I MEET LE GAIRE

My hand touching her own seemed to work a sudden transformation. She was instantly upon her feet facing me, drawing back a little against the grape arbor.

"Do not take my words so seriously," she exclaimed. "I am excited, almost hysterical to-night. To-morrow I shall regret much I have done and said. But you must go, Lieutenant; every moment of delay adds to your peril and mine. No; please do not touch me or speak to me again; only listen--there is a bridle path leading directly from the farther corner of the stable to the river; a gate will let you out of the orchard lot; now go!"

"You will not even shake hands?" "I--I--yes, of course, I will do that." Our fingers clasped, and we stood face to face, our eyes meeting through the darkness. The thrill of contact, the wild hope that this girl really cared unusually for me, became almost overpowering. I longed to crush her in my arms, to pour into her ears the passionate words that burned on my lips. I forgot everything except her presence, her nearness, the soft pressure of her hand.

"Billie! Billie!"

"No! No!" and she had instantly released herself. "You forget yourself; you forget my position. Now it is good-bye."

"You positively mean this?"

"I do. I am a soldier's daughter, Lieutenant Galesworth, and I am trusting you to act as a soldier and a gentleman."

Under the cloak of darkness my face burned, feeling the reproof of this appeal, realizing that I merited the sting. For the instant my actions, my presumption, seemed contemptible. I had taken advantage of her kindness, her sympathy, her trust, and openly misconstrued womanly friendliness into a stronger emotion. The rebuke was perfectly just; I could not even find words of apology, but turned away silently. And she made no effort to stay me, either by word or motion.

I had crept forward as far as the low fence before the numbness left me, before I came back to full comprehension of my situation, and the serious work confronting me. Then the soldier spirit reawoke into alert action, my thought intent upon escape, my nerves steadying down for the coming trial. I recall glancing back, imagining I saw the white glimmer of her dress against the dark shrubbery, and then I resolutely drove all memory of her from my mind, concentrating every instinct to the one immediate purpose of overcoming the stable guard. This was not altogether new work to one inured as a scout, but sufficiently serious to call forth every precaution. Cautiously I crept along the fence until I discovered an opening large enough to crawl through, scarcely rustling the concealing leaves, and resting flat on the opposite side while I surveyed the prospect. I was not far now from the south wall of the stable, which loomed black and shapeless against the sky. Not a movement revealed the whereabouts of the guard, and, with the girl's description to guide me, I concluded the fellow would be stationed at the other extremity of the building. Convinced as to this probability I dragged my body slowly forward until I could touch the log wall. I could see better now, being myself in the denser shadow, and knew the passage was clear to the corner.

Assured of this I rose to my feet, revolver in hand, and pressing close against the side of the building, advanced quickly and silently. At the corner I peered about, scarcely daring to breathe, but with heart pounding, as I caught sight of the fellow, not over three feet distant. He was seated on an overturned bucket, his back toward me, both hands clasping a musket, his head bent slightly forward. He seemed listening to some noise in the distance, totally unconscious of my approach. The man's fingers were nowhere near the trigger of his gun, and my straining eyes could perceive no sign of any other weapon. This had to be silent work--silent and swift. With one step forward I had my revolver pressed hard against his cheek, my other hand crushing his fingers to the musket.

"Keep quiet, man! Not a move! I'll blow your head off if you lift a hand!"

"Oh! Good God!"

He was but little more than a boy; I could see his face now under the slouch hat, and I had already frightened the life half out of him.

"Drop your gun! Now stand up!" He obeyed like an automaton, his brain seemingly paralyzed. There was nothing to fear from this fellow, yet I knew better than to become careless--terror has been known to drive men crazy. I caught him by the collar, whirling him about, my Colt still at his ear.

"Go straight to the stable door, son!"

"Who--who are you? W--what do you want?"

"Don't stop to ask questions--you trot, unless you want to get hurt. Do you hear me?--the stable door! That's it; now undo the button, open the door, and go inside."

I held him like a vice, assured his belt contained no weapons, and thrust him forward against the wall. He was so helpless in my grasp that it was like handling a child.

"Feel along there--higher up--and tell me what you find. Well, what is it?"

"A--a bridle," his voice barely audible.

"Halter strap on it?"

"Yes, sir."

"Take it off, and hand it back here. Now go on, and feel the next stake."

"There's a blanket, and--and a rope halter."

"Good! give me that; now, son, put both hands back here, cross the wrists. Come, stand up to it; this is better than getting killed, isn't it? Now here is a nice soft spot to lie on, and I guess you'll remain there for a while. Do you want me to gag you, or will you keep still?"

"I'll--I'll keep still!"

"Well, be sure you do; your life isn't worth a picayune if you raise any row."

I arose to my feet, confident the boy had been safely disposed of, and feeling blindly around in the darkness, seeking to locate the stalls. At that instant a horse neighed outside; then I heard the sound of hoofs pounding on soft soil. Whoever the fellow was, he was almost there--coming up at a trot, just back of the stables. My brain worked in a flash--there was but once chance to stave off discovery. With a bound I was beside the boy, and had jerked off his hat, jamming it down on my own head, as I muttered in his ear, "One word from you now, and you'll never speak again--don't take the chance!"

I leaped for the door, and grasped the musket, barely straightening up, as the oncoming horseman swung around the corner. It was a desperate chance, yet in this darkness he could scarcely distinguish color of uniform or shape of features. It might work; it was worth trying. I saw the dim outlines of horse and rider in a red glow, as though the latter held a cigar between his lips; then I swung forward my gun.

"Halt! who comes?"

Startled by the sudden challenge, the horse reared to the sharp jerk at the reins, the man uttering an oath as he struggled to control the beast.

"Hell! What's this?"

"A sentry post; answer up, or I'll call the guard--who are you?"

"An officer on special service." "Dismount, and give the word."

He swung reluctantly down, growling, yet with sufficient respect for my cocked musket to be fairly civil, and stepped up against the lowered barrel, his horse's rein in hand.

"Atlanta," he whispered.

My gun snapped back to a carry, my only thought an intense anxiety to have him off as quickly as possible.

"Pass officer on special service."

He paused, puffing at his cigar.

"What's the best way to the house, sentry?" he asked with apparent carelessness, "along the fence there?"

"The road runs this side, you can't miss it," I replied civilly enough, but stepping back so as to increase our distance.

"Ah, yes--thanks."

He flipped the ash from his cigar, drawing at the stub so fiercely the red glow reflected directly into my eyes. He stared a moment, then turned, and thrust a foot into the stirrup.

"I've seen you somewhere before, my man."

"I was at the gate when you came through just before dark."

"Oh, yes," he replied, apparently satisfied, and swung up lightly into the saddle. "So you recognize me, then?"

"Captain Le Gaire, is it not? The sergeant said so."

He believed he had me completely deceived, that I entertained no suspicion he had also recognized me, and that therefore he could play me a sharp trick. I was not sure, for the man acted his part rarely well, only that I knew it was not in Le Gaire's nature to be so excessively polite. What was his game, I wondered, gripping my musket with both hands, my eyes following his every motion. Would he venture an attack alone, or ride on and report me to the guard? I had little enough time in which to speculate. He gathered up the reins in one hand, his horse cavorting; he had probably found somewhere a fresh mount. I stepped aside, but the animal still faced me, and with high-flung head partially concealed his rider. Suddenly the latter dug in his spurs, and the beast leaped straight at me, front hoofs pawing the air. I escaped as by a hair's breadth, one iron shoe fairly grazing my shoulder, but, with the same movement, I swung the clubbed musket. He had no time to dodge; there was a thud as it struck, a smothered cry, and the saddle was empty, a revolver flipping into the air, as the man went plunging over. I sprang to the horse's bit, the frightened animal dragging me nearly to the fence before I conquered him. But I dare not let go--once free he would join the troop horses, his riderless saddle sure to alarm the guards. With lacerated hands, and shirt torn into shreds, I held on, jerked and bruised by the mad struggle, until the fellow stood trembling. Using the bridle rein for a halter strap I tied him to the fence, and, sore all over and breathing hard from exertion, went back to discover what had become of Le Gaire.

The excitement of encounter had, for the instant, banished all recollection of the young woman hidden beneath the shadow of the grape arbor. My entire mind had concentrated on the fight, which, even now, might not be ended. I knew I had struck the fellow hard with the full, wide swing of the musket stock; I had both felt and heard the blow, and the impact had hurled him clear from the horse. Beyond doubt he was helpless, badly hurt perhaps, and there suddenly came to me a fear lest I had actually killed him. I had struck fiercely, impelled by the instinct to save myself, but I had had no desire to take the man's life. I had no reason to like Le Gaire; I believed him a bully, a disagreeable, boasting cur, but he was something to Willifred Hardy, and I could not afford to have his blood on my hands. I thought of her then, casting a swift glance back toward the shadows beyond the fence, and then went straight toward where the fellow lay, afraid to learn the truth, yet even more intensely afraid to again meet her without knowing. He had evidently fallen upon his shoulder, and still lay in a huddled heap. I had to straighten out his form before I was able to decide whether he was living or dead. I bent down, undoing his jacket, and placed my ear to his heart. It beat plainly enough, almost regularly--the man was alive; I doubted if he were even seriously injured. This discovery was such a relief that I muttered a "Thank God," and began rubbing his chest as though in effort to restore the fellow to consciousness. Then my senses came back, my realization of the situation. Let Le Gaire lie where he was; others would take care of him soon enough. I must get away; I could use his horse, pretend to be him, if necessary, and before daylight be safely across the river. I sought along the ground until I found the dropped revolver, thrust it into my belt, and ran over to where the horse was tied.

I had loosened the rein, my hand on the pommel, when the thought came that I must tell her first before I rode away. Even though the delay was a risk to us both, yet she must understand the truth, be informed of Le Gaire's condition, and why I had attacked him. At the instant this last seemed more important than all else. It would require but a moment, and then I could go, confident the man's injury would be no additional barrier between us, would never cause her to suspect that I had attacked him wantonly, actuated by personal motives. He might try to make her think so, if he were the kind I believed, his mind already suspicious of her interest in me. Her very sympathy for his wounds would make her easily influenced; this natural sympathy must not be inflamed by doubt of my motives and the thought that I had deliberately sought the man's life. It may have been two rods between the fence and the grape arbor, and I called to her softly.

CHAPTER XIV
ACROSS THE RIVER

She came toward me swiftly, slipping through the night like a shadow, instantly recognizing my voice.

"You--you are not hurt, Lieutenant Galesworth?" she asked, her voice trembling.

"No; merely bruised, and shaken up--the horse did that."

"Oh; was it you who had that struggle with the horse? I--I thought he would surely kill the man."

"The poor fellow was frightened," and I stroked his neck softly, "and certainly gave me a hard tussle. But that's all over now. I want to explain what has happened before I leave."

"Yes."

"I owe you that, do I not, wearing your colors?"

I could not perceive the expression of her face, but the tone of her voice was not altogether encouraging.

"They were but expressive of my best wishes; of course I wished you to succeed."

"I wonder--will you continue your good wishes after hearing my story?"

"What do you mean? You have not killed any one?"

"No; but I have hurt one who seems to have some claim upon you."

She drew in her breath quickly, clasping her hands.

"Who?--tell me! Can you mean Captain Le Gaire?"

"I regret to say 'yes'; this was his horse. Now don't blame me until you hear the whole story. I will tell it all in very few words, and then go."

"But--but you are sure he is not seriously hurt?"

"He may have a rib or collar-bone broken, and is still unconscious; nothing that will keep him out of mischief long. I wanted to tell you all about the affair myself--I don't trust Le Gaire."

"Why say that to me?"

"Because I must. If I understand the man the very first thing he will do will be to poison your mind against me--"

"He? Why?"

"Miss Hardy," I said soberly, "what use is there for us to play at cross-purposes? You realize that Captain Le Gaire suspects that you have an interest in me, that you have helped in my escape. He doesn't like me any the better for that. Men will do strange things when they are in love--such men as Le Gaire. Do you suppose I intend permitting him to thus influence you against me, when I am where I cannot defend myself?"

"But he would never do that; I am sure, he never would."

"Possibly not, but I prefer you should have my version to compare with what he may say. We have met strangely, in a manner which could only happen in time of war, and one day and two nights of adventure together have already made us better acquainted than would a year of ordinary social intercourse. I value your good wishes, and feel more gratitude than words can express. I am not going away leaving you to think me unworthy. I will tell you this exactly as it occurred, and you are to believe me, no matter what is said later."

My earnestness made an impression and as I paused her lips parted.

"Yes--I am going to believe you."

"I felt sure you would. Now listen, for I must be away, and Le Gaire attended to."

I told it simply, clearly, making no attempt except to bring out the important facts, realizing that her own imagination would supply the details. She clung to the fence, our eyes meeting as I spoke swiftly, making no comment until I concluded.

"Could I have done otherwise?"

"No; you are not to be blamed, but I am so sorry it happened to be Captain Le Gaire."

"You mean because--"

"He has been much to me," she interrupted, "perhaps still is, although--" she paused suddenly, catching her breath,--"yet this can make no difference."

"But it does."

She remained silent, and, I thought, drew slightly back.

"You do not wonder?" I asked, unable to restrain myself, "you do not ask why? May I not tell you?"

"I prefer you should not," very quietly. "I am not foolish enough to pretend that I do not understand. We are going to part now, and you will forget."

"Is it then so easy for you?"

"I need not confess, only I see how utterly foolish all this is. The conditions bringing us together in a few hours of intimacy have been romantic, and, perhaps, it is not strange that you should feel an interest in me. I--I hope you do, for I shall certainly always feel most kindly toward you, Lieutenant Galesworth. We are going to part as friends, are we not? You will remember me as a little Rebel who served you once, even against her conscience, and I will continue to think of you as a brave soldier and courteous gentleman. Isn't that worth while? Isn't it even better than dreaming an impossible dream?"

"But why impossible?"

"Surely you know."

"You mean Le Gaire?"

"I mean everything. Captain Le Gaire may be partially responsible, but there is much besides. Need we discuss this further?"

I should have hesitated, but I simply could not consent to be dismissed thus completely. Through the obscuring mist of the night I saw her face dimly, and it fascinated me. Behind the quiet decision of her voice there was a tremulousness which yielded courage. I could not part with her like this.

"Billie," I said, and she started at the familiarity of the name, "I am going to risk even your good opinion rather than leave in doubt. Don't treat me like a boy." Her hand was upon the fence, and I placed both of my own upon it. "Be honest with me. Forget the uniform, this sectional war, and let us simply be man and woman--can you not?"

She did not answer, her hand yet held in mine, so startled by my sudden outburst as to be helpless.

"I must know," I went on heedlessly, the very touch of her flesh making me reckless. Our position, the danger of the night, all vanished, and I saw only the whiteness of her face. Perhaps, had I been able to read her eyes, their expression might have served to curb my tongue, but nothing else could have held me silent. "I am going away, going into the lines of a hostile army; I may not reach there alive, and, if I do, I may fall in the first battle. I must tell you the truth first--I must. Don't call it foolish, for it is not. Dear, I may be a Yankee, but I am also a man, and I--"

"Oh, stop! please stop!" her fingers clasping me, her form closer. "I can not--I will not permit you to say this. I have no right. You have made me disloyal to my country; you shall not make me disloyal to all else. If I should listen I would have no self-respect left. For my sake be still, and go."

"But I know you are not indifferent; you cannot conceal the truth."

"Then be content, be satisfied, be generous."

"If you will only say one thing."

"What?"

"That I may come to you--after the war."

She stood a moment motionless, and then withdrew her hand.

"That would be equivalent to a hope which I cannot give," she returned soberly. "When the war ends I shall probably no longer be Willifred Hardy." My heart beat like a trip-hammer; I could hear it in the silence.

"The man yonder?"

She bent her head.

"You will not," my voice firm with swift conviction. "If that is all, I am not afraid. If you loved him would you be standing here even to say a word of farewell? Whatever pledge may be between you, on your part it is not love. You cannot deny this--not to me! Yes, and you are already beginning to know him. Remember, I have had to listen to some conversation between you--I know his style. Ah, yes, I will go, because I dare not keep you out here longer, but, if God lets me live, I am going to find you again. Yes, I am; don't doubt that, little girl. I could stand back for a real man, but not for Le Gaire; that's not in human nature. See, I have your ribbon yet, and am going to wear it."

"Without my permission?"

I reached out my arm and drew her gently against the fence barrier, so close I could look down into her eyes, gazing up into mine startled by the sudden movement.

"Lip permission, yes--I prefer to read consent elsewhere."

"And do you?"

"I shall believe I do. See, here is the ribbon; will you take it?"

"Of course not. Why should I care if you have that? It has no value to me. But I will not stay and talk longer. Let me go, Lieutenant! yes, you must. What shall I do to help--to help Gerald?"

"Go straight into the house, and report to the guard. You were walking in the garden for a breath of air, and overheard the struggle. They will find him. Goodbye, Billie."

I held out my hand, and she extended her own without a moment's hesitation.

"Good-bye," she said. "Shall I not wait here a few moments until you are across the road?"

I touched my lips to her fingers.

"What, with Gerald lying there!" happily. "Oh, Billie, are you so anxious as that for me to get safely away?"

"I--I am certainly not anxious to have you caught--not now. But you are almost impertinent; indeed you are. I cannot say a word you do not misinterpret. Please do not attempt to tease me; let us part friends."

The tone in which she said this meant far more than the mere words; I had ventured enough, and recognized the limitation to her patience. However strong her interest in me might already be, no acknowledgment was probable under present circumstances. I would but waste time, perhaps seriously injure my standing with her, were I to continue. The future must be left to work out its own miracle--to reveal her heart, and to prove the worthlessness of Le Gaire. For me to linger longer, holding her there in constant peril of discovery, would be simply madness.

I led the horse back, past where the disabled Confederate lay, pausing an instant to look down on the dim figure. He groaned, and turned partially over on one side, evidence that consciousness was returning. The man was not badly hurt, and I felt no deep regret at his condition. I could distinguish the narrow bridle path by my feet, and knew I would be less conspicuous out of the saddle. However, nothing opposed our progress, and we even succeeded in crossing the road without being observed. Here a long slope, rutted, and partially covered with low bushes, led directly down to the river, and we pushed through the tangle, keeping well hidden. Once on the bank of the stream all above was concealed from view, but I listened in vain for any sound indicative of pursuit. The night was mysteriously still, unbroken, even the air motionless. Obsessed now by the one controlling impulse to get away safely, I drove the horse into the water, and as he reached swimming depth, grasped a stirrup leather, and compelled him to strike out for the opposite shore. It was not a hard struggle, nor were we long at it, although the current was swift enough to bear us down a hundred feet, or more, before we struck bottom, wading out at the mouth of a small creek, the low banks offering some slight concealment. I looked back through the darkness, across the dim water, and up the shrouded hill on the opposite side. Lights were winking here and there like fire-flies. I stared at them, light-hearted, confident I had every advantage; then I patted the horse, and adjusted the stirrups.

"She waited until we were safe across, old fellow," I said, too pleased to remain still. "Now we'll ride for it."

He turned his head, and rubbed his nose along my arm. The next moment I was in the saddle, spurring him up the bank.

CHAPTER XV
I MEET AN EX-SLAVE

In this narrative of adventure it would but waste the reader's time to indulge in any extended description of military movements. The interest of my story centres around individuals rather than the great events of history, and I will touch these but briefly, so as to make the surrounding conditions sufficiently clear. It was noon the following day when I reached headquarters with my report, only to find that rumors of the combined movements of Johnston's and Beauregard's forces had already penetrated our lines. I could merely add details to the information previously received. The result was the immediate strengthening of our position to repel any possible attack. None occurred however, except desultory skirmishing. Later we learned the reason to be the failure of Chambers to appear, his march having been retarded by heavy rains.

At the end of this period of waiting our army was well prepared for action, the troops eager to test the strength of the enemy. Impatient of delay, and suspecting the probable cause of the Confederate quietness, we finally took the aggressive, determined to regain our former position south of the river. An. early morning attack won us the bridge and the town beyond, while heavy forces rushed the available fords, and after some severe fighting, obtained foothold on the opposite bank. Hastily throwing up intrenchments these advance troops succeeded in repulsing two charges before nightfall. This brought an end to hostilities. During the hours of darkness reinforcements were hurried across the stream. By dawn the opposing forces were about evenly mated, and every man in either line knew a battle was imminent.

In this emergency the need of every soldier was felt, and I was returned to my regiment for duty. We were the first to trot over the recaptured bridge, and through the deserted streets of the village. Impelled by a curiosity which could not be resisted I wheeled my horse and rode up the gravelled driveway to Judge Moran's door, but to my vigorous knocking there was no response. The shades were drawn at the windows, the house silent, and yet I felt convinced the old partisan was within, watching from some point of vantage. Yet if I believed this, the same silence and refusal to respond also served to convince me that Miss Hardy was no longer there. She was a vastly different type, and would exhibit interest even in the coming of the enemy. Ay! and she would have seen me, and not for one moment could I be made to believe that she would treat me with contempt.

I rode back slowly to rejoin the column of horsemen, glancing over my shoulder at the house, my mind busily occupied with the stirring events which had transpired there. She had gone with the Confederate troops, and had probably already been safely returned to her own home. Moran might have departed also, but more likely he remained to look after his property. I wondered who was her escort for the long ride--would it be Captain Le Gaire, sufficiently recovered from his injuries for this service, yet scarcely capable of active military duty? If so, he was with her still, a guest at "The Gables," sufficiently an invalid to be interesting, and to require attention, but with tongue in good repair. I was glad I had told my story first; the gentleman would experience some difficulty in changing Miss Willifred's opinion of the affair.

The gray dust cloud hung about us, almost obscuring the files of plodding troopers; to right and left the flankers showed dark against the green of the fields, and far in front an occasional carbine barked as some suspicious scout fired at a skulking figure. Once this would have been full of interest, but now it was mere routine, the sturdy veterans of the Ninth riding soberly forward, choked with dust, their hats drawn low over their eyes, wearied by a long night in the saddle. I glanced proudly down those ranks of fighting men, glad to be with them once again, but my thought drifted back to Billie, for this was the road we had travelled together. It seemed a long while ago, and much might happen before we should meet again, if ever we did. I might be killed in battle, or Le Gaire might insist upon an immediate marriage. This last was what I most feared, for I believed that if this could only be sufficiently delayed, she would learn to know the man better, and refuse to be sacrificed. The engagement rather mystified me, for it was clear enough no blind love on her part was responsible for its existence; at least she had begun to perceive his shallowness, and resented his attempt at bullying. I even began to believe that some one else had now come into her life, whose memory would serve to increase the feeling of dissatisfaction. Le Gaire was not the kind that wears well--he could not improve upon acquaintance; and, while I was no connoisseur of women, yet I could not persuade myself that her nature was patient enough not to revolt against his pretensions. I was no egotist, no lady-killer, but I recognized now that I loved this girl, and had read in her eyes the message of hope. Mine was, at least, a fighting chance, and fighting was my trade. I liked it better so, finding the lady more alluring because of the barrier between us, the zest of combat quickening my desire. Already I began to plan meeting her again, now that the campaign had turned our faces southward. Back beyond those wooded hills some freak of fate must lead me right, some swirl of fortune afford me opportunity. I was of the school of Hope, and Love yielded courage.

I looked back down the long hill, so silent and deserted that gray morning when we were driving together, but now dark with the solid masses of marching troops. It was a stirring scene to soldier eyes, knowing these men were pressing sternly on to battle. They seemed like a confused, disorganized mob, filling the narrow road, and streaming out through the fields; yet I could read the meaning of each detached movement, as cavalry, artillery, infantry, staff and wagon trains, met and separated, swinging into assigned positions, or making swift detour. Hoarse voices shouted; bugles pealed; there was the rumble of wheels, the pounding of hoofs, the tramp of feet, and over all the cloud of dust, through which the sun shone redly. The intense vividness of the picture gave me a new memory of war. Suddenly a battery of artillery, out of sight on the distant crest, opened fire, the shrieking shells plunging down into the ploughed field at our left, and casting the soft dirt high in air. Our advance spread wide into skirmish line, the black dots representing men flitting up the steep side of the hill, white spirals of smoke evidencing their musket fire. Behind them was a grim mass of infantry, silent and ominous, swinging forward like a huge snake. The men of the Ninth straightened up, their eyes glowing, but it was soon over with--the snake uncoiled, flinging a tail gleaming with steel over the ridge, and the troopers sank back wearily into their saddles.

As I turned again to glance over my shoulder I noticed a man riding at the right of the second file. His face was new to me, and so peculiar was it that I continued to stare, unable to determine whether the fellow was white or colored. He was in private's uniform, but carried no arms, and for head covering, instead of the hat worn by the Ninth, had an infantry cap perched jauntily on his curly black hair. But his face was clear, and his cheeks rosy, and he sat straight as an arrow in the saddle. I drew back my horse and ranged up beside him, inspired by curiosity. The eyes turned toward me undoubtedly betrayed negro blood.

"I do not remember seeing you before," I said, wiping the dust from my lips. "Are you a new recruit?"

"I'se Col'nel Cochran's man," he answered, without salute, but with the accent of education oddly mixed with dialect.

"Oh, I see--what has become of Sam?"

"He done took sick, an' de col'nel wanted a man right away, so he picked me."

"Did you belong around here?"

"Well, no, not exactly belong round yere, but I'se travelled dese parts some considerable. I was born down in Louisiana, sah."

"Not so very long ago either," I ventured, feeling a peculiar interest in the fellow. "Were you a slave?"

His rather thin lips closed over his white teeth, and his fingers gripped the saddle pommel.

"Yes,"--the word snapped out. "I'se nineteen, sah, an' my mother was a slave. I reckon my father was white 'nough, but that don't count fo' much--I'se a nigger just de same. Dat's bad 'nough, let me tell yo', but it's worse to be yo' own father's nigger."

I had nothing to say to this outburst, feeling that back of it were facts into which I had no right to probe, and we rode along quietly. Then he spoke, glancing aside at me:

"Dey won't be no 'portant fightin' long yere, sah, not fo' 'bout ten miles."

"How do you figure that out?"

"'Cause de lay ob de groun' ain't right, fo' one thing, an' 'cause all de Confed intrenchments was back yander."

"Yonder--where?"

"In behind de log church at de Three Corners--done know dat country mighty well."

I turned and faced him, instantly suspicious.

"Now see here; you do know that country, and a bit too well for a man riding in the ranks. Where did you come from? Were you in the Confederate service? Let's have this straight."

"Suah," with frankness. "I done tol' de col'nel all how it was. I was wid my Massa from Louisiana, an' he was a captain, sah! 'Bout two weeks ago he lef' me down yander on de pike wid orders fo' to stay dere till he done come back. But it wa'n't no job fo' me, sah, an' so I skipped out de first night, an' joined up wid de Yanks. I reckon I knows 'bout whar I belongs in dis yere fightin', an' I ain't nobody's slave no mor'."

The lad's earnestness impressed me, and beneath his words was evident a deep smouldering resentment, not so much against slavery as against the individual who had owned him.

"What is your name, my boy?"

"Charles Le Gaire, sah."

CHAPTER XVI
A CALL TO DUTY

The family name was an uncommon one, and, coupled as it was with "Louisiana," and the title "Captain," could refer only to Gerald Le Gaire. I wanted to question, the lad, but refrained, spurring my horse ahead so as to remove the temptation. Even the little already said plainly revealed that he resented bitterly his position in life, and determined to remain no longer in slavery to his own father. His father! That would be Le Gaire! The thought added fuel to the flame of dislike which I already cherished against the man. Of course legally this former relationship between master and slave meant nothing; it would be considered no bar to legitimate marriage; perhaps to one brought up in the environment of slavery it would possess no moral turpitude even, yet to me it seemed a foul, disgraceful thing. Whether it would so appear to Miss Willifred I could not even conjecture; she was of the South, with, all the prejudice and peculiarity of thought characteristic of her section. Pure-hearted, womanly, as I believed her to be, this earlier alliance still might not seem to her particularly reprehensible. Certainly it was not my part to bring it to her attention, or to utilize my knowledge of the situation to advance my cause, or injure Le Gaire. Nor would I question the ex-slave further; I already knew enough, too much possibly, although curiosity was not dormant, and I wondered what had become of the mother, and from what special cause had arisen the intense hatred in the heart of the son.

We rode steadily forward all day, under fire twice, and once charging a battery. All that opposed our advance however was a thin fringe of troops, intent merely upon causing delay, and making a brief stand, only to fall back promptly as soon as we flung forward any considerable body of men. By night-fall we had attained a position well within the bend of the river, the centre and left wing had achieved a crossing, and our entire line had closed up so as to display a solid front. The Ninth bivouacked in the hills, our rest undisturbed, except for the occasional firing of the pickets. With dawn we were under arms, feeling our way forward, and, an hour later, the two armies were face to face. Nearly evenly mated, fighting across a rough country, neither side could claim victory at the end of the day. While we on the right forced our line forward for nearly five miles, leaving behind us a carpet of dead, the left and centre met with such desperate resistance as to barely retain their earlier position. It required an hour of night fighting to close up the gap, and we slept on our arms, expecting an early morning assault. Instead of attempting this the enemy fell back to their second line of intrenchments, and, after waiting a day to determine their movements and strengthen our own line, we again advanced, feeling our way slowly in, but finally meeting with a resistance which compelled a halt.

The details of this battle belong to history, not to these pages. The Ninth bore no conspicuous part, hovering on the extreme right flank, engaged in continuous skirmishing, and scouting along miles of front. The morning of the third day found the armies fronting each other, defiant yet equally afraid to join battle, both commanders seeking for some point of strategy which would yield advantage--we of the North fearful of advancing against intrenchments, and those of the South not daring to come forth into the open. For the moment it was a truce between us--the truce of two exhausted bull-dogs, lying face to face with gleaming teeth, ready to spring at the first opening.

We of the Ninth were at the edge of an opening in the woods, with low hills on either hand, our pickets within easy musket-shot of the gray-clad videttes beyond the fringe of trees. Knowing our own success we could not comprehend this inaction, or the desperate fighting which held back the troops to the east, and we were impatient to go in. I was lying on my back in the shelter of a slight hollow, wondering at the surrounding stillness, wishing for anything to occur which would give action, when the major rode up, accompanied by another officer in an artillery uniform. I was on my feet in an instant saluting.

"Lieutenant Galesworth, this is Captain Kent, an aide on General Sheridan's staff. He desires you to accompany him to headquarters."

My heart bounding with anticipation, within five minutes I was riding beside

him, back to the river road, and along the rear of our extended line. He was a pleasant, genial fellow, but knew nothing of why I had been summoned, his orders being
simply to bring me at once. Two hours of hard riding, and we came to a double log
cabin, with a squad of horsemen in front, and a considerable infantry guard near by.
A sentry paced back and forth in front of the steps, and several officers were sitting
on the porch. Dismounting, my companion handed the reins of both horses to a
trooper, and led the way in. A word to the sentinel, and we faced the group above.
One, a sharp-featured man, with very dark complexion, rose to his feet.

"What is it, Kent?"

"This is Lieutenant Galesworth, of the Ninth Illinois Cavalry. The general will
wish to see him at once."

The dark-featured man glanced at me, and turned back into the house, and
Kent introduced me to the others, none of whom I recognized. This was not Sheridan's staff, but before I could question any of them, the messenger returned, and
motioned for me to follow. It was a large room, low-ceilinged, with three windows,
the walls of bare logs whitewashed, the floor freshly swept, the only furniture a
table and a few chairs. But two men were present, although a sentinel stood motionless at the door,--a broad-shouldered colonel of engineers, with gray moustache
and wearing glasses, sitting at a table littered with papers, and a short stocky man,
attired in a simple blue blouse, with no insignia of rank visible, his back toward
me, gazing out of a window. I took a single step within, and halted. The short man
wheeled about at the slight sound, his eyes on my face; I recognized instantly the
closely trimmed beard, the inevitable cigar between the lips, and, with a leap of the
heart, my hand rose to the salute.

"Lieutenant Galesworth?"

"Yes, General."

"Very well; you may retire, Colonel Trout, and, sentry, close the door."

His keen gray eyes scrutinized my face, betraying no emotion, but he advanced
closer, one hand upon the table.

"General Sheridan informs me he has found you a valuable scout, always ready
for any service, however dangerous."

"I have endeavored to carry out my orders, General," I answered quietly.

"So I am told," in the same even voice. "The army is full of good men, brave men, but not all possess sufficient intelligence and willingness to carry out an independent enterprise. Just now I require such a man, and Sheridan recommends you. How old are you?"

I answered, and barely waiting the sound of my voice, he went on:

"You have scouted over this country?"

"I have, sir."

"How far to the south?"

"About five miles beyond the Three Corners."

"Not far enough, is it, Parker?" turning to the officer at the table.

"The house is below," was the response, "but perhaps I had better explain the entire matter to Lieutenant Galesworth, and let him decide for himself whether he cares to make the attempt."

The general nodded approval, and walked back to the window, his hands clasped behind his back. Parker spread out a map.

"Just step over here, Lieutenant. This is our present position, represented by the irregular blue line; those red squares show the enemy's forces as far as we understand them. The crosses represent batteries, and the important intrenchments are shown by the double lines. Of course this is imperfect, largely drawn from the reports of scouts. Their line is slightly shorter than our own, our right overlapping, but they have a stronger reserve force protecting the centre. Now notice the situation here," and he traced it with his pencil. "Your regiment is practically to the rear of their main line of defence, but the nature of the ground renders them safe. There is a, deep ravine here, trending to the southeast, and easily defended. Now note, ten miles, almost directly south of Three Corners, on the open pike, the first building on the right-hand side beyond a log church, stands an old plantation house. It is a large building, painted white, in the midst of a grove of trees, and in the rear is a commodious stable and a dozen negro cabins. The map shows this house to be somewhat to the right of the Confederate centre, and about five miles to the rear of their first line."

I bent over, intent on the map, endeavoring to fix each point clearly in my mind. Parker paused in his speech, and the general turned about, his eyes fastened upon us.

"I understand," I said finally.

"Very well. Deserters informed us last night that Johnston had taken this house for his headquarters. This morning one of our most reliable scouts confirms the report, and says the place can be easily approached by a small party using the ravine for concealment, coming in past the negro cabins at the rear."

My eyes brightened, as I straightened up, instantly comprehending the plan.

"What guard have they?"

"A few sentinels at the house, and a squad of cavalry in the stable. Naturally they feel perfectly safe so far to the rear of their own lines. It is the very audacity of such an attempt which makes success possible."

The general stepped forward.

"Don't take this as an order, Lieutenant," he said bluntly. "It will mean a desperate risk, and if you go, you must comprehend thoroughly the peril involved. You were recommended as the best man to lead such a party, but we supposed you already knew that country."

"I can place my hand on a man who does know every inch of it," I replied, my mind clear, and my decision reached. "I thank you for the privilege."

"Good; when?"

"To-night, of course; there is ample time to prepare."

"How many men will you require?"

I hesitated, but for barely an instant.

"Not to exceed ten, General--a small party will accomplish as much as a larger one, and be less liable to attract attention. All I need will volunteer from my own company."

Apparently his own thought coincided with mine, for he merely looked at me a moment with those searching gray eyes, and then turned to the map, beckoning me to join him.

"Familiarize yourself with every detail of the topography of the region," he said, his finger on the paper. "Colonel Parker will explain anything you may need to know." He straightened up, and extended his hand, the cigar still crushed between his teeth. "I believe you are the right stuff, Lieutenant; young enough to be reckless, old enough to know the value of patience. Are you married?"

I shook my head, with a smile, yet conscious my cheeks were flushed.

"Then I am going to say to you--go, and do the best you can. Parker will give you any other instructions you desire. Good-bye, my lad, and good luck."

He turned and left the room, my eyes following him until the door closed.

CHAPTER XVII
BEGINNING THE NIGHT ADVENTURE

The colonel of engineers did not delay me long, and, eager to be away, I made my necessary questions as brief as possible. Riding back through the encampment of troops, hampered more or less by the irregularity of the different commands, I had ample time in which to outline the night's adventure. I comprehended fully the danger of the mission, and that the probability was strongly against success. Reckless audacity, coupled with rare good fortune, might result in our return with the prisoner sought, but it was far more likely that we would be the ones captured, if we escaped with our lives. Yet this knowledge caused no hesitancy on my part; I was trained to obedience, and deep down in my heart welcomed the opportunity. The excitement appealed to me, and the knowledge that this service was to be performed directly under the eye of the great General of the West, was in itself an inspiration. If I lived to come back it meant promotion, the praise of the army, a line on the page of history--enough surely to arouse the ambition of youth.

It was early in the afternoon when I reached the position of my regiment, and reported to the colonel, asking the privilege of selecting a detail. Then, as I sat at mess, I studied my men, mentally picking from among them those best adapted to the desperate task. I chose those I had seen in action, young, unmarried fellows, and for "non-com," Sergeant Miles, a slender, silent man of thirty, in whom I had implicit confidence. I checked the names over, satisfying myself I had made no mistake. Leaving Miles to notify these fellows, and prepare them for service, I crossed to the colonel's tent in search of the ex-slave. He was easily found.

"Le Gaire," I began, choking a bit at the name, "do you remember a big white house, on the right of the pike, the first beyond a log church, south from the Three

Corners?"

He looked up from his work with sparkling eyes.

"I suah does; I reckon I could find dat place in de dark."

"Well, that is exactly what I want you to do, my man. I have some work to do there to-night."

"How yo' goin' to git dar?"

I explained about the ravine, the positions of the Confederate lines, and where I understood the special guards were stationed. The boy listened in silence, his fingers, clinching and unclinching, alone evidencing excitement.

"Will that plan work?" I asked, "or can you suggest any better way?"

"I reckon it'll work," he admitted, "if yo' don't git cotched afore yo' git dar. I knows a heap 'bout dat ravine; I'se hunted rabbits dar many a time, an' it ain't goin' to be no easy job gittin' through dar in de dark."

"Will you show us the way?"

"Well, I don't just know," scratching his head thoughtfully. "Maybe de col'nel wouldn't let me."

"I can arrange that."

"Den I don't want fo' to go to dat house; dat's whar I run away from."

"But I thought you belonged to the Le Gaires of Louisiana?"

"Dat's what I did, sah; but I done tol' yo' I come up yere wid de army. I was left dere till de captain come back; dose folks was friends o' his."

"Oh, I see; well, will you go along as far as the end of the ravine?"

He looked out over the hills, and then back into my face, his eyes narrowing, his lips setting firm over the white teeth. I little realized what was taking place in the fellow's brain, what real motive influenced his decision, or the issues involved.

"I reckon I will, sah, providin' de col'nel says so." There was, of course, no difficulty in obtaining the consent of that officer, and by nine o'clock we were ready to depart, ten picked men, young, vigorous lads, though veterans in service, led by Miles, together with the negro Le Gaire and myself. Taking a lesson from the guerillas we were armed only with revolvers, intending to fight, if fight we must, at close quarters; and the brass buttons, and all insignia of rank liable to attract attention had been removed from our blouses. Upon our heads we wore slouch hats. I had decided to make the attempt on foot, as we could thus advance in greater silence.

Without attracting attention, or starting any camp rumor, we passed, two by two, out beyond the pickets, and made rendezvous on the bank of the river. It was a dark night. As soon as the sergeant reported all were present, I led the way up stream for perhaps a mile until we came to the mouth of the ravine. Here I called them around me, barely able to distinguish the dim figures, although within arm's length, explained my plans and gave strict orders. As I ceased speaking I could plainly hear their suppressed breathing, so deathly still was the night.

"If any man has a question, ask it now."

No one spoke, although several moved uneasily, too nervous to remain still.

"Le Gaire, here, will go first, as he knows the way, and I will follow him; the rest drop in in single file, with the sergeant at the rear. Keep close enough to distinguish the man in front, and be careful where you put your feet. No noise, not a word spoken unless I pass back an order; then give it to the next man in a whisper. Don't fire under any conditions except by command." I paused, then added slowly: "You are all intelligent enough to know the danger of our expedition, and the necessity of striking quick and hard. Our success, our very lives, depend on surprise. If each one of you does exactly as I order, we've got a chance to come back; if not, then it means a bullet, or a prison, for all of us. Are you ready?"

I heard the low responses, and counted them--ten, the negro not answering.

"All right, men," then, my voice hardening into a threat: "Now go ahead, Le Gaire, and remember I am next behind, and carry a revolver in my hand. Make a wrong move, lad, and you'll never make another."

I could faintly discern the whites of his eyes, and heard one of the men snicker nervously.

"Lead off! Fall in promptly, men."

It was a rocky cleft through the hills, perhaps a hundred yards wide here where it opened on the river, with a little stream in its centre fringed with low trees, but narrowing gradually, and becoming blocked with underbrush as it penetrated deeper into the interior. For a mile or more the course was not entirely unknown to me, although the darkness obscured all familiar landmarks. The negro, however, apparently possessed the instinct of an animal, or else had night eyes, for he never hesitated, keeping close along the edge of the stream. The tree-branches brushed our faces, but our feet pressed a well defined path. Farther in, the shadows becoming more dense, this path wound about crazily, seeking the level spots; yet Le Gaire moved steadily forward, his head lowered, and I kept him within reach of my arm, barely able to distinguish the cautious tread of feet behind. Clearly enough he knew the way, and could follow it with all the certainty of a dog. Relieved as to this, and confident the fellow dare not play us false, I could take notice of other things, and permit my thoughts to wander. There was little to be seen or heard; except for the musical tinkle of the stream, all to the right was silence, but from the other side there arose an occasional sound, borne faintly from a distance--a voice calling, the blare of a far-off bugle, the echo of a hammer pounding on iron. Once through the obscuring branches the fitful yellow of a camp-fire was dimly visible, but the ravine twisted so that I could not determine whether this was from Federal or Confederate lines. Anyhow no eye saw us creep past, and no suspicious voice challenged. Indeed we had every reason to believe the ravine unguarded, although pickets were undoubtedly patrolling the east bank, and there were places we must go close in under its shadow.

So intent had I been upon this adventure, my mind concentrated on details, that the personal equation had been entirely forgotten. But now I began to reflect along that line, yet never for a moment forgetting our situation, or its peril. I was going down into the neighborhood where Willifred Hardy lived--to which she had probably already returned. I was going as an enemy to her cause, guided by an ex-slave of Le Gaire's. It was rather an odd turn of Fate's wheel, and, while there was no probability of our meeting, yet the conditions were suggestive. My eyes were upon the dim form in advance, and I was strongly tempted to ask if he knew where Major Hardy's plantation was. Beyond doubt he did, but this was no time for dalliance with love, and I drove the temptation sternly from me, endeavoring to concentrate my mind on present duty. But in spite of all Billie would intervene, her blue-gray eyes challenging me to forget, and the remembrance of her making my step light. I was going to be near her again, at least, if only for an hour; perhaps, whether I succeeded or failed, she would hear my name mentioned. Even that would be better than forgetfulness, and she was one to appreciate a deed like this. I should like to see her eyes when they told her--when they spoke my name. I wondered where Captain Le Gaire was, and whether he had been her escort back through the Confederate lines. Most probably yes, and perhaps he had remained at the Hardy house, still incapacitated from duty by the blow I had struck him--an interesting invalid. Even this thought did not trouble me as it might have done otherwise, for I believed Billie had already begun to see the real man behind the fellow's handsome face; if so, then time and companionship would only widen the breach between them-- perhaps my memory also.

It was a hard three hours' travel, practically feeling a passage through the darkness, for the narrow path extended but little beyond a mile, after losing which we stumbled forward through a maze of rock and underbrush. This finally became so dense that the negro veered to the left, where there was a grassy ledge, along which we made more rapid progress, although facing greater danger of discovery. However, the night was black, and to any picket looking down from above the ravine must have appeared a dark, impenetrable void, while our feet in the grass scarcely made a sound. Once we saw a moving figure above us, barely visible against the sky-line, and halted breathlessly, every eye uplifted, until the apparition vanished; and once, warned by the cracking of a twig, we lay flat on our faces while a spectral company went past us on foot, heading at right-angles across our path. I counted twenty men in the party, but could distinguish nothing as to uniform or equipment. We waited motionless until the last straggler had disappeared. By this time we were well behind the Confederate lines, with troops probably on either side, for this gash in the surface had both narrowed and veered sharply to the east. It still remained sufficiently deep to conceal our movements, and, as we had circled the picket lines, we could proceed with greater confidence. We were beyond the vigilance of sentinels, and could be discovered now only through some accidental encounter. I touched Le Gaire on the shoulder, and whispered in his ear:

"How much farther is it?"

"'Bout half a mile, sah," staring about into what to me was impenetrable darkness. "Yo' see de forked tree dar on de lef'?"

I was not sure, yet there was something in that direction which might be what he described.

"I guess so--why?"

"I 'members dat tree, for dar's a spring just at de foot ob it."

"Is the rest of the way hard?"

"No, sah, not wid me goin' ahead of yo', for dar's a medium good path from de spring up to de top o' de hill. I'se pow'ful feared though we might run across some ob dem Confed sojers 'round yere."

I tried to look at him, but could see only the whites of his eyes, but his voice somehow belied his words--to my mind there was no fear in the fellow. I passed back word along the line, and found all the men present. Not a sound came out of the night, and I ordered the ex-slave to lead on.

CHAPTER XVIII
OVERHEARD CONVERSATION

It was a little gully, hardly more than a tramped footpath, leading down the bank up which we crept until we attained the level. With eyes sharpened by the long night vigil we could perceive the dim outlines of buildings, and a glow or two of distant lights. I felt of the face of my watch, deciding the time to be not far from half-past twelve. Our tramp had seemed longer than a trifle over three hours, and it was a relief to know we still had so much of darkness left in which to operate. I touched the man lying next me, unable to tell one dark form from another.

"Who are you?"

"Wilson, sir."

"Where is the guide?"

"Right yere, sah," and the speaker wriggled toward me on his face. "Dis yere is de place."

"I supposed so, but it is all a mere blur out there to me. What are these buildings just ahead of us?"

"De slave quarters, sah; dey's all deserted, 'cept maybe dat first one yonder," pointing. "I reckon Aunt Mandy an' her ol' man are dar yet, but de field hands dey all done cleared out long time ago. De stable was ober dar toward de right, whar dat lantern was dodgin' 'round. Yo' creep 'long yere, an' I'll point out de house--see, it's back o' de bunch o' trees, whar de yaller light shows in de winder. I reckon dar's some of 'em up yet."

From his description I received a fair impression of the surroundings, questioning briefly as I stared out at the inanimate objects faintly revealed, and endeavoring to plan some feasible course of action. The stable was a hundred yards to the rear of the house, a fenced-off garden between, the driveway circling to the right. Between the slave quarters and the mansion extended an orchard, the trees of good size and affording ample cover. We were to the left of the house, and the light seen evidently streamed through one of the windows of the front room. Where the guard was stationed no one of us could guess, yet this had to be determined first of all. I called for Miles, and the sergeant, still holding his position at the rear, crept forward.

"I am going in closer to discover what I can," I said quietly. "I may be gone for half an hour. Advance your men carefully into the shadow of that cabin there, and wait orders. Don't let them straggle, for I want to know where they are." I bent lower and whispered in his ear, "Don't let that negro out of your sight; but no shooting--rap him with a butt if necessary. You understand?"

"Sure; I'll keep a grip on his leg."

I paused an instant thinking.

"If luck helps me to get inside, and I find the way clear, I'll draw that shade up and down twice--this way--and you can come on. Move quickly, but without noise, and wait outside for orders, unless you are certain I am in trouble."

"Yes, sir; we'll be there."

"Have one man watch that light all the time; don't let him take his eyes off it. Be careful no prowling trooper stumbles on you; keep the men still."

I saw the dim movement as he saluted and felt no doubt of obedience,--he was too old and tried a soldier to fail. I crept forward, scouted about the cabin to make sure it was unoccupied, and then advanced into the shadows of the orchard. I was all nerves now, all alertness, every instinct awake, seeing the slightest movement, hearing the faintest noise. There were voices--just a mumble--in the direction of the stable, and, as I drew in closer toward the house I could distinguish sounds as though a considerable party were at table--yet even the tinkle of knife and plate was muffled; probably the dining-room was on the opposite side. However, this would seem to indicate the presence of the one we sought, although so late a supper would render our task more difficult of execution. I was tempted to try the other side first, but the open window with the light burning inside was nearer, and I wished first to assure myself as to that. I could see no sentries, but the embers of a fire were visible on the front driveway. Whatever guard might be about the steps, none patrolled this side; I must have waited several minutes, lying concealed in the dense shrubbery, peering and listening, before becoming fully convinced. The omission brought a vague suspicion that Johnston might not be present after all--that this was instead a mere party of convivial officers. If so, the sooner I could convince myself the better, to make good our safe return. The thought urged me forward.

A small clump of low bushes--gooseberries, I judged from the thorns--was within a few yards of the house, the balance of the distance a closely trimmed turf. The bottom of the window through which the light shone was even with my eyes when standing erect, but I could perceive no movement of any occupants, a small wooden balcony, more for ornament than for practical use, shutting off the view. I grasped the rail of this with my hands and drew my body slowly up, endeavoring to keep to one side out of the direct range of light. This effort yielded but a glimpse of one corner of the seemingly deserted interior, and I crouched down within the rail, cautiously seeking to discover more. Fortunately the wooden support did not creak under my weight. The apartment was apparently parlor and sitting-room combined, some of the furniture massive and handsome, especially the centre-table and a sofa of black walnut, but there was also a light sewing-table and a cane-seated rocker, more suggestive of comfort. At first glance I thought the place empty, although I could plainly hear the murmuring sound of voices from beyond; then I perceived some one--a woman--seated on a low stool before the open fire-place. She sat with back toward me, her head bent upon one hand. I was still studying the figure in uncertainty when a door, evidently leading into the hall, opened and a man entered. He was in Confederate field uniform, the insignia on his collar that of a major,--a tall, broad-shouldered man, with abundant hair and an aggressive expression. The woman glanced up, but he closed the door, shutting out a jangle of voices, before speaking.

"What was it? You sent for me?"

She rose to her feet, and came a step forward,--my heart leapt into my throat, my fingers gripped the rail.

"Yes," she said quietly, looking into his face, "I have decided I cannot do it."

"Decided! What now?" and his surprise was beyond question. "Why, what does all this mean? No one has sought to coerce or drive you; this was your own choice. Surely you have had ample time in which to consider!"

"Oh, yes," wearily, her hand pressing back her hair, "but--but I really never understood myself until to-night; I am not sure I do even now."

"A girlish whim," he broke in impatiently. "Why, daughter, this is foolish, impossible; all arrangements are made, and even now they are toasting the captain in the dining-room. Under no other conditions could he have got leave of absence, for his injuries are trivial. Johnston told me as much before he left, and I know we shall need every man to-morrow if we force the fighting."

"Why does he accept leave then, if he is needed here?" she asked quickly.

"For your sake and mine, not fear of battle, I am sure. There will be no heavy action at this end of our line, as we shall fall back to protect the centre. But the movement as contemplated will leave all this ground to be occupied by the Yankees; they'll be here by to-morrow night beyond doubt; even now we retain only a skeleton force west of the pike. I cannot leave you here alone, unprotected."

"Is that why you have pressed me so to assent to this hurried arrangement?"

"Yes, Billie," and he took her hands tenderly. "Captain Le Gaire suggested it as soon as we learned this region was to be left unguarded, and when he succeeded in getting leave to go south it seemed to me the very best thing possible for you. Why, daughter, I do not understand your action--by having the ceremony to-night we merely advance it a few months."

"But--father," her voice trembling, "I--I am not so sure that I wish to marry Captain Le Gaire at--at all."

"Not marry him! Why, I supposed that was settled--you seemed very happy--"

"Yes, once," she broke in. "I thought I loved him--perhaps I did--but he has not appeared the same man to me of late. I cannot explain; I cannot even tell what it is I mean, but I am afraid to go on. I want more time to decide, to learn my own heart."

"You poor little girl, you are nervous, excited."

"No, it is not that, papa. I simply doubt myself, my future happiness with this man. Surely you will not urge me to marry one I do not love?"

"No, girlie; but this decision comes so suddenly. I had believed you very happy together, and even to-night, when this plan was first broached, there was no word of protest uttered. I thought you were glad."

"Not glad! I was stunned, too completely surprised to object. You all took my willingness so for granted that I could find no words to express my real feelings. Indeed I do not believe I knew what they were--not until I sat here alone thinking, and then there came to me a perfect horror of it all. I tried to fight my doubts, tried to convince myself that it was right to proceed, but only to find it impossible. I loathe the very thought; if I consent I know I shall regret the act as long as I live." "But, Billie," he urged earnestly, "what can have occurred to make this sudden change in you? Captain Le Gaire belongs to one of the most distinguished families of the South; is wealthy, educated, a polished gentleman. He will give you everything to make life attractive. Surely this is but a mere whim!"

"Have you found me to be a nervous girl, full of whims?"

"No, certainly not, but--"

"And this is no whim, no mood. I cannot tell, cannot explain all that has of late caused me to distrust Captain Le Gaire, only I do not feel toward him as I once did. I never can again, and if you insist on this marriage, it will mean to me unhappiness--I am, sure of that."

"But what can we do at this late hour! Everything is prepared, arranged for; even the minister has arrived, and is waiting."

She stood before him, her hands clasped, trembling from head to foot, yet with eyes determined.

"Will you delay action a few moments, and send Captain Le Gaire to me? I--I must see him alone."

He hesitated, avoiding her eyes and permitting his glance to wander about the room.

"Please do this for me."

"But in your present mood--"

"I am perfectly sane," and she stood straight before him, insistent, resolute. "Indeed I think I know myself better than for months past. I shall say nothing wrong to Captain Le Gaire, and if he is a gentleman he will honor me more for my frankness. Either you will send him here to me, or else I shall go to him."

The major bowed with all the ceremony of the old school, convinced of the utter futility of further argument.

"You will have you own way; you always have," regretfully. "I shall request the captain to join you here."

CHAPTER XIX
LE GAIRE FORCES A DECISION

He left the room reluctantly enough, pausing at the door to glance back, but she had sunk down into the rocker, and made no relenting sign. Every sense of right compelled me to withdraw; I could not remain, a hidden spy, to listen to her conversation with Le Gaire. My heart leaped with exultation, with sudden faith that possibly her memory of me might lie back of this sudden distrust, this determination for freedom. Yet this possibility alone rendered impossible my lingering here to overhear what should pass between them in confidence. Interested as I was personally I possessed no excuse to remain; every claim of duty was elsewhere. I had already learned General Johnston was not present, and that an attack was projected against our left and centre. This was news of sufficient importance to be reported at headquarters without delay. To be sure the withdrawal of troops from this end of the Confederate line made our own return trip less dangerous, still, even if I ventured to remain longer, I must early despatch a courier with the news.

I drew silently back from the window, flinging one limb over the balcony rail, preparing to drop to the ground below. Her back was toward me, and she heard nothing; then a man came round the end of the house, walking slowly and smoking. I could see the red glow of his cigar, and inhale the fragrance of the tobacco. I hung on desperately, bending my body along the rail, and he passed directly beneath, yet so shadowed I could merely distinguish his outline. The fellow--an officer, no doubt, seeking a breath of fresh air--strolled to the opposite corner, and then turned off into the orchard. I dared not risk an attempt to drop and run, for I knew not what might await me in the darkness. Yet where I clung I was exposed to discovery, and, when he turned his back, I sank down once more within the shelter of the balcony. He stopped under the trees, apparently having found a seat of some kind, although I could see nothing except the tip of the burning cigar, as he flipped aside the ashes. I had almost forgotten what might be occurring within, until aroused by the sound of Le Gaire's voice.

He certainly looked a handsome fellow, standing there with hand still on the knob of the door, dressed in a new uniform tailored to perfection, his lips and eyes smiling pleasantly, never suspecting the reason for which he was summoned.

"What is it, Billie?" he asked easily. "A last word, hey?"

"Yes," she answered, lifting her eyes to his face, but not advancing. "I--I have been thinking it all over while waiting here alone, and--and I find I am not quite ready. I sent for you to ask release from my promise, or, at least, that you will not insist upon our--our marriage to-night."

The man's dark face actually grew white, his surprise at this request leaving him gasping for breath, as he stared at her.

"Why, good God, girl, do you realize what you are saying?" he exclaimed, all self-control gone. "Why, we are ready now; Bradshaw just arrived and every ar-rangement has been made for our journey. It cannot be postponed."

"Oh, yes, indeed, it can," and she rose, facing him. "Surely you would not force me against my will, Captain Le Gaire? I do not desire to rebel, to absolutely refuse, but I hope you will listen to me, and then act the part of a gentleman. I presume you desire me for your wife, not your slave."

I thought he had lost his voice he was so long in answering; then the tones were hoarse, indistinct.

"Listen! Yes! I want you to explain; only don't expect too much from me."

She looked directly at him, her cheeks flushing to the insolence of his accent.

"I am hardly likely to err in that way any more," rather coldly, "but I do owe you an explanation. I have done wrong to permit this affair to go so far without protest, but I did not comprehend my own feelings clearly until to-night. I merely drifted without realizing the danger, and now the shock of discovery leaves me al-most helpless. I realize distinctly only one thing--I can not, I will not, marry you.

"Do these words seem cruel, unjust?" she went on, strangely calm. "Perhaps they are, yet it is surely better for me to speak them now than to wreck both our lives by remaining silent longer. You came to me a year ago, Captain Le Gaire, at a time when I was particularly lonely, and susceptible to kindness. You were an officer in the army, fighting for a cause I loved, and your friendly attentions were very welcome. My father liked you, and we were constantly thrown together. I have lived rather a secluded life, here on this plantation since my school days, meeting few men of my own station, and still young enough to be romantic. I thought I loved you, and perhaps the feeling I cherished might have truly become love had you always remained the same considerate gentleman I first believed you to be. Instead, little by little, I have been driven away, hurt by your coarseness, your lack of chivalry, until now, when it comes to the supreme test, I find my soul in revolt. Am I altogether to blame?"

I do not think he comprehended, grasped the truth she sought to convey, for he broke forth angrily:

"Very pretty, indeed! And do you think I will ever stand for it? Why, I should be the laughing stock of the army, a butt for every brainless joker in the camp. I am not such a fool, my girl." He stepped forward, grasping her hands, and holding them in spite of her slight effort to break away. "I am a frank-spoken man, yes, but I have never failed to treat you with respect."

"You may call it that, but you have repeatedly sworn in my presence, have ordered me harshly about, have even arranged this affair without first consulting me. If this be your manner before marriage, what brand of brutality could I expect after?"

"Poof! I may be quick-tempered; perhaps we are neither of us angels, but you choose a poor time for a quarrel. Come, Billie, let's kiss and make up. What! Still angry? Surely you are not in earnest?"

"But I am--very much in earnest."

"You mean to throw me down? Now at the last moment, with all the fellows waiting in the next room?"

She had her hands freed, and with them held behind her, stood motionless facing him.

"Would you marry me against my wish?" she asked. "Would you hold me to a promise I regret having made? I sent for you merely to tell you the truth, to throw myself on your generosity. I am scarcely more than a girl, Captain Le Gaire, and acknowledge I have done wrong, have been deceived in my own feelings. You have my word--the word of a Hardy--and we keep our pledges. I suppose I must marry you if you insist, but I implore you as a man of honor, a Southern gentleman, to release me."

Her voice faltered, and Le Gaire laughed.

"Oh, I begin to see how the wind blows. You do stand to your promise then. Very well, that's all I ask."

"I do not love you; I do not think I even respect you."

"Nevertheless you cannot shake me off like that. It's only a whim, a mood, Billie; once married I'll teach you the lesson over again. You were loving enough a month ago."

"I was in the midst of a girl's dream," she said slowly, "from which I have awakened--won't you release me, Captain Le Gaire?"

"I should say not," walking savagely across the room. "Come, Billie, I'm tired of this tantrum. A little of this sort of thing goes a long way with me. You're a head-strong, spoiled girl, and I've already put up with enough to try the patience of Job. Now I'm going to show my authority, insist on my rights. You've promised to marry me, now, to-night, and you are going to do it, if I have to go to your father and tell him plainly just what is the matter with you."

"With me! the only matter is that I have ceased to care for you."

"Yes, in the last week! Do you think I am blind? Do you suppose I don't know what has changed your mind so suddenly? Do you imagine I'm going to let you go for the sake of a damned Yankee?"

She fairly gasped in surprise, her fingers clinched, her cheeks flaming.

"A Yankee! Captain Le Gaire, are you crazy?"

"No," his temper bursting all control. "That's what's the matter with you. Oh, of course, you'll deny, and pretend to be horrified. I saw into your little game then, but I kept still; now you are carrying it too far."

"What do you mean? I am not accustomed to such language."

"I mean this: You think you are in love with that sneaking Yankee spy--I don't know his name--the fellow you helped through our lines, and then hid at Moran's. Now don't deny it; I asked some questions before I left there, and you were with him out under the grape arbor. I saw the imprint of your feet in the soft dirt. By God, I believe you knew he struck me, and permitted me to lie there while he got away."

"Captain Le Gaire--"

"Now you wait; this is my turn to talk. You thought you had fooled me, but you had not. Under other conditions I might accede to your request, but not now--not to give you over to a Yank. I've got your promise, and I propose to hold you to it."

"But it is not that," she protested. "I--I am not in love with Lieutenant Galesworth."

"So that is the fellow's name, is it--Galesworth," sneeringly. "I thought you pretended before you did not know."

She remained silent, confused.

"I'm glad to know who he is; some day we may have a settlement. Well, all I know about the affair is this, but that's enough--you rode with him all one night, hid him all the next day, and then helped him escape. You lied to me repeatedly, and now you want to break away from me at the last minute. It's either this Galesworth or somebody else--now who is it?"

Billie sank back into a chair, but with her eyes still on the man's face.

"It is no--one," she said wearily. "It is not that at all; I--I simply do not care for you in that way any longer."

"Poof! do you mean you won't keep your word?"

"I mean I want to be released--at least a postponement until I can be sure of myself."

"And I refuse--refuse, do you understand that? You either marry me to-night or I go to your father with the whole story. He'll be pleased to learn of your affair with a Yankee spy, no doubt, and of how you helped the fellow through our lines. And I've got the proofs too. Now, young lady, it is about time to stop this quarrel, and come down to facts. What are you going to do?"

"You insist?"

"Of course I do."

Her head sank upon her hand, and even from where I peered in upon them, helpless to get away, equally helpless to aid, I could see her form tremble.

"Then there is no escape, I suppose; I must keep my promise."

He touched her on the shoulder, indifferent to her shrinking away, a sarcastic smile on his lips.

"I knew you would. I don't take this Yankee business seriously, only I wanted you to know I understood all about it. You're too sensible a girl to get tangled up that way. We'll drop it now, and I'll show you how good I can be. May I kiss you?"

"I--I would rather not--not yet. Don't be angry, but I--I am not myself. Where were you going?"

"To tell your father it is all settled. You must be ready when we come back."

He paused with hand on the door looking back at her. There was a moment's breathless silence; then her lips whispered:

"Yes."

I turned to look out into the black orchard, and then gazed back into the lighted room. I knew not what to do, how to act. My remaining where I was could be of no possible service to her, indeed my discovery there would only add to her embarrassment, yet I had no reason to believe the officer had left his seat yonder, and therefore dare not drop to the ground. My heart ached for the girl, and I longed to get my hands on that cur of a Le Gaire, yet might venture to approach neither. It was a maddening situation, but I could only stand there in the dark, gripping the rail, unable to decide my duty. Perhaps she did love me--in spite of that vigorous denial, perhaps she did--and the very possibility made the blood surge hot through my veins. Could I help her in any way? Whatever her feeling toward me might be, there remained no question as to her growing dislike for Le Gaire. Not fear, but a peculiar sense of honor alone, held her to her pledge. And could I remain still, and permit her to be thus ruthlessly sacrificed? Would Major Hardy permit it if he knew?--if the entire situation was explained to him? Le Gaire never would tell him the truth, but would laugh off the whole affair as a mere lovers' quarrel. Could I venture to thrust myself in? If I did, would it be of any use? It would cost me my liberty, and the liberty of my men; probably I should not be believed. And would she ever forgive me for listening? I struggled with the temptation--swayed by duty and by love--until my heart throbbed in bewilderment. Then it was too late. Fate, tired of hesitancy, took the cards out of my hands. Billie had been sitting, her head bowed on the table, the light above glistening on her hair. Suddenly she arose to her feet, her face white and drawn, her hands extended in a gesture of disgust. Attracted by the open window, and the black vista of night beyond, she stepped through onto the balcony, and stood there, leaning against the rail.

CHAPTER XX
WE ARRIVE AT A CRISIS

I remained there, pressed into one corner, unable to move, scarcely venturing to breathe, her skirt brushing my leg, the strands of her hair, loosened by the night wind, almost in my face. She was gazing straight out into the night, utterly unconscious of my presence, so deeply buried in her own trouble that all else seemed as nothing. For a moment she remained motionless, silent; then her hands pressed against her forehead, and her lips gave utterance to a single exclamation:

"Oh, God! I can never, never stand it! What shall I do?"

Perhaps I moved, perhaps some sense of the occult revealed my presence, for she turned swiftly, with a sharp gasp of the breath, and looked straight into my eyes. The recognition was instant, bewildering, a shock which left her speechless, choking back the cry of alarm which rose into her throat. She gripped the rail and stared as though at a ghost.

"Don't cry out," I entreated quickly. "Surely you know whom I am."

"Yes, yes," struggling to regain her voice. "I--know; but why are you here? How long have you been here?"

"It is a story too complex to repeat," I said earnestly, "but I have been here since your father first came--don't blame me, for I couldn't get away."

"Then--then you heard--"

"Yes; I heard everything. I tried not to; I pledge you my word it was all an accident. I was here for another purpose, a military purpose. I did not even know this was your home. I am trapped on this balcony, and dare not attempt to get away--I had to listen. You will believe what I say?"

I was pleading so desperately that she stopped me, one hand grasping my sleeve.

"Yes, of course. I am sure you could never do that purposely. But I do not know what to say, how to explain. You must go at once. Can you not realize my position if you are discovered here? What--what Captain Le Gaire would say?"

"Very easily," my voice insensibly hardening at the memory, "and I should like to remain to meet him, if that were the only danger. No, please stand exactly where you are, Miss Hardy, so as to keep me in the shadow. Thank you. There is a man sitting on a bench yonder just within the orchard. He has been there for the last twenty minutes, and it is his presence which has made it impossible for me to get away. Can I escape in any manner through the house?"

She shook her head, her glance wandering from the lighted room out again into the night.

"No; there is only the one door."

"Who are here besides Le Gaire and your father?"

"A half-dozen officers, two from the Louisiana regiment, the rest belonging to the staff; they are just ending up a feast in the dining-room."

"And is the house under guard?"

She hesitated, looking me now squarely in the eyes, her face clearly revealed as the light from within fell upon it.

"Why do you ask?--for military reasons?"

"No; that is all passed and gone. We came hoping to capture General Johnston, as scouts informed us this was his headquarters for the night. But he is not here, and you will do your cause no harm by telling me all I ask."

"I do not think there are any guards posted," she answered, convinced that I spoke the truth. "I have not been out, but I am sure there are no soldiers about the place, except the officers' servants at the stable with the horses. The general departed before dark, and took his bodyguard with him."

She had no reason to deceive me, and her sincerity was beyond question. This was better than I had dared hope, and instantly a new plan leaped into my mind, the very audacity of which made me gasp. Yet it might work, carried out with sufficient boldness, although only to be resorted to as a last desperate necessity. As I stood there, revolving this new thought swiftly through my mind, the old fear seemed to return to her.

"Did--did you hear--everything?" she asked again.

"I am afraid I did," I confessed humbly, "but I am going to forget."

"No, that is not necessary. I am not sure I am altogether sorry that you over-heard."

"But I am--at least, a part of what I overheard struck me rather hard."

"What was that?"

"Your reference to me. Billie, I had been dreaming dreams."

Her eyes dropped, the long lashes shading them.

"But I had previously warned you," she said at last, very soberly. "You knew how impossible such a thought was; you were aware of my engagement."

"Yes, and I also knew Le Gaire. All I hoped for was time, sufficient time for you to discover his character. He is no bug-a-boo to me any longer, nor shall any tie between you keep me from speaking. As I have told you I did not come here expecting to meet you--not even knowing this was your home--yet you have been in my mind all through the night, and what has occurred yonder between you and that fellow has set me free. Do you know what I mean to do?"

"No, of course not; only--"

"Only I must believe what you said about me to him; only I must continue to respect an agreement which has been wrung out of you by threat. I refuse to be bound. I know now the one thing I wanted most to know, Billie--that you do not love him. Oh, you can never make me think that again--"

"Stop!" and she was looking straight at me again. "I shall listen to you no longer, Lieutenant Galesworth. I cannot deny the truth of much which you have said, but it is not generous of you to thus take advantage of what was overheard. It was merely a quarrel, and not to be taken seriously. He is coming back, and--and I am going to marry him."

There was a little catch in her voice, yet she finished the sentence bravely enough, flinging the words at me in open defiance.

"When? To-night?"

"Yes, immediately, as soon as Captain Le Gaire can confer with my father."

I smiled, not wholly at ease, yet confident I knew her struggle.

"You might deceive some one else, Miss Billie," I said quietly, "and perhaps if I were not here this programme might indeed be carried out--I believe Le Gaire is cur enough to insist upon it. But I am here, and you are not going to marry him, unless you tell me with your own lips that you love the man."

She stared into my eyes, as though doubting my sanity.

"Will you consent to say that?"

"I deny your right to even ask."

"Yet I shall take silence as a negative, and act accordingly. No, you will not hate me for it; you may imagine you do for the moment, but the time will come when your heart will thank me for interference, for saving you from a foolish sacrifice. You do not love Le Gaire; you cannot look me in the eyes and say that you do."

"You are impertinent, ungentlemanly. I simply refuse to answer a question you have no right to ask."

"I assume the right in accordance with a law as old as man."

"What law?"

"The law of love," I returned earnestly, "the love of a man for the one woman."

I could see her slight form sway as the full significance of these words came to her; her cheeks flamed, but there was no shadowing of her eyes.

"I am going in, Lieutenant Galesworth," she said finally, drawing back to the open window. "You have forgotten yourself, forgotten the respect due me."

"But I have not, Billie," and in my earnestness I neglected all caution, stepping forward into the full glare of light. "The highest respect is the basis of true love, and, little girl, I love you."

She clung to the frame of the window, rendered speechless by my audacity, struggling with herself.

"Oh, don't say that! I cannot listen; I must not. Believe me, Lieutenant Galesworth, I do not altogether blame you, for I have been indiscreet, foolish. I--I have not meant to be; I merely endeavored to prove kind and friendly, never once dreaming it would come to this. Now it must end, absolutely end; even if you despise me for a heartless coquette, there is no other way. My path is laid out for me, and I must walk in it. It may not be altogether pleasant, but I made my choice, and it is too late now for retreat. I want you to help me, not make it any harder."

"By going away, you mean? By leaving you to be coerced?"

"I was not coerced; it was my own free choice."

We were both so interested as to forget everything except ourselves, utterly oblivious to the situation, or to what was occurring without. My eyes were upon her face, endeavoring to read the real truth, and I knew nothing of the two men at the edge of the orchard. Like a shot out of the night broke in a voice:

"Billie, who is that you have with you?"

I saw her reel against the side of the window, every trace of color deserting her face, her eyes staring down into the darkness. She gasped for breath, yet answered, before a thought flashed through my brain:

"Only a friend, papa. Did you suppose I would consent to remain alone long?"

"Le Gaire said he just left you."

She leaned out over the rail, half concealing me from view.

"Oh, that must have been fifteen minutes ago," and she laughed. "It is never safe to leave me as long as that. You know that, papa, and now I warn Captain Le Gaire."

The older man echoed her laugh, striking his companion lightly on the shoulder.

"I fear the little witch is right, Gerald," he said pleasantly. "Come, we'll go in, and uncover the whole conspiracy."

Their backs were toward us, and she straightened up, grasping me by the hand. She was shaking from head to foot, even her voice trembled.

"You must not be found here, and we have but a moment. Drop to the ground as soon as they turn the corner. Don't hesitate; don't compromise me."

"But what will you tell them?"

"Oh, I do not know--anything that comes into my head. Don't mind me, I'll take care of myself."

"But you will not; that is the whole trouble--if I go now I lose you forever. Billie, let me stay!"

She broke from me, stepping back into the room, yet there was a look in her eyes which made me desperate. She did not love Le Gaire, she despised him. I was certain of that, and more than half convinced her heart was already mine. Should I run from the fight like a coward, sneak away in the night, leaving her to be sacrificed? The very thought sickened me. Better to meet the issue squarely--and I believed I knew how it could be done. I grasped the curtain, drew it down twice in signal, and stepped into the room.

"I am going to take command here now, Billie," I said with new sternness. "All you need to do is obey orders."

CHAPTER XXI
WE CAPTURE THE HOUSE

If she was startled and frightened before, she was doubly so now at this sudden revolt on my part. But I had no time then for explanation, only for the stern exercising of authority. If I was right, if deep down in the girl's heart there was love for me, she would forgive this action as soon as she realized its purpose-- aye! she would respect me the more for daring the deed.

"Don't attempt to interfere now, my girl; go over to the big chair and sit down."

My revolver was in my hand, and she saw it, her eyes wide open.

"You--you are not going to hurt them?"

"No, not if they use any sense, but this is not going to be boys' play. Will you do as I say?"

She sat down, gripping the arms of the chair, and leaning forward, half inclined to scream, yet afraid to utter a sound. Without taking my eyes from her, I slipped across the room to where I would be partially concealed as the door opened. I knew what I was going to do, or, at least, attempt to do, and realized fully the risk I ran, and the chance of failure. It would require daring and coolness to capture those in the house, without raising any alarm, and likewise the prompt cooperation of my men. If they had seen my signal, and if I could disarm these first two, the rest should be comparatively easy. There were steps in the hall, and the jingle of spurs. Hardy entered first, his head turned backward as though he spoke to Le Gaire. I saw the girl rise to her feet, but my whole attention was concentrated upon the two men. The instant the space was sufficient, I forced the door shut, and stood with my back against it, the black muzzle of my Colt staring them in the eyes.

"Hands up, gentlemen!" I said sternly, "a movement means death."

They presented two astounded faces, Hardy's absolutely blank, so complete his surprise, but Le Gaire recognized me instantly, his mouth flying open, his eyes glaring.

"Good God!--you!"

"Yes; hands up, Le Gaire! Don't be a fool."

His dark complexion was yellow with pallor, and I knew him for a coward at heart, yet his very hatred of me made him dangerous. Hardy was different, realizing his helplessness, but eying me coolly, his hands held over his head.

"What does all this mean?" he asked quietly. "Who the devil are you?"

"He's that damned Yank Billie's been so interested in," broke out the captain, "the same fellow who knocked me off my horse at Jonesboro."

Major Hardy glanced toward his daughter inquiringly, but before she could utter a word in explanation I cut in:

"This has nothing to do with Miss Hardy. She is as much a prisoner as you are. Now, Captain, hand me your revolver--butt first, please. Major Hardy, I will also trouble you. Now both of you back up slowly against the wall."

Their faces were a study, Hardy rather seeming to enjoy the experience, his thin lips smiling grimly, but Le Gaire was mad, his jaw set, his eyes glaring at me.

"I should rather like to know what all this means, young man," said the former. "Do you expect to capture the house single-handed?"

"Hardly, but I've made a good start," now fully at ease, with a revolver in each hand, the third thrust in my belt. "However I've no time now to explain."

Without turning my face from them I sidled over to the window, speaking quietly into the darkness without: "Come in, men, one at a time."

Almost to my surprise they came over the rail like so many monkeys, scarcely a sound revealing the movements. I saw the smile fade from off the major's lips, and my eyes caught Billie's wide open in astonishment. The fellows hustled in behind me, not knowing what was expected of them, but ready enough for anything. I glanced at them, beckoning to Miles.

"All here, Sergeant? Then draw down the shade. Wilson, you and Carney come over here, and keep an eye on these two men. Miles, let me speak to you a moment."

I led him into one corner, outlining the situation in a dozen words.

"There may be half a dozen in the dining-room--yes, just across the hall--including a preacher--armed, of course, but they don't suspect there is a Blue-coat within ten miles. They're out for a good time, and have been having it. If you can get the bunch covered first, there need be no fight. Don't fire a shot; just lay the iron down on them. Take all the men along, except the two I need here. You know your business."

"Sure," grinning, "and what then?"

"Scout around the house. I don't believe there are any guards set, but it will be safer to make sure."

"There's some cavalrymen at the stable, sir; we heard 'em singin' out there."

"A few officers' servants; you can attend to them easily enough after you are certain about the house. By the way, who is the best man to send back?"

"Into our lines, sir? Young Ross would be all right."

There was a desk in one corner, with writing materials on it, but I was most anxious just then to be assured we controlled the situation. Some of those fellows across the hall might become restless, and stroll in here at any moment, to discover the cause for delay.

"Very well, Miles; leave Ross here, and carry out your orders; that should give you seven men--why, no, it doesn't! Where is the negro?"

"He said you told him he didn't need go beyond the head of the ravine, sir," explained the sergeant, "and as one of the men heard you say so, I didn't feel like making him come along. He started back for camp."

"I believe I did promise something like that," I admitted, "and he wouldn't have been much assistance anyway. Well, six men and yourself ought to do the business. Watch the windows, so none get away."

Perhaps I should have gone myself, but I was disinclined to leave the room, desirous of getting off my despatch without delay, and possessed implicit confidence in the promptness and discretion of the sergeant. He drew his revolver, the men silently following his example, and the little party slipped quietly out into the hall, the last man closing the door behind him. Evidently they encountered no one in the passageway. Listening intently I heard the dining-room door thrown back violently, a confused noise of feet, of chairs hurriedly pushed aside, a voice uttering a stern order, the sound of a brief struggle, ended by a blow and the thud of a body striking the floor, then numerous voices speaking excitedly, followed by silence. Convinced the work had been accomplished, and that the house was now entirely in our possession, I walked across the room to the desk. Miss Hardy still sat where I had ordered, and I was compelled to pass her chair. Her eyes met mine coldly.

"Would you permit me to go across to my father?" she asked.

"Most certainly; you are in no sense a prisoner, except I shall have to ask you to remain in the room for the present."

She inclined her head ever so slightly.

"I shall ask no further favor, and thank you for granting this."

I sank into the chair at the desk, and watched her cross the room. Her words and actions hurt me, and yet it was scarcely to be expected that she would be pleased with the sudden change in affairs. To see me thus in complete control of the situation, her father and Le Gaire prisoners, all their plans frustrated, was maddening, particularly so as she realized that this result came largely through her own indiscretion. I began myself to doubt the complete success of my scheme. Without question I had the power now to prevent her marriage, yet I might have gone too far, and caused a revulsion of feeling. She had been interested in me before--for it had been her part to help me in times of danger, and sympathy lies very close to love--but now the conditions were changed, and she might feel very different toward my interference. Perhaps I was destined to lose rather than gain, yet it was too late now to draw back--I must play the game out to its ending. I wrote rapidly, utterly ignoring her conversation with Hardy, yet someway conscious that Le Gaire sought to join in, and was answered in a single swift sentence, the girl not even turning to glance at him. The simple action caused my heart to leap to my throat--could it be the lady played a part, her coldness to me intended to deceive others? It was a hope, at least, and I went to my task with fresh courage. I told it all in a dozen sentences--Johnston's plans for the morrow; the withdrawal of Confederate troops from our left, and their concentration in reserve of the enemy's centre; our capture of the Hardy house, and my hope to retain possession until the right of our line could be flung forward. Then I called Ross, and he came across the room, looking scarcely more than a boy, but with a serious face.

"Can you find your way back down the ravine to our lines, my lad?"

"Yes, sir."

"Then don't lose any time. The Confederate troops have been withdrawn, but you must watch out for stragglers. Give this to Colonel Cochran, and tell him it must be forwarded to headquarters at once. Explain to him the situation here. Now be off." He saluted, wheeled sharply about, and went out the window. I heard him strike the ground. Then I sat silently looking at the others in the room, wondering how the sergeant was getting along, and slowly realizing that I had a white elephant on my hands. I was endeavoring to play two games at once, love and war, and the various moves were confusing. It might be possible even for my little squad to hold this advance position until reinforcements arrived, but what could be done with the prisoners? Billie might forgive me--realizing the motive--for all which had occurred thus far, but if I were to turn her father and Le Gaire over to the hardships of a Northern prison, I could expect no mercy. I cared little as to the fate of the others, they had taken the chances of war, but these two must be liberated before our troops came up. I could not catch the girl's eyes; she sat with averted face, talking earnestly to her father. Uneasy, and puzzled how best to straighten out the tangle, I went out into the hall, and glanced in at the room opposite. A bunch of gray-clad men were against the wall, disarmed and helpless, even their tongues silent, and three watchful troopers guarded them, revolvers in hand. All stared at me as I stepped forward.

"Where is the sergeant?"

"At the stable, sir."

"Oh, yes; hope he has as good luck there--got them all?"

"Every bloomin' one of 'em, sir. They was quite nice about it."

An indignant voice spoke from the gray line.

"Blamed if it ain't Atherton! Say, Major, what does all this mean?"

I laughed, stepping forward so as to see the speaker's face.

"Captain Bell, isn't it? Thought I recognized your voice. I'm not Atherton, although I believe I was introduced to you under that name once. I have wanted to thank you ever since for bearing testimony in my favor."

His jaw fell, his eyes staring.

"Who the devil are you then?"

"A Federal officer; my name is Galesworth."

"And this is no joke?"

"Well, hardly, Captain. I shouldn't advise you to take the affair that way. These fellows here might not appreciate the humor of it."

I turned back, and met Miles in the hall, just as he came in through the front door. He grinned at sight of me, evidently well pleased.

"Got every mother's son of 'em, sir," he reported. "Easy job too; never had to fire a shot, and only hit one fellow; he started a shindy in there," with a glance toward the dining-room. "There were five gray-jacks out in the stable, all asleep, an' they was like lambs. The blamed fools never had a guard set."

"They felt safe enough, no doubt, back here," I returned. "The last thing they thought about was any Yankees getting this far. Do you know what they were gathered here for?"

He shook his head.

"It was intended for a wedding party, until we butted in."

"Hell! not that pretty girl back in there?"

"Yes," for somehow I felt I had better tell him enough of the truth to make the situation clear. He was an honest, clear-headed fellow, and I needed help. "And that Confederate Captain--Le Gaire--was to be the bridegroom. I am going to tell you the whole story, Sergeant, and then you'll see what sort of a fix I'm in."

I went over it hastily, yet with sufficient detail so as to make it all clear to his mind. He listened soberly at first, and then his eyes began to twinkle, and he interrupted with numerous questions. Apparently he found the tale most amusing.

"Well, if that ain't the rummest story ever I heard! It beats a novel by 'bout a mile. I never was married myself, sir, but I've got a blamed pretty girl waitin' for me back in ol' Illinoy, an' I reckon I know what she'd want me to do in a case like this. Sure, I'm with you until the cows come home, and so are the rest o' the boys. Lord, this is the kind o' sojerin' I like; somethin' happenin' every minute. What's next, sir?"

"Perhaps I better look over the house first," I said thoughtfully, "and see where we can stow away these prisoners without needing all our men to guard them. You take charge in there while I am gone, Miles, and let the girl go anywhere she pleases so she promises not to leave the house."

"All right, sir," and the sergeant saluted, his eyes shining, as I started for the stairs.

CHAPTER XXII
MISS WILLIFRED DECLARES HERSELF

I glanced at the various rooms up stairs, but nothing seemed exactly suitable for our purpose, and, finally, taking a trooper along to hold a light, explored the basement with better results. Here I found a considerable cellar, divided into two sections, the floor of stone slabs, and the walls well bricked. Iron bars, firmly set, protected the small windows, and altogether the place appeared favorable for our purpose. To be sure, desperate prisoners could not be confined in such quarters for any length of time, but it would answer temporarily, providing we left a guard within. Satisfied as to this, after fixing up a stout bar across the door, I returned to the first floor, and gave orders to have the men taken below. We could not differentiate between officers and privates, but robbed the rooms up stairs of bed-clothing, and thus made them as comfortable as possible. Bell and the clergyman made voluble protests, but yielded to the inevitable, being persuaded by the revolvers of the guards to accompany the others. So far as arms went we were now well supplied, having added to our original equipment the officers' pistols, and the carbines of the men captured in the stable. This matter settled I turned to the consideration of the case of the two men remaining in the front parlor.

Here was a more serious problem, for I could not herd Major Hardy with those fellows below, nor was I willing to humiliate Le Gaire by any such treatment. Not that I thought him too good to associate with these others, but Billie must not think I was actuated by any feelings of revenge. I talked the situation over with the sergeant, who proved a hard-headed, practical man, and we decided upon an upstairs room, over the kitchen, which had only one small window, through which a man of ordinary size could hardly crawl. I went up to examine this more carefully, and to nail down the window frame. As I came out into the hall again, rather dreading the impending interview in the parlor, I saw her coming alone up the broad stairway. She did not see me until her foot was upon the last step, and then she stopped, suddenly, one hand gripping the rail, her cheeks burning. One glance into her eyes caused me to nerve myself for an unpleasant session.

"I have been waiting for you to return," she said very coldly, yet with a slight falter in the voice, "and when I spoke to the sergeant, he said you were up here."

I bowed, hat in hand, and waited, unwilling to speak until I knew something of her purpose.

"Lieutenant Galesworth, what is the meaning of all this? What do you propose doing with my father and Captain Le Gaire?"

"Did they send you to me to find out?"

"No; father merely supposed I was going to my own room after something I needed."

"And Le Gaire?" I insisted.

She looked at me frankly, her eyes utterly fearless.

"We have scarcely spoken, and--and he certainly would never have advised my coming to you. I came of my own volition, because--well, because you claimed this was all a service to me. I--I do not understand what you meant, or--or why you hold us prisoners."

I thought I saw light now. She forced herself to be angry with me, but face to face was unable to carry out the programme.

"Will you come up here, Miss Billie?" I asked. "Let us take this settee a moment, and I will endeavor to explain. We are alone here, and I would not care to talk freely before the others. I prefer them to think this is purely a military affair, don't you?"

She hesitated, biting her lip, and standing motionless. My hand was extended, but she ignored it, yet, after a moment, she stepped up beside me, her hand on the settee.

"It--it is not a military affair then?"

"Only incidentally--I told you the truth before."

"I--I do not remember."

"Perhaps I failed to make all clear; indeed, I was a little hazy myself, events crowded upon us so rapidly. Won't you sit down while I talk?"

She sank upon the settee, as though to an order, looking into my face, with an expression in her eyes I was unable to comprehend.

"I have wanted to see you alone," I began, determined there should be no lack of courage on my part. "There is no longer need of any secrets between us. We have met only once before to-night, but that meeting was of such a character that we were instantly acquainted. To be sure we were working at cross-purposes, and you outwitted me, but later you squared all that by saving me from capture."

"Why go over that unfortunate occurrence?" she interrupted. "Do you not suppose I regret that enough already?"

"I doubt if you regret it at all."

"But I do--I haven't had a moment's peace since."

"Indeed! Why?" and I bent lower, eager to read her eyes. "Because even in that little time you had learned to care for me?"

"Your words are insolent," rising to her feet, proudly, but I remained directly in her path.

"No, Miss Willifred," earnestly, "they are not, because they come from the heart. You are a woman, and therefore you understand. You cannot be angry with me, no matter how hard you try. You are endeavoring to deceive yourself, but the effort is useless. You do care for me--that was why you waited for me to get safely across the river; that was why you have come to me now. Ever since I left you in the grape arbor I have been in your thoughts."

"And why I was also about to marry Captain Le Gaire, I suppose," she interposed defiantly, but with eyes unable to meet mine.

"I can comprehend that easily enough, helped by what I overheard. You cannot tell me you desired to marry Captain Le Gaire--can you?"

"No," for I stopped, and thus compelled an answer. "It would be useless to deny that."

"I was so sure of this that I acted, took the one course open to me to prevent your doing this wrong. I deliberately determined to risk your displeasure rather than permit the sacrifice. You were marrying him merely because you had promised, because you could not explain to your father why your feelings had changed--you were afraid to confess that you loved a Yankee."

"But I didn't--it was not that!"

"Then what was it?"

She remained silent, but now I was fully aroused.

"Billie," my voice low, and barely reaching her ear. "When I rode away that night I knew I loved you. I was a Yankee soldier, but I had been captured by a Rebel. I scarcely possessed a hope then of meeting you again, but I did believe you already realized what kind of a man Le Gaire was. I could not conceive that you would marry him, and I swore to myself to seek you out at the earliest moment possible. Don't draw back from me, dear, but listen--you must listen. This means as much to you as to me."

"But I cannot--I must not."

"What is there to prevent? Your pride of the South? Your adherence to the Confederacy? I care nothing for that; we are not Rebel and Yankee, but man and woman. As to Le Gaire, I have no respect for his claim upon you, nor would your father have if he knew the truth. It is all an accident our meeting again, but it was one of God's accidents. I thought I was sent here to capture Johnston, but my real mission was to save you. I've gone too far now to retreat. So have you."

"I?" in half indignant surprise.

"Dear, do you suppose I would dare this if I doubted you?--if I did not believe your heart was mine?"

"And if convinced otherwise, what would you do?"

The tone in which this was spoken, the swift question startled me.

"Do? Why, there would be nothing to do, except return."

"Leaving your prisoners?"

I glanced out through the nearest window, noting the sky growing gray in the east, and suddenly realized that, if we succeeded in getting away ourselves now, the transporting of Confederates under guard would be scarcely possible. She seemed to read all this in my face, before I could frame an answer.

"I have listened to you, Lieutenant Galesworth," she burst forth, "because I had to. You have had everything your own way thus far, but now it is my turn. I am a woman, a woman of the South, a soldier's daughter, and am not likely to surrender my heart, my principles, my life before such an assault. You have taken too much for granted; because I have not wished to hurt you, you have believed my silence indicative of love; you have construed friendship into devotion. Now it is my turn to speak. I did like you, and helped you; without doubt I was indiscreet, but I thought only of friendship, supposing we would part then, never to meet again. Under those circumstances," and her voice faltered slightly, "it may be that I said and did more than I should, enough--well, enough to encourage you. But--but I thought it all over with. You knew of Captain Le Gaire, and that should have been sufficient. Yet you come here, in face of all this, and--and dare to make love to me."

"But you are forgetting what I overheard--the fact that I know your real feelings toward Le Gaire."

"No, I do not forget, but that was nothing--nothing to do with you. It was merely the result of a mood, a whim, a lovers' quarrel. No, don't speak, don't stop me. I am not going to lie. It was not a mood, nor a whim. I had been analyzing my own heart, and discovered Captain Le Gaire was not what I had believed him to be. The very fact that both he and my father so took everything for granted, arranged all details without consulting my wishes, made me rebellious. But your dictation is even worse than theirs. They had some right, while you have none, absolutely none, Lieutenant Galesworth--have you?"

"I--I hardly know," confused by this direct question, and the flash of her eyes. "I supposed I had."

"Yet with nothing but imagination to build upon. Have I ever told you I did not care for Captain Le Gaire, or that I loved you?"

"No," I admitted, feeling myself driven relentlessly to the wall.

"I am not angry at you, for I understand how all this has occurred. I believe you have been inspired by the highest motives, and a desire to serve me. If I am angry at any one, it is myself. I have permitted you to go too far, to assume too much. Now it ends, for I am going to marry Captain Le Gaire."

She stood up straight before me, her head poised proudly, her cheeks flushed, her eyes bright with excitement. Never before had she appeared more attractive, and the love that swelled up into my heart seemed to choke all utterance. Could I have mistaken everything? Could I have deceived myself so completely? Did these hard words represent her true purpose, or were they merely wrung out of her by stress of circumstance? I could not determine, but I knew this--I could not turn about now and retreat. If I did that I would certainly lose, while if I fought it out there was still hope. No woman--at least no woman like Willifred Hardy--ever loved a coward, or a quitter, and I was determined she should not catalogue me in either class. All this came to me rather in instinct than thought, yet I was ready enough when she began questioning.

"Now you will go away, won't you?"

"Go away?"

"Yes, back to your own people, and leave us alone. There is no reason why you should stay here longer. You are not serving me, nor your cause. Release your prisoners, and get away safely before you yourself are captured."

"Did Le Gaire tell you to make this proposition?"

"Certainly not," indignantly, "I have not spoken to Captain Le Gaire."

"Well, Miss Billie," soberly, "I accept your words just as they are spoken, and will trouble you no longer with my attentions. But this has become a military matter now. It is too late for us to attempt getting back, but I have sent a man for reinforcements, and we shall hold this house until they come. I do not propose to release a single prisoner, or permit a rumor of what has occurred here to reach Confederate headquarters. You are also a prisoner, although I will accept your parole."

She flung back her head defiantly.

"Which I refuse to give."

"Then obey my orders; is that your room yonder?"

"Yes."

"I will trouble you to go in there."

She stared at me, biting her lip, with foot tapping the carpet, but I had spoken sternly.

"Do you mean that?"

"Every word. I hope I shall not have to call one of my men, and place you under guard."

There could be no doubt she was angry, yet I was the master, and, after one glance into my face, her eyes burning, she swept by me, and entered the room designated. I gave a glance about its interior, marking the distance to the ground; then took the key and inserted it in the outer lock. She stood silently facing me, her face flushed, her bosom rising and falling swiftly.

"I regret very much this necessity," I apologized, "but you have left me no alternative."

"I have no desire to be spared," she returned, "and no favors to ask, Lieutenant Galesworth."

Our eyes met, mine, I am sure, as resolute as her own, and I stepped back into the hall, closing and locking the door.

CHAPTER XXIII
THE CHALLENGE

I went slowly down stairs, swayed by a conflict of emotions. Had I indeed gone too far, been too stern and abrupt? Still it was surely better to err in this direction than to exhibit weakness, and it was only between these two that I had any choice remaining. What lay between us and our own lines was uncertain--possibly Confederate pickets, surely bands of stragglers, renegades from both armies. Now that we had waited so long, it would be a desperate chance to attempt to traverse that ravine in daylight. We were far safer here, hidden away, but must guard well that no knowledge of our presence be scattered abroad. Billie had defied me, threatened, and refused to accept parole; nothing remained but to hold her prisoner. Besides her words had stung and angered me. Even while I doubted their entire truth they still hurt, serving to increase my bitterness toward Le Gaire.

I was in this mood as I paused a moment to glance out at the gray dawn. The smooth pike was at least a hundred yards away, barely visible here and there through the intervening trees. Everything about was quiet and deserted--war seemed a long way off. Standing there alone, hearing the birds singing in the branches, and gazing out across the green, closely trimmed grass, I could scarcely realize our perilous position, or the exciting events of the past night. I felt more like a guest than an invader, and was compelled to bring myself back to realities with an effort. I was helped by the sudden appearance of Miles in the hallway.

"Thought I better take another look down stairs, sir," he explained, as I turned, facing him. "They are quiet enough in there."

"I was just going in," I said. "We will have to put those two with the others at present. Our people should be up here before night, and meanwhile we must remain quiet. Anything happened in there?"

"Nothing important. The old major fell asleep after the girl left, but the other fellow is pacing back and forth like a caged tiger, and cursing. He's asked me some leadin' questions 'bout you, an' where Miss Hardy's gone. Were you goin' in, sir?"

"Yes; you better wait."

I opened the door, and stepped into the parlor, the sergeant following, evidently anticipating a scene. The room showed some signs of disorder, the furniture disarranged, and one chair overturned. Wilson sat in front of the window, the shade of which had been drawn down, and the other guard was near the door. Both men had their revolvers drawn, and, from their positions, and Le Gaire's attitude, apparently trouble was anticipated. He was in the middle of the room, with hands clinched and eyes blazing, and wheeled to face me as I entered.

"Oh, it's you, is it!" he exclaimed, sudden anger sweeping away every vestige of control. "I may be a prisoner, but I'll be damned if I'll keep still. This whole affair is an outrage. What have you done with Miss Hardy?"

"The lady has gone to her own room up stairs, Captain Le Gaire," I replied courteously enough.

"But not until after seeing you, you sneaking Yankee hound," he burst forth, striding forward. "What does this all mean? What influence have you got over the girl?"

The major sat up suddenly.

"See here, Le Gaire, you leave my daughter's name out of this."

The enraged captain favored him with a glance.

"I know more about this affair than you do, Hardy. This blue-bellied puppy was with Billie before, and I knew there was some infernal scheme on the moment I saw him here to-night. The girl helped him to get away once before, and there's some trick being worked off now."

The older man was upon his feet instantly.

"Hold on there; not another word; whatever my girl has done she is not going to be condemned in my presence without a hearing."

"Major Hardy," I broke in, and stepped between them. "This is my quarrel, and not yours. Your daughter has done nothing for which she can be criticised. All her connection with me has been accidental, and during our last interview she merely begged for your release. When I refused to grant the request, she repudiated her parole, and I locked her in her own room as a prisoner. I did not even know this was your home, or that Miss Willifred was here, when I came. When Captain Le Gaire insinuates that there was any arrangement between us he lies."

"Were you not on the balcony alone, talking together?"

"Yes, she caught me there, by coming out suddenly."

"And protected you, you coward--drew us into the trap."

"Miss Hardy had no knowledge of what I proposed doing, nor that I had any men with me. Indeed, I myself acted merely on the spur of the moment."

"What were you sneaking about there in the dark for then?" he sneered. "You are nothing but a contemptible spy."

I was holding my temper fairly well, yet my patience was near the breaking point.

"I may as well tell you," I answered at last, "and my men will corroborate all I say. We came here under special orders hoping to capture General Johnston, who, we were informed, was quartered here for the night. We had no other object--"

"Until you saw Billie."

I wheeled upon him so fiercely that the fellow took a step backward.

"Captain Le Gaire, you have said enough--all I shall permit you to say. Miss Hardy had no connection whatever with this affair. If it is true that you are engaged to the lady, then you should be defending instead of attacking her."

"I should hardly come to you for instructions."

"Then take them from Major Hardy."

"Oh, hell, Hardy don't understand. He's as blind as a bat, but you cannot pull the wool over my eyes, Mr. Yankee spy. I've seen some of your fine work before. If I wasn't a prisoner under guard I'd give you a lesson you'd remember as long as you lived."

I stood holding my breath, looking at him, scarcely less angry than he, yet outwardly cool.

"You would give me a lesson?"

"I spoke plainly enough, I hope. This is a personal matter between us, and you know it, and a Southern gentleman settles his own affairs. Only a Yankee coward would hide behind his authority."

"And you think I do?"

He glanced about, with a wave of the hand at the guards.

"Doesn't it look like it?" he asked sarcastically.

The sneer cut me to the quick, cut me so sharply I replied before stopping to reflect. If he wished to fight me I would give him a chance; either he must make good his boasting or have his bluff called. And there was but one way. I looked at the two troopers, who were staring at us in deep interest; at Miles' grinning appreciation of the scene, and at Hardy, puzzled, but still angry at the use of his daughter's name. Then my eyes met the captain's.

"I am greatly inclined to accommodate you, Captain Le Gaire," I said quietly, "and give you any opportunity you may desire on equal terms. Sergeant, take the men into the hall."

They passed out reluctantly enough, and I stepped over to make certain the door was securely closed. Then I came back, and fronted the fellow. He had not changed his position, although the major had again risen to his feet.

"Well," I asked, "now what is it you wish to say?"

"Am I no longer a prisoner?"

"Not so far as our personal relations are concerned. My men will prevent your leaving these grounds, or sending out any message before night. Otherwise you are at liberty. Now what do you propose doing?"

My unexpected promptness dazed him, but in no way diminished his anger.

"Will you fight me?"

"I see no occasion for it."

"Then I will furnish one."

Before I could recoil, or even realize his purpose, he sprang the single necessary step forward and, with open hand, struck me in the face.

"Even a blue-belly should understand the meaning of that," he exclaimed hotly.

I did understand, the hot blood surging to my cheeks, yet in some mysterious way I never in my life felt cooler, more completely in control of myself. Every nerve tingled, yet not a muscle moved, and I smiled into his face, truly glad it had come to this.

"Personal combat is not a habit with us, Captain Le Gaire," I said coldly. "But in this case you will not find me seeking escape. I am very much at your service."

"Now?" his eyes blazing.

"The quicker the better. Who seconds you?"

"Major Hardy, of course--"

"I'm damned if I will, Le Gaire," burst in the staff-officer indignantly, thrusting himself forward. "You forced this matter with an insult no gentleman could take, and besides have dragged my daughter's name into the affair."

"You refuse to act for me?"

"Emphatically, yes! In the first place I don't believe in your damned Louisiana code, and in my opinion, you've acted like a confounded bully. So far as I can see Galesworth has done his duty, and nothing more. I'd go out with him, under the circumstances, before I would with you."

"I could not think of asking such a favor," I blurted out in astonishment.

"You do not need to ask--I volunteer, if you can use me."

I do not believe I shall ever forget the expression on the dark, scowling face of Le Gaire. He had not expected this, that he would be deserted by his own people, yet the fact merely served to increase his bitterness, harden his purpose. The twist of his lips left his teeth exposed in an ugly grin.

"All right, Hardy," he said, at last, "I'll not forget this, and I reckon the story won't help you any in our army. I'll get the Yank, second or no second, if the fellow doesn't back out."

"You need have no fear on that score," I replied soberly. "I am no believer in the duel, and this will be my first appearance on the field, but you have got to fight now. Moreover you shall have all your rights guarded." I stepped to the door, and opened it.

"Sergeant, go down to the prisoners and bring Captain Bell here."

He was back in another moment, grasping the arm of the surprised Confederate, who stared about at us in silent wonderment.

"Captain Bell," I asked, "I presume you have some acquaintance with the duelling code?"

He bowed gravely, waiting for me to explain.

"Captain Le Gaire has seen fit to strike me in the face with his open hand, and I have agreed to meet him at once. Will you act for the gentleman?"

"Why not Major Hardy?"

"Because he will represent my interests."

Bell turned his eyes toward the major, puzzled and uncertain.

"This looks rather queer to me, Hardy. Has Le Gaire done something which will prevent my acting in his behalf?"

Hardy stroked his chin, and squared his shoulders.

"Captain Le Gaire made some reflections on my family, sir, which I resent. I refused to act for him on that ground, but I know of no reason why you could not honorably serve. I merely prefer to assist Galesworth."

Bell hesitated, feeling, no doubt, there was something behind all this he did not comprehend. It was also evident enough that he was no admirer of Le Gaire, the latter gazing at him without a word.

"Am I perfectly free to act?"

"Yes--on parole of the grounds."

"Very well, I accept; I presume my man Is the challenged party?"

Both Hardy and myself bowed.

"Then I will ask Captain Le Gaire to accompany me to the dining-room. I shall return in a few moments."

We watched them pass out, and then Hardy and I turned, and looked into each others' faces.

CHAPTER XXIV
I BECOME A FAMOUS SWORDSMAN

Sergeant," I said shortly, "I think you can be of greater service in the hall." He disappeared reluctantly enough, and, as the door closed, I extended my hand to the major.

"I certainly appreciate your assistance," I began warmly. "I know very little about these affairs, or how they are conducted."

He took my hand, yet with no great cordiality, plainly enough already somewhat doubtful as to his course.

"I presumed as much, sir, but first, and before we proceed further, I should like to have some explanation of the trouble between you and Le Gaire. You are doubtless aware that I am the father of Willifred Hardy."

"Yes, Major, and I am perfectly willing to tell you the whole story. Shall I send for Miss Hardy to corroborate whatever I may say?"

"No, sir. You are a Yankee, but a gentleman, and I accept your word. I prefer Billie should know nothing of what is occurring."

I told it swiftly from the beginning, yet was careful to leave no impression that she had performed anything more than a mere friendly service to an enemy in danger. Even then it was difficult for the Confederate to appreciate fully the girl's motives, and his face clearly expressed disapproval. As I came to an end, after telling of her effort to gain his release, and my locking her within her own room, he paced back and forth across the floor, scowling down at the carpet.

"By Gad, you tell the story all right," he exclaimed, "but that doesn't seem like Billie; whatever got into the girl to make her do a trick like that?"

"You mean helping me?"

"Yes, against Le Gaire. I can understand how she took you through to Jonesboro; that was necessary. But all the rest is a puzzle. Did you know she was engaged to Captain Le Gaire?"

"Yes; but evidently she did not think it would help him any to betray me, and she was careful enough I should not escape in time to do any harm to your army. There was no treason in her act, Major, only she felt sympathy toward me."

"But she permitted your attack on the man."

"She knew nothing of it, until it was all over with." I hesitated, but why should I? Surely he must already begin to perceive the truth. "That she should have left him lying there until I was safely across the river is the only act which tells hard against Le Gaire. No woman could have done that, Major Hardy, if she really loved the wounded man."

He did not reply, evidently endeavoring to realize all my meaning.

"This is where you have made your mistake," I went on convincingly. "Nothing is holding your daughter to Le Gaire but her promise. I was obliged to overhear their conversation after you left, and he appealed to her pride, to the honor of the Hardys, in order to gain her consent to the marriage. She told him she no longer loved him, that he was not the man she had supposed him to be--actually begged for release. I can understand the situation, and, it seems to me, you ought to now. He is a handsome fellow, dashing and reckless, the kind to make an impression. She was flattered by his attentions, and deceived into the thought that she really cared for him. Then she saw his true nature--his selfishness, brutality, cowardice, even--and revolted. I doubt if I had anything to do with this change--it was bound to come. You are a man, Major Hardy, and must know men--is Le Gaire the kind you would want your daughter to marry?"

"By Gad! the way you put it--no!" emphatically. "I've thought well enough of him until to-night; probably he's kept his best side turned toward me, and, besides, it never once occurred to me that Billie didn't want him. I've heard stories about the man, pretty hard ones at that, but he appeared like a gentleman, and I naturally supposed them largely fairy tales. Because I felt sure Billie liked him, I did also, but to-night he has shown me the other side of his character. Still, I don't know that I wonder much at his hating you."

"I have given him all the cause I could--would gladly give more if possible."

Hardy's eyes twinkled.

"I reckon your heart is all right, even if your uniform is the wrong color. But, young man, this affair puts me in a queer box. I spoke up rather hastily a while back, and now here I am seconding a damned Yankee in a fight against one of our own men--it don't just look right."

"I merely accepted your own offer; no doubt my sergeant would act."

"Oh, I'll stay. The fact is, I rather like you, Lieutenant--eh, what is the name? Oh, yes, Galesworth--you see Billie never even so much as mentioned having met you. Anyway, I'm in this affair, and am going to stick, although if all they tell about Le Gaire is true I wouldn't give much for your chances of coming out whole."

"He is a duellist then?"

"Notorious; although, as near as I can learn, he has not had a serious affair for some time. He assured me once, when I ventured to question him, that he was through with that sort of thing. It's common practice among the Louisiana hot-bloods, and I supposed he had got his senses. Probably Billie never even heard of his reputation in this respect. What do you do best--shoot or fence?"

"Shoot, although I am hardly an expert at either."

"Le Gaire will name swords," he said soberly. "He's a fine swordsman, and probably the only question is how badly he'll try to hurt you."

"A pleasant prospect surely."

"For him, yes, but as your second I propose impressing Captain Bell, when he arrives, with the idea that you are particularly expert with the sabre, which happens to be the only sword weapon present. If I succeed he may decide that pistols will be better."

I stared at him with full appreciation, realizing the man was really seeking to serve me.

"May make it too," he went on calmly. "You're a stronger man than Le Gaire, and that means something with the sabre. If I can convince Bell, he'll make Le Gaire decide in favor of the gun. There he comes now. Well, Bell, you've been long enough about it--must be your first case."

The infantryman bowed rather coldly, his back against the closed door, as he surveyed us both.

"I have not had much experience in such affairs, Major Hardy, and I desired some understanding of the circumstances before finally consenting to act," he replied stiffly. "I am informed that Captain Le Gaire is the challenged party."

"Well, that might be a question, but we will waive the technicalities. Le Gaire provoked the fight, and was rather nasty about it in my judgment, but all we are anxious about now is to get the preliminaries over with as soon as possible. We acknowledge that your man was the one challenged."

"Then, sir, we demand an immediate meeting, and name swords as the weapons."

Hardy turned to me, a smile of delight illumining his face.

"Good enough," he exclaimed, sufficiently loud to reach the ears of the astonished captain. "Not so bad, hey, Galesworth?"

I nodded, but without venturing a reply, and Bell exhibited his surprise in his face.

"Is--is Lieutenant Galesworth an expert with the sabre?" he asked, after a moment's silence.

"Is he!" echoed Hardy. "Do you mean to say Le Gaire has never heard of him?"

"I--I think not."

"That's odd. Why, we of the staff knew all about those sabre trials in the Federal camp. I naturally supposed Le Gaire wished to try his skill with the champion for the honor of the South. Such a struggle ought to be worth seeing, but Galesworth would have the advantage of weight, and length of arm."

Bell evidently did not know either what to say or do. This threw an entirely new light on the situation, and left him in an awkward position. He shuffled uneasily about.

"Would--would you gentlemen mind my consulting Captain Le Gaire again?" he questioned doubtfully. "I think he should fully understand his opponent's skill."

Hardy laughed, completely at ease, and enjoying the other's dilemma.

"Well, I hardly know about that, Bell. Under the laws of the code we can hold you to your first choice, and I'm inclined to do so. Great joke on Le Gaire. However, I am willing to leave it to my man. What do you say, Galesworth?"

I had retired to the opposite side of the room, and was leaning with one arm on the mantel. In spite of the seriousness of the affair, it was impossible not to be amused by this sudden turn. Bell's eyes shifted questioningly toward me.

"Surely Lieutenant Galesworth will not desire to take any undue advantage," he ventured.

"Was not that Captain Le Gaire's idea?" I returned sharply. "He has the reputation of expert swordsmanship."

"He is a swordsman, yes, but does not profess to excel with the sabre."

I waited a moment in silence, permitting my hesitancy to become plainly apparent.

"Well, Captain Bell, much as I prefer the weapons already named, I will nevertheless consent to a change. I am ready to concede anything if I can only compel your man to fight."

"Do you mean to question Captain Le Gaire's courage, sir?" hotly.

"He seems to be fairly solicitous about his own safety, at least," chimed in Hardy. "Go on, Bell, and talk it over with him--this is not our row."

The little captain backed out still raging, and the major followed him to the door, lingering there as though listening. I watched curiously until he straightened up, struggling to keep back a laugh.

"That's some liar you've got for a sergeant, Galesworth," he said genially. "Bell ran up against him in the hall, and stopped to ask a question. He wasn't exactly certain we had been telling the truth. Your man must have been primed for the occasion the way he turned loose. Would like to have seen Bell's eyes pop out as the fellow described your exploits. Makes me proud to know you myself."

"Did Miles say I was an expert with the sabre?" I questioned in astonishment.

"Did he! Champion of the Army of the Tennessee; undefeated for two years, both afoot and on horse-back; described a wonderful stroke that caught them all; told about how you accidentally drove it an inch too far once, and killed your opponent. Oh, he was great. It will be pistols when Bell comes back; don't doubt that, my boy, and I know the very spot--out back of the stable, level ground, and no interference."

The interest which Major Hardy was exhibiting, as well as the promptness with which he had espoused my side of the quarrel, made me suspicious that he was not altogether sorry to be thus easily rid of Le Gaire. I could not venture questioning him on so delicate a matter, but without doubt he also saw the Louisianian in a new light, and began to comprehend the change in his daughter. Moreover the humor in the situation appealed to him, and, having once volunteered to serve me, he became thoroughly loyal to that purpose. His very presence gave me courage, and his words stiffened me for the coming ordeal. This was my first occasion of the kind and, as the earlier anger wore off, I found myself looking forward with some dread to the encounter. It was not fear, but the newness of the experience jarred my nerves. I paced back and forth across the room, only partially aware of what he was saying, endeavoring to straighten matters out in my own mind. Was I doing right? Was I justified in this course of action? I had followed the impulse of passion, the sting of Le Gaire's blow driving all other memory from me. But now I realized the peril in which my action might involve others, the men under my command, for instance, and wondered what Billie would think and say when the news of the quarrel reached her. She would understand the real cause, yet, with her father upon my side, I was not likely to suffer greatly. Anyway the die was cast; it was too late now to regret. Bell returned full of apology and explanation, expressing a desire that the weapons be changed to pistols. Hardy arose from his chair, his eyes twinkling behind heavy lashes.

"Sure; Galesworth is easily satisfied. I have two derringers up stairs exactly alike; my father was out with them twice! Quite a fad duelling was in his day, but the guns haven't been used for years. Come handy now. By the way, Lieutenant, you shoot equally well with either hand, I believe? Very valuable accomplishment; never could myself. We will meet you, Captain Bell, back of the stable in fifteen minutes. Sorry we have no surgeon present. That is all, is it not?" as the infantryman still lingered. "The minor details can be arranged on the field."

CHAPTER XXV
THE END OF THE DUEL

The sun was slightly above the horizon, still showing round and red through the slight mist of early morning, as the major and I passed down the deserted front steps, and circled the house on our way to the place of meeting. Under his arm was the leather case containing the derringers, and we crossed the intervening turf without exchanging a word. I was myself in no mood for conversation, and Hardy appeared equally inclined to silence. I glanced across at him, noting how straight he stood in his well-worn uniform, how gray his hair was, and the stern manliness of his face. From head to foot he was the gentleman and the soldier. By some chance our eyes met, and, with a quick glance back at the house, he stopped suddenly.

"Galesworth," he said quietly, his glance searching my face, "I do not wish you to have any misunderstanding about my exact position in this affair. The war is not personal with me. We differ politically, and I am as loyal to the South as any one, and you wear the Blue with just as much honor as I wear the Gray. But when it comes to men I stand with the one I believe to be nearest right. Le Gaire forced this quarrel on you deliberately; he was threatening to do it before you came in. In fact, his manner ever since our capture has disgusted me, and when he finally dared to drag Billie's name into the controversy, I naturally rebelled. If there is anything I despise in this world, sir, it is a bullying duellist, and, by Gad! that's what the fellow looks like to me."

"I comprehend perfectly, Major Hardy," I said, as he paused. "You are merely doing as you would be done by."

"Well, yes, that's a partial explanation. I prefer to see fair play. Yet I am going to confess that isn't all of it. I rather like you, young man--not your damned uniform, understand--and the way you've acted toward my girl. You've been honorable and square, and, by Gad, sir, you're a gentleman. That's why I am going to see you through this affair. If all I hear is true, Le Gaire came back to me with a lie, and that is something I have never taken yet from any man."

He stood straight as an arrow, his shoulders squared, his slender form buttoned tightly in the gray uniform coat. The sun was upon his face, clear-cut, proud, aristocratic, and his eyes were the same gray-blue as his daughter's. Then he held out his hand and I clasped it gladly.

"I cannot express the gratitude I feel, Major Hardy," I faltered. "One hardly expects such kindness from an enemy."

"Not an enemy, my boy--merely a foeman. I am a West Pointer, and some of the dearest friends I have are upon the other side. But come, let us not be the last on the field."

He tried to talk with me pleasantly as we crossed the garden, and approached the stable, and I must have answered, yet my mind was elsewhere. This was all new to me, and my mood was a sober one. My father was an old-time Puritan to whom personal combat was abomination, and even now I could feel his condemnation of my course. I regretted myself the hot headedness which had led me on, but without the faintest inclination to withdraw. Yet that earlier hatred of Le Gaire had left me, and his blow no longer stung. No desire for revenge lingered, only a wish to have the whole matter concluded quickly, and a hope that we both might leave the field without serious injury. It was in this frame of mind that I turned the corner of the stable, and saw the chosen duelling ground. It was a smooth strip of turf running north and south, with the stable to the left, and a grove of trees opposite. The building cast a shadow over most of the space, and altogether it was an ideal spot, well beyond view from the windows of the house. Hardy opened the leather case, placing it upon the grass, and I saw the two derringers lying against the plush lining, deadly looking weapons, with long steel-blue barrels, and strangely carven stocks. Someway they fascinated me, and I watched while he took them up and fondled them.

"Rather pretty playthings, Galesworth," he said admiringly. "Don't see such often nowadays, but in my father's time they were a part of every gentleman's belongings. He would as soon have travelled without his coat. I've seen him practise;

apparently he never took aim," he held the weapon at arm's length. "Wonderfully accurate, and the long barrel is better than any sight; just lower it this way; there's almost no recoil."

The sound of a distant voice caused him to drop the pistol back into its place, and rise to his feet. Then Le Gaire and Bell turned the corner of the stable, stopping as they perceived us standing there. The major removed his hat, his voice coolly polite.

"I believe everything is prepared, gentlemen. Captain Bell, if you will examine the weapons, we will then confer as to the word and the method of firing."

"I prefer choosing my own pistol," broke in Le Gaire bluntly, "and loading it as well."

Hardy's face flushed, his eyes hardening.

"As you please, sir," he retorted, "but I might construe those words as a reflection on my integrity."

"When a Confederate officer takes the side of a Yank," was the instant angry response, "he can hardly claim much consideration."

"Captain Le Gaire," and Hardy's voice rang, "you have enough on your hands at present without venturing to insult me, I should suppose. But don't go too far, sir."

"Gentlemen," broke in Bell excitedly, "this must not go on. Le Gaire, if you say another word, I shall withdraw entirely."

The Louisianian smiled grimly, but walked over to the weapon case, and picked up the two derringers, testing their weight, and the length of barrel. Hardy stared at him, his lips compressed.

"Well," he burst forth at last, "are you satisfied, sir?"

"I'll choose this," insolently, and dropping the other back into its place. "Where is the powder and ball?"

The major pointed without daring to speak.

"All right; don't mind me. I always load my own weapon, and just now I am anxious to shoot straight," and he looked across at me sneeringly.

If it was his purpose by all this theatrical display to affect my nerves, he failed utterly, as instead, the very expression of his face brought me back to a fighting spirit. Hardy saw this, and smiled grimly.

"Step this way a moment, Bell," he said quietly, "while we arrange details. I reckon those two game-cocks will wait until we are ready."

The two officers moved away a dozen paces and stopped in the shadow of the trees, conversing earnestly. I endeavored to keep my eyes off from Le Gaire, and remain cool. It seemed to me I saw every movement of a leaf, every dropping of a twig, yet could scarcely realize the position I was in. I was about to face that man yonder--now carefully loading his weapon--to deliberately fire upon him, and receive in return his fire. I felt as though it were a dream, a nightmare, and yet I was conscious of no fear, of no desire to avoid the ordeal. I can recall the scene now, clearly etched on my memory--the outlines of the trees silhouetted against the sky, the dark shadow of the stables, the green, level turf, the two figures--the one short and stout, the other tall and slender--talking earnestly; the deep blue of the sky overhead, the steel gleam of the derringer in the open case, and Le Gaire loading carefully, his eyes now and then glancing across at me. Then the two men wheeled with military precision, and walked back toward us. I saw Hardy take up the second pistol, and load it in silence, while Bell whispered to Le Gaire, the latter with his weapon tightly clasped. A moment later the major thrust the carved stock into my hand, and I looked at it curiously.

"Gentlemen," he said clearly, stepping to one side, "we will make this as simple as possible. You will take positions here, back to back."

The sound of his voice, the sharp ring of authority in it, awoke me to the reality as though I had received an electric shock. I felt the fierce beat of my heart, and then every muscle and nerve became steel. Without a tremor, my mind clear and alert, I advanced to the point designated, and stood erect, facing the south; an instant, and Le Gaire's shoulders were touching mine.

"Now listen closely," said Hardy, his voice sounding strangely far off, yet each word distinct. "I am to give the first word, and Bell the second. When I say 'forward' you will take ten paces--go slowly--and halt. Then Bell will count 'one, two, three'; turn at the first word, and fire at the third. If either man discharges his weapon before 'three' is spoken, he answers to us. Do you both understand?"

We answered together.

"Very well, gentlemen, are you ready?"

"I am."

"Go on."

There was a moment's pause, so still I could hear my own breathing, and the slight noise Le Gaire made as he gripped his derringer stock more tightly.

"Forward!"

I stepped out almost mechanically, endeavoring not to walk too fast, and regulating each stride as though I were measuring the field. At the end of the tenth I stopped, one foot slightly advanced for the turn, every nerve pulsing from strain. It seemed a long while before Bell's deep voice broke the silence.

"One!"

I whirled, as on a pivot, my pistol arm flung out.

"Two!"

Le Gaire stood sideways, the muzzle of his derringer covering me, his left hand supporting his elbow. I could see the scowling line between his eyes, the hateful curl of his lip, and my own weapon came up, held steady as a rock; over the blue steel barrel I covered the man's forehead just below his cap visor, the expression on his face telling me he meant to shoot to kill. I never recall feeling cooler, or more determined in my life. How still, how deathly still it was!

"Th--"

There was a thud of horses' hoofs behind the stable, Bell's half-spoken word, and the sharp bark of Le Gaire's levelled derringer. I felt the impact of the ball, and spun half around, the pressure of my finger discharging my own weapon in the air, yet kept my feet. I was shocked, dazed, but conscious I remained unhurt. Then, with a crash, three horsemen leaped the low fence, riding recklessly toward us. I seemed to see the gray-clad figures through a strange mist, which gradually cleared as they came to a sharp halt. The one in advance was a gaunt, unshaven sergeant, lifting a hand in perfunctory salute, and glancing curiously at my uniform.

"Mornin', gentlemen," he said briefly. "Is this the Hardy house--Johnston's headquarters?"

The major answered, and I noticed now he had Le Gaire gripped by the arm.

"This is the Hardy house, and I am Major Hardy, but Johnston is not here. Who are you?"

"Couriers from Chambers' column, sir. He is advancing up this pike. Where will we find Johnston?"

"Take the first road to your right, and inquire. When will Chambers be up?"

"Within four or five hours. What's going on here? A little affair?"

Hardy nodded. The sergeant sat still an instant, his eyes on me as though puzzled; then evidently concluded it was none of his business.

"Come on, boys!" he said, and with a dip of the spurs was off, the two others clattering behind. Hardy swung Le Gaire sharply around, his eyes blazing.

"You damned, sneaking coward!" he roared, forgetting everything in sudden outburst. "By Gad, Bell, this fellow is a disgrace to the uniform--you know what he did?"

"I know he fired before I got the word out," indignantly.

"The blamed curb--yes; and when those fellows rode up he tried to blurt out the whole situation. Good God, Le Gaire, aren't you even a soldier?" shaking the fellow savagely. "Haven't you ever learned what parole means? Damn you, are you totally devoid of all sense of personal honor?"

"I never gave my parole."

"You lie, you did; you are here on exactly the same terms as Bell and I--released on honor. Damned if I believe there's another man in Confederate uniform who would be guilty of so scurvy a trick. Were you hurt, Galesworth?"

"No, the ball struck my revolver case, and made me sick for a moment."

"No fault of Le Gaire's--the noise of the horses shattered his aim. Lord! how I despise such a cowardly whelp!"

He flung the man from him so violently he fell to his knees on the ground. The look of amazement on Le Gaire's face, his utter inability to comprehend the meaning of it all, or why he had thus aroused the enmity of his brother officers, gave me a sudden feeling of compassion. I stepped toward him. Perhaps he mistook my purpose, for he staggered partially erect.

"Damn you!" he yelled. "I'm fighting yet!" and flung the unloaded derringer with all the force of his arm at my face.

CHAPTER XXVI
MISS WILLIFRED SURPRISES US

The butt struck me fairly, and I went down as though felled by an ax. If I lost consciousness it could have been for scarcely more than a moment, but blood streamed into my eyes, and my head reeled giddily. Yet I knew something of what occurred, heard voices, caught dimly the movement of figures. Le Gaire ran, rounding the end of the stable, and Hardy, swearing like a trooper, clutching at his empty belt for a weapon, made an effort to follow. Bell sprang to me, lifting my head, and his face looked as white as a woman's. He appeared so frightened I endeavored to smile at him, and it must have been a ghastly effort. My voice, however, proved more reassuring.

"I'm all right," I insisted thickly. "Just tapped a little. I--I wasn't looking for anything like that."

"I should say not. Here, can you sit up? By Heavens! I hope Hardy catches him."

"He hardly will," I answered, struggling into sitting posture, a vision of the chase recurring to mind. "He was too mad to run."

Bell laughed nervously.

"I never supposed Le Gaire was that kind of a cur," he said regretfully. "I never liked the fellow, or had much to do with him. Blamed if I could understand why Miss Hardy--"

"Oh, he played nice enough with her up until the last week at least," I broke in, aroused by the name. "Le Gaire is good looking, and pleasant also when things are going his way. It's when luck is against him that he gets ugly. Besides, he had the major on his side."

"I happen to know something about that," returned Bell dryly. "It was talked over at headquarters. Le Gaire is rich, and Hardy hasn't much left, I reckon, and the captain filled him up with fairy tales. Some of them drifted about among the boys. There were others told also not quite so pleasant, which Hardy did not hear. You see, none of us cared to repeat them, after we realized Miss Willifred was interested in the man."

"You mean duelling?"

"No, that was rather mild; fellows in his regiment mostly cut him dead, and say he is yellow; generally in the hospital when there's a battle on. But Forsdyke tells the worst story--he heard it in New Orleans. It seems Le Gaire owned a young girl--a quadroon--whom he took for a mistress; then he tired of the woman, they quarrelled, and the cowardly brute turned her back into the fields, and had her whipped by his overseer. She died in three months."

"I guess it's all true, Bell," I said, and I told him of the boy. "He was our guide here last night, and it is just as well for Le Gaire the lad did not know he was present. Help me up, will you?"

I leaned on his arm heavily, but, except for the throbbing of my head, appeared to be in good enough condition. With slight assistance I walked without difficulty, and together we started for the house. At the edge of the garden Hardy appeared, still breathing heavily from his run. He stared at me, evidently relieved to find me on my feet.

"Broke the skin, my lad--a little water will make that all right. Glad it was no worse. The fellow out-ran me."

"He got away?"

"Well, the fact is, Galesworth, I do not really know where he went. The last glimpse I had he was dodging into that clump of bushes, but when I got there he was gone."

"Ran along the fence," broke in Bell, pointing. "You couldn't see him for the vines. See, here's his tracks--sprinting some, too."

We traced them easily as long as we found soft ground, but the turf beyond left no sign. Yet he could not have turned to the left, or Bell and I would have seen him. The fellow evidently knew this, yet if he ran to the right it would take him to the house. It hardly seemed possible he would go there, but he had been a guest there for some time, and probably knew the place well; perhaps realized he would be safer within--where no one would expect him to be--than on the road. This was the conception which gradually came to me, but the others believed he had gone straight ahead, seeking the nearest Confederate outpost. Able to walk alone by this time, I went in through the back door, and bathed my face at the sink, leaving Hardy and Bell to search for further signs of the fugitive.

As I washed I thought rapidly over the situation. Le Gaire knew that Chambers' force would be along the pike within a few hours--probably long before the appearance of any Federal advance in the neighborhood, as he was unaware that I had sent back a courier. The house was the very last place in which we would seek for him, and the easiest place to attain. Once inside, stowed away in some unused room, he could wait the approach of Chambers' troops, escape easily, and become a hero. The whole trick fitted in with the man's type of mind. And he could have come in the same way I had, sneaking through the unguarded kitchen--why, in the name of Heaven, had Miles neglected to place a guard there?--and then up the servants' stairs. I dried my face on a towel, rejoicing that the derringer blow had left little damage, and opened the door leading to the upper story. It was a narrow stairway, rather dark, but the first thing to catch my eye was a small clod of yellow dirt on the second step, and this was still damp--the foot from which it had fallen must have passed within a very short time. I had the fellow--had him like a rat in a trap. Oh, well, there was time enough, and I closed the door and locked it.

I talked with the sergeant, and had him send Foster to watch the kitchen door, and detail a couple of men for cooks, with orders to hurry up breakfast. Miles had seen nothing of Le Gaire, and when Hardy and Bell returned, they acknowledged having discovered no trace of the fugitive. I let them talk, saying little myself, endeavoring to think out the peculiar situation, and determine what I had better do. Already there was heavy cannonading off to the right, but at considerable distance. The battle was on, and might sweep this way before many hours, yet I could no longer doubt the complete withdrawal of Confederate troops from the neighborhood. Not a gray-jacket or flash of steel was visible, and everything about was a scene of peace. Yet when Chambers came this house would hardly escape without an overhauling. Of course he might not come this way, for Johnston could easily despatch a courier to advise another road, yet probably the line of march would not be changed. Should I wait, or withdraw my little force, at least as far as the shelter of the ravine? I cared nothing about retaining the prisoners, indeed was anxious to release both Hardy and Bell. Nor was I any longer worried about Le Gaire--especially his relations with Miss Willifred. I could trust the major to relate the story of the past hour to his daughter, and the captain would scarcely venture to face her again. It seemed to me we ought to go, as it would be no service to our cause to retain the house. However there was no hurry; we had ample time in which to breakfast, and--and, well I wanted to see Billie again, to leave behind me a better impression. I gave the major the key to her room, and asked him to call her for the morning meal, already nearly ready. She came down a few moments later, freshly dressed, and looking as though she had enjoyed some sleep. Her father must have given her some inkling of the situation, for she greeted me pleasantly, although with a certain constraint in manner which left me ill at ease.

Our breakfast passed off very nicely, the food abundant and well cooked, although we were compelled to wait upon ourselves. I asked Miles to join us, but he preferred messing with the men, and so the four of us sat at table alone. As though by mutual consent we avoided all reference to the war, or our present situation, conversation drifting into a discussion of art and literature. I realized later that Miss Willifred had adroitly steered it that way, but if it was done to test me, she could scarcely have chosen a better topic. I had come from the senior class of a great college into the army, and was only too delighted to take part again in cultured conversation. Bell had taken an art course, and Miss Hardy had apparently read widely, and the discussion became animated, with frequent clashes of opinion. I was happy to know that I surprised the lady by the extent of my information, and her flushed cheeks and brightening eyes were ample reward. The major said little, yet when he occasionally spoke it was to reveal that he was a man of unusual learning.

I shall recall the details of that meal as long as I live--the peculiar conditions, and the faces of those present. It was all so little like war, the only suggestion of conflict the uniforms we wore, and the dull reverberation of that distant cannonading. For the time, at least, we forgot we were upon the very verge of a battle, and that we were politically enemies. Prisoners were in the basement beneath, guards were patrolling the hall without, yet we laughed and joked, with never a reference to the great conflict in which all present bore part. Of course much of this was but veneer, and back of repartee and well-told story, we were intent upon our own problems. With me, now that I had decided upon my plans, everything centred upon Miss Willifred. I would search the house for Le Gaire, endeavor to have one word with her alone, and then retire to a place of greater safety with my men. The quicker I might complete these arrangements the better, and I could trust those present with some knowledge of my intention.

"Gentlemen," I said, as the party was preparing to rise, "just a moment. I am going to ask you to respect your parole for only a very short time longer. Of course this does not include Miss Hardy as she has refused all pledges to me. So soon as my men complete their breakfast, and a few details are looked after, we shall withdraw in the direction of our own lines. Naturally I have no desire to be captured by Chambers. I am merely going to request that you remain within doors until we depart. After that you may release the prisoners, and rejoin your commands."

The eyes of the two men met, and the major replied:

"Certainly, Lieutenant, we have no reason to complain."

"And Miss Hardy?"

"Oh, I will answer for her."

"That is hardly necessary, papa, as I will answer for myself," and her eyes met mine across the table. "I was angry last night, Lieutenant Galesworth, and unreasonable. If you will accept my parole now I give it gladly."

I bowed with a sudden choking of the throat, and Hardy chuckled.

"A very graceful surrender--hey, Bell? By Gad, this has been quite a night for adventure. Fact of it is, Galesworth, I'm mighty grateful to you for the whole affair, and, I reckon, Billie is also."

She arose to her feet, pausing an instant with her hand upon the back of the chair.

"Lieutenant Galesworth has merely made apparent to you what I had discovered some time ago," she said quietly. "I am sure he needs no thanks from me--perhaps might not appreciate them. I am going to my room, papa, until--until the Yankees leave."

"An unreconstructed Rebel," he exclaimed, yet clearly surprised. "Why, I thought you and Galesworth were great friends."

"Has he made that claim?"

"Why--eh--no. It was what Le Gaire said."

"Oh! I should suppose that by this time you would rather doubt the statements of that individual. Lieutenant Galesworth probably understands that we are acquaintances, and--enemies."

She left the room, without so much as glancing at me, Hardy calling after her,

"I'll come up as soon as I smoke a cigar with Bell."

The door closed, and his eyes met mine.

"What the devil is the trouble, my boy? That wasn't like Billie; I never knew her to harbor an unkind thought in her life. Have you done something to anger her?"

"Not to my knowledge, Major," I answered honestly. "Perhaps I was harsh last night, but I merely intended to be firm. This is all a great surprise to me."

He shook his head, and the two men left the room. I waited until certain they were safely out of the way. I was perplexed, hurt, by the girl's words and action. What cause had I given her for treating me with such open contempt? Surely not my avowal of love, however inopportune that might have been, nor my holding her prisoner. Could something have occurred of which I knew nothing? Could Le Gaire have poisoned her mind against me with some ingenious lie? It was all too hazy, too improbable, for me to consider seriously--but she must explain before we went away. With this in mind I passed into the hall, and began to ascend the stairs.

CHAPTER XXVII
THE BODY OF LE GAIRE

Miles had stationed a sentry just inside the front door, but he was the only one of our men visible, nearly all of the others being at breakfast in the kitchen. I felt no need of any help however, for Le Gaire was unarmed, and not of a nature to make serious resistance. Besides, if I was mistaken as to his hiding place in the house I preferred making the discovery alone. My exploration during the night had made me familiar with the arrangement of the front rooms, but not the extension to the rear. I stopped, in the silence, at the head of the stairs, to glance about, and decide where I had better begin. Miss Hardy's door was closed, even the transom lowered, and I instantly decided not to disturb her until the very last. Yet I was soldier enough to take the other rooms in rotation, realizing the danger of leaving an enemy in my rear. These were soon disposed of, although I made a close search, disarranging beds, delving into closets, and leaving no nook or corner big enough to conceal a man, unrevealed. I endeavored to accomplish all this quietly, yet must have made some noise, for as I rolled back a bed in the third room entered, I heard the door creak and sprang to my feet to confront Billie. I hardly know which was the more startled, for the girl staggered back, one hand thrown out.

"You! Oh, I thought--" she drew her breath quickly.

"You thought what?"

"Oh, nothing--only I heard the noise, and--and wondered who it could be." She looked about at the confusion. "What--what are you doing? Hunting for some one?"

"A needle in a haystack," I answered, suddenly suspicious that she might know something of the fugitive. "Will you help me search?"

"I--I hardly appreciate your humor," haughtily. "Is--is it Captain Le Gaire?"

"Why do you suspect that, Miss Willifred? Is it because you imagine the man may be here?"

"Because I know he got away; because I know your feeling toward him, your effort to take his life."

"You know! What is all this?" so stunned I could scarcely articulate. "Surely your father--"

"I know of no reason why my father should be dragged into this affair."

"But he was present; he surely told you what occurred."

"He said the two of you went out to fight; that it was a dishonorable affair. He gave me no particulars, and I asked none--I already knew what had taken place."

"Then you have seen Le Gaire since--is that so?"

She turned her back toward me, and stepped into the hall. The action was defiant, almost insulting.

"Miss Willifred, I insist on an answer."

"Indeed," carelessly, "to what?"

"To my question--have you seen Le Gaire since?"

"I refuse to tell you."

It was an instant before I found my voice, or could control my words. This was all most confusing, and yet the light was coming. Here was the secret of her sudden dislike for me. Her hand was already upon the knob of her own door, and she did not so much as glance back. What could I say? What ought I to say? Beyond doubt, uncertain as to her real feelings toward Le Gaire, Hardy had not revealed to her the fellow's disgraceful action. Some way, his brief explanation had merely served to confirm her previous opinion that the captain had been the one injured--such an impression she could have derived only from Le Gaire. It was equally clear I could not explain. She would scarcely believe any effort to defend myself. Why should she think me capable of a dastardly act? Why believe Le Gaire's hasty lie, and refuse me even a hearing? The thought left me so indignant that for the moment I felt indifferent even to her good opinion.

"Well, Miss Hardy," I said at last, conscious my voice trembled, "I am going to find this man if he is in the house, even if the search takes me to your own room."

"Then begin there," and she stood aside, the door flung open. "It must require great bravery to hunt down an unarmed man."

"I only know you are going to regret those words when you learn the truth. There is a mistake here, but one others must rectify. Your actions merely confirm my belief that Le Gaire sought refuge in this building. I am going to know before I withdraw my men."

She was not quite so defiant, not quite so certain, yet she did not move.

"Will you tell me--has he been here?"

"Why do you want to know?"

I hesitated, not really knowing myself, suddenly made aware that I had no true purpose in the search. My embarrassment confirmed her suspicion.

"Revenge, wasn't it?" scornfully. "A desire to complete the work begun yonder. I'll answer if you wish me to. Captain Le Gaire came here to me wounded, and seeking shelter. I helped him as I would any Confederate soldier. But he is not here now--see, the room is empty; yes, search it for yourself."

It was useless arguing, useless denying--the girl was in a state of mind which no assertions of mine could combat.

"Then where is he now?"

"I have no means of knowing--safely away from the house, I hope. I--I left him here when I went down stairs; when I came back he was gone."

"And you say he was wounded?"

"Certainly--you ought to know, the blow of an assassin, not a soldier."

She looked straight at me, her cheeks red, her eyes burning with indignation. Then, as though she could bear my presence no longer, she swept into the room, and closed the door in my face. It was an action of such utter contempt that I actually staggered back, grasping the rail of the stair. What in the name of Heaven had gained possession of the girl? What infernal lie had been told her? By all the gods, I would find Le Gaire, and choke the truth out of him. My head ached yet with the blow he had dealt me, but this hurt worse. I had a reason now for running the man down. Wherever he had gone, even into the Confederate camp, I vowed I would follow. But first the house: I could conceive of no way in which he could have gotten out--there was a guard in front, and I had locked the rear door. I went at the task deliberately, coolly, determined to overlook nothing. There was something of value at stake now, and my mind was as busy as my hands and eyes. How did he ever succeed in getting to Billie? I had locked her door, and taken away the key. It was not until I invaded the last room on the main floor that I solved this riddle--the two apartments formed a suite with connecting door between. However he was not there now, and all that remained to search was the servants' ell.

The hallway narrowed, and was lower by a single step, the back stairs at the left. There was no window, and with all the doors closed, I could see down only a portion of the way. The hallway itself was gloomy, the shade of the rear window being closely drawn. This, with the stillness all about, enabled me to hear the voices of the men in the kitchen below, and to become aware that the firing, sounding from a distance since early morning, seemed now much closer at hand. It was not altogether artillery any longer, but I could plainly distinguish the volleys of musketry. What could this signify? Were the Confederates being forced back? If so would the Hardy house be caught in the maelstrom of retreat? The possibility of such a result only made haste more imperative. There were three doors at the right, and two opposite. I opened these cautiously, half expecting Le Gaire to dash out, with any weapon he might have secured, desperate enough to fight hard. But nothing occurred, the rooms showed no sign of having been lately occupied. I was at the one next to the last when a board creaked somewhere behind me, and I wheeled about instantly, and ran back to the head of the stairs. There was nothing visible, and a glance down the front hall proved it also deserted--only the door of Miss Willifred's room stood slightly ajar. She was watching me then, fearful lest the fellow had failed to get away. This discovery added to my anxiety, and my anger. He should not get away--not if I could prevent it--until he confessed to her the truth. I ran back into the ell, fearful now that he had escaped through a window, yet determined to examine that last room. There was a rag carpet along the back hall, and, in the semi-darkness, I tripped, falling heavily forward, striking the floor with a crash, my revolver flying from my hand, and hitting the side wall. I was on my knees in an instant, thoughtless of everything except that I had come into contact with a body. The shock numbed me, nor could my fingers alone solve the mystery. I sprang erect, and threw open the nearest side door, permitting the light to stream in. Then I saw the man's face, upturned, lifeless--the face of Gerald Le Gaire. It seemed to me I could not move, could not even breathe, as I stared down at the motionless form. Then I touched his wrist, feeling for a pulse which had ceased to beat. A noise at my back caused me to start, and glance behind. Billie stood at the end of the narrow hall.

"What is it? Have--have you killed him?"

I whirled, facing her, indignant at the words, and yet understanding as swiftly the reason for her suspicions.

"It is Captain Le Gaire. I have just found him lying here."

"Found him! Yes, but not lying there; I heard the noise, the fall of his body. Is--is he dead?"

She stood grasping the stair-rail, shrinking back from closer approach, her white face horror-stricken. I drew a quick breath, fairly quivering under the sting of her words.

"Yes, he is dead, Miss Hardy," I said, knowing I must end the suspense, "but not by my hand. I tripped and fell in the darkness, causing the noise you heard. I am going to ask you to return to your room; you can be of no service here. I will have your father and Captain Bell help me with the body."

She never moved, her eyes on my face.

"Then--then will you permit my father to come to me?"

"Certainly--perhaps we will know then how this occurred."

"Is that your revolver lying there?"

I had forgotten the weapon, but perceived it now, on the floor just beyond Le Gaire's head.

"Yes, it was dropped when I fell," I took a step toward her. "You will go back, will you not?"

She seemed to shrink from my approach, and moved backward, still facing me, until she came to her own door. There she remained a moment, clinging to the knob, but as I emerged into the full light of the front hall, she stepped into the room, and closed the door. Some way, her action hurt me worse than any words could have done, yet I walked past to the stairs in silence, and called to the guard below.

Miles came up with the two Confederates, and a dozen words of explanation sufficed. Together we picked up the body, bore it into a near-by room, and placed it upon the bed. The man had been struck back of the ear, apparently by the butt of a revolver or the stock of a gun, the skull crushed. Death had been instantaneous;

possibly he never knew what hit him. We examined the wound, and then looked into each others' faces utterly unable to account for the condition.

"By Gad, I don't see how he ever got that," said Hardy. "Nor this ugly cut here on the forehead. What do you make out of it, Galesworth?"

I shook my head, thoroughly mystified.

"I've told you all I know; he was lying there in the open when I found him--there was nothing he could have struck against in falling."

"That was a blow struck him," insisted the sergeant, "either by a square-handled pistol, or a carbine stock. I've seen that sorter thing before; but who the hell ever hit him?"

No one attempted to answer. Then I said,

"The only thing I have noticed which might be a clue is this: when I first came in through the kitchen I discovered a clod of fresh clay dirt on the back stairs. I supposed it had dropped from Le Gaire's boots. But there's no sign of yellow clay on his boots now. It must have been some one else."

"Trailin' the poor devil," ejaculated Miles. "But who was he? An' where is he now?"

None attempted a guess, looking blankly into each others' faces, and down upon the ghastly features of the dead man. We were all accustomed to death, and in terrible form, but this was different, this held a horror all its own. I could hear the heavy breathing, we stood so motionless.

"Major Hardy,"--and it was like sacrilege to break the silence,--"we can never clear the mystery standing here. I've examined every room on this floor, and there is not so much as a rat in any of them. Whoever the murderer was, he has either got away, or is hidden on some other floor--is there an attic?"

"Yes, but with no stairs; the only way to get there is by the kitchen roof. What do you propose to do?"

"Take a moment and see if I can think it out," I said, drawing a sheet up over the dead face. "There must be some simple way to account for all this if we can only get on the right trail. Come, gentlemen."

We passed out together, and stopped in front of the closed door. The firing without was growing so much heavier that all noticed it, Bell striding to the end of the hall, and thrusting his head out of the window. Still it was not close enough as yet to be alarming, and my thought was upon other things.

"Major, I wish you would go in and speak to your daughter," I said. "I told her you would come and tell her all you knew."

I watched him cross to the door, knock, and enter.

CHAPTER XXVIII
I FORCE BILLIE TO LISTEN

There was a narrow settee against the wall, and I sat down upon it, to think and to wait for Hardy's return. Eager as I was to discover the cause of Le Gaire's death, yet it seemed almost more important that Billie be brought to an understanding of conditions. Her father could scarcely fail this time to relate in full the details of our encounter, and the girl would realize at once her injustice toward me. I hardly knew what I dared hope as a result, but she was impulsive, warm-hearted, and would surely endeavor to make amends. Bell came back from the front of the house.

"Some fight going on out there," indicating the north and east, "and seems to be drifting this way."

"Our fellows are driving you," I replied. "Have been noticing that all the morning; looks as if your left and centre were giving way."

"Wait until Chambers gets up, and you'll hear another tune," his pride touched. "What's the sergeant doing?"

"Evidently going to get a look at the attic." Then, deciding quickly,--"I am going to turn you all loose, and try to get back to our lines, as soon as we can gain some understanding of this death mystery, Bell. It looks as though the battle would end up somewhere about here, and I can hardly expect to fight the entire Confederate army with ten men and a sergeant. It's a dignified retreat for me. Where now?"

"To help your man. I am crazy to get away. I'm a soldier, Galesworth, and they're wondering out there why I am not in my place. The earlier you say go, the better pleased I'll be."

He clambered out the window to where Miles was perched on the steep roof, and I was left alone, with no noise in my ears but the continuous firing, the reverberations already jarring the house. I found it difficult to collect my thoughts, or to reason out the situation. Everything had occurred so swiftly, so unexpectedly, as to leave me confused--the surging of battle our way, the affair with Le Gaire, his strange death, the thought which had taken possession of Billie, the skulking murderer hid somewhere within the house--all combined to leave me in a state of perplexity. I should have withdrawn my men before daylight; there was no sign of any Federal troops advancing up the ravine, and probably my messenger had failed to get through. It looked as though we were left to our fate. Every moment counted, and yet I could not leave until this mystery was made clear, and Miss Willifred convinced of my innocence. I was so involved in the tangled threads that to run away was almost a confession, and must risk remaining, moment by moment, in hope some discovery would make it all plain. Yet the longer I thought the less I understood. Le Gaire had come to Billie wounded--but how? His very condition had appealed to her as a woman. She had pitied, sympathized, and he had taken advantage of her natural compassion to falsely charge me with the whole trouble. How far he had gone, what foul accusation he had made, could not be guessed, yet he had sufficiently poisoned her mind against me. Then circumstances had combined to make the case still blacker. Doubtless to her it was already conclusive. I had been seeking the fellow alone, revolver in hand. She had overheard what must have sounded like a struggle, and there was the dead man, his skull crushed by a blow. Everything pointed directly toward me from her point of view--motive, opportunity. Who else could it be? Even I, anxious as I was, could not answer that question. I had seen no one, was not aware the dead man had an enemy about the place, could discover no clue except that bit of damp clay on the stairs. Yes, and my own boots were stained with it also--only I knew that lump never came from mine. These thoughts swept across my mind in lightning-like flashes, but brought no solution to the problem. Then Major Hardy suddenly appeared, closing the door, and mopping his face with a handkerchief. His eyes met mine.

"By Gad, Galesworth," he began, "woman is the hardest creature to comprehend on this foot-stool. I've been trying to understand them for fifty years, and am still in the primary class. You'd never have thought that girl of mine cared anything for Le Gaire to hear her talk last night, yet, now the fellow is dead, she is crazy. Lying in there on the bed, crying, and won't say a word. Only thing she asked me when I came in was what he had been killed with. I said it looked as if he had been struck from behind with a pistol butt, and then she collapsed. Couldn't get a thing out of her--just cried, and begged me to go away; said she'd be all right, if left alone. Blamed if I know what to do with a woman like that--over such a fellow as Le Gaire too! By Gad, I supposed Billie had more sense. When she wouldn't talk to me I proposed sending you in to explain matters. You should have seen her eyes, Galesworth, through the tears. Mad! I never waited to hear what she was trying to say. I reckoned the best thing to do was to leave her alone a while."

"You explained nothing?"

"No--what was there to explain?"

"Major," I said, every nerve braced for conflict, "with your permission I am going in there and have a talk with your daughter--may I?"

"Certainly, as far as I am concerned, but I don't envy you the job."

"I'll assume all risk, but I am not willing to leave her like this. Perhaps I understand the situation better than you do. You stay where I can call you if necessary, and look after the search for whoever got Le Gaire. Bell and Miles are out on the roof trying for the attic. I won't be gone long."

I have gone into battle with less trepidation than I approached that door, but never with greater determination to bear myself as became a man. Billie was going to know the truth just as clearly as I could tell it to her. I could not convince myself it was love for Le Gaire which had so affected her. I doubted if she had ever loved him. The fellow had played upon her sympathy, her pity, and circumstances had conspired to cause her to believe I was his murderer. This was amply sufficient to account for her feeling of horror, her evident desire to escape further contact with me. Hardy had been blind and blundering--had made things worse, rather than better; now I must see what I could do. I rapped at the panel, and thought I heard a faint response. A moment later I stood within, and had closed the door behind me. She was on a couch at the opposite side of the room, but arose to her feet instantly, her face white, one hand sweeping back the strands of ruffled hair.

"You!" she exclaimed incredulously. "Why have you come here? I supposed it would be my father."

"Major Hardy told me how you were feeling; that he could do nothing for you--"

"Did he understand I wished to confer with you?"

"No, but--"

"You decided to invade my room without permission. Do you not think you have persecuted me quite long enough?"

"Why do you say persecuted?"

"Because your acts have assumed that form, Lieutenant Galesworth. You persist in seeking me after I have requested to be left alone."

"Miss Hardy," and my eyes met hers, "has it ever occurred to you that you may be the one in the wrong, the one mistaken? I am simply here to explain, to tell you the truth, and compel you to do justice."

"Indeed! how compel? With the revolver in your belt?"

"No; merely by a statement of facts, to be proven, if necessary, by the evidence of your father and Captain Bell. I am not asking you to believe me, but surely they have no occasion for falsifying. Why have you not listened to them?"

"Listened!" startled by my words. "I would have listened, but they have said nothing. They have seemed to avoid all reference to what has occurred. I thought they were trying to spare me pain, humiliation. Is there something concealed, something I do not know?"

"If I may judge from your words and action the entire truth has been kept from you," and I advanced a step or two nearer. "I am not the one to come with an explanation, but your father has failed, and I am not willing to go away until this matter is made clear. Whether you believe, or not, you must listen."

She stared at me, still trembling from head to foot, and yet there was a different expression in her eyes--puzzled doubt.

"You--you will have much to explain," she said slowly. "If--if I were you I should hardly attempt it."

"Which must mean, Miss Hardy, that you are already so prejudiced a fair hearing is impossible. Yet I thought you, at least, a friend."

A deep flush swept into her cheeks, to vanish as quickly.

"You had reason to think so, and I was," earnestly. "I was deceived in your character, and trusted you implicitly. It seems as though I am destined to be the constant victim of deceit. I can keep faith in no one. It is hard to understand you, Lieutenant Galesworth. How do you dare to come here and face me, after all that has occurred?"

She was so serious, so absolutely truthful, that for the moment I could only stare at her.

"You mean after what you said to me last night? But I am not here to speak of love."

"No," bitterly. "That is all over with, forgotten. In the light of what has happened since, the very memory is an insult. Oh, you hurt me so! Cannot you see how this interview pains me! Won't you go--go now, and leave me in peace."

"But surely you will not drive me away unheard!--not refuse to learn the truth."

"The truth! It is the truth I already know, the truth which hurts."

"Nevertheless you are going to hear my story. If I have done a wrong to you, or any one, I want it pointed out, so it may be made right. I shall not leave this room, nor your presence, until I have uttered my last word of explanation. I should be a coward to turn away. Will you sit down and listen? You need not even speak until I am done."

She looked at me helplessly, her eyes full of questioning, yet, when I extended a hand, she drew back quickly.

"Yes--I--I suppose I must."

She sank back upon the couch, these words barely audible, and I drew a deep breath, hardly knowing where to begin.

"I am a Federal officer, Miss Hardy, and my uniform is no passport to your favor, yet that is no reason you should be unjust. I do not think I have ever been guilty of but one ungentlemanly act toward you, and that was unavoidable--I mean listening to your conversation with Captain Le Gaire."

She shuddered, and gave utterance to a little cry.

"I loved you; with all my heart I loved you," I went on swiftly, driven by a sudden rush of passion. "What you said then gave me a right to tell you so."

"And was it because I was unwilling to listen that--that you did what you did later?" she broke in hastily.

"Did later! You mean that I consented to meet Le Gaire?"

"Yes--that you compelled him to fight you; that you--Oh, God! Why bring this all up again?"

"Merely because nothing occurred of which I am ashamed. Without doubt it was my love for you which caused the trouble. But I was not the aggressor. Did you suppose otherwise? Le Gaire deliberately struck me across the face."

She rose again to her feet, her cheeks blazing.

"It was the answer of a gentleman to an insult given the woman he was to marry," proudly.

"The answer to an insult! What insult?"

"You know; I shall not demean myself to repeat the words."

So this was what she had been told! Well, I could block that lie with a sentence.

"Miss Hardy," I asked soberly, "are you aware that your father refused to act for Captain Le Gaire, but went to the field as my second?"

"No," her whole expression indicative of surprise. "Impossible!"

"But it was not impossible, for it was true. Captain Bell had to be send for to second Le Gaire, and he did it under protest. Do you imagine your father would have taken my part if I had uttered one word reflecting upon you?"

She attempted to speak, but failed, and I took advantage of the silence.

"Major Hardy is in the hall, and will corroborate all I say. Perhaps I ought not to attempt my own defence, but this misunderstanding is too grave to continue. There is too much at stake in your life and mine. From what you have already said it is evident you have been deceived--probably that deception did not end merely with the commencement of the quarrel."

"Did--did Major Hardy truly second you?" she interrupted, apparently dazed. "I--I can hardly comprehend."

"He did; he even volunteered to do so. Le Gaire charged you with being unduly intimate with me, and your father resented his words. The man began threatening as soon as I entered the room, and finally struck me across the face, daring me to an encounter. I am no duellist; this was my first appearance in that role; but I could never have retained my self-respect and refused to meet him."

"You--you forced him to accept pistols?"

"In a way, yes. Your father convinced him I was an expert swordsman, and consequently he chose derringers, believing they would be to his advantage. The truth is, I am not particularly skilled in the use of either."

She looked at me a moment as though she would read clear down into the depths of my soul; then she leaned over against the head of the couch, her face hidden in her arm.

"I--I will listen," she said falteringly, "to all you have to say."

CHAPTER XXIX
THE MYSTERY DEEPENS

It was a task I distinctly shrank from, but could not escape.

"Shall I not call in your father, and ask him to relate the story?"

"No; I would much rather hear it from you--tell me everything."

My heart throbbed at these simple words, and the thought suddenly occurred that possibly it was her loss of faith in me, rather than the death of Le Gaire which had brought such pain. If she had actually believed all the man had told her, it must have proven a shock, yet how could I now best counteract his story? It was not my nature to speak ill of any one, least of all the dead, but I must justify myself, win back her respect. Only the whole truth could accomplish this. There was a hassock nearby and I dropped down upon it. She did not move, nor turn her face toward me.

I began with my orders to report at General Grant's headquarters, so as to thus make clear to her the reasons bringing me to the Hardy plantation. I told about our night trip up the ravine, explained my ignorance of who occupied the house to which I had been, despatched, and how circumstances compelled me to remain concealed on the balcony, and thus overhear her conversation with her father and Captain Le Gaire. I even referred to our quadroon guide, and then it was she suddenly turned her face toward me.

"A quadroon--and claiming to have once lived here? Who could that be?"

"A servant slave of Le Gaire's."

"Oh, yes! Charles. I remember now--he ran away."

Somehow she seemed more like the Billie of old now, and I went on with greater confidence, barely touching on my sudden determination to prevent her wedding, the capture of the house, and our subsequent conversation together. As

I approached the unpleasant interview in the parlor she sat up, brushing back her hair, and with questioning eyes on mine, exhibited the deepest interest. I told the rest, word by word, act by act, determined to thus impress upon her the full truth of the narrative. I could tell by her aroused interest that I was succeeding, while her questions gave me some inkling as to what she had been previously led to believe. After my account of the duel and Le Gaire's escape I stopped to ask,

"Miss Billie, do you believe all this?"

"Oh, I must! You surely would not dare say what you have, unless certain my father would sustain you."

"But is it hard to believe?"

"Yes and no. I--I wish to believe, because--well, because it is so disagreeable to lose confidence in any one who has been esteemed as a friend. Perhaps I am too loyal, too easily convinced. But--but I was told such a different story, and it seemed so real, and every fact with which I was acquainted appeared to confirm it. If all you tell me now is true, Lieutenant Galesworth, I hardly know how I dare look you in the face."

"Forget that, and let us understand fully. Will you tell me all,--how you came to protect Le Gaire, and what it was he told you?"

She was silent, her eyes shaded, and I waited, wondering if she meant to speak.

"Perhaps if you consent to do this," I urged, "it may help to clear up the mystery of his death."

"You have not told me about that."

"I know little beyond the discovery of the body," gravely, "and should prefer to understand all that passed between you before going on with my own tale. I have taken you already as far as I have witnesses to corroborate me--beyond that you will have to trust my word alone."

Her long lashes uplifted, the blue-gray eyes looking directly into my own.

"What is all that firing?" she questioned. "The house fairly quakes; is it a battle?"

"Yes; the contending forces have been gradually drawing nearer ever since daylight. The Confederate lines are being forced back, and when Chambers arrives in support this point may prove the centre of struggle. I am eager to get away, Miss

Billie, to protect the lives of my men, but I could not leave with you feeling as you did--believing me a coward, a murderer."

"But I am ashamed to tell you--ashamed to confess I could ever have thought it true."

I touched her hand with my fingers, and she did not shrink away, or seem to observe the action.

"I am bound to learn sometime--wouldn't you rather tell me yourself?"

"Yes, for, perhaps, I can make it seem less bad, more natural. I was angry when you left me, locked here in this room. I was indignant at what you had said and done, and did not realize the military necessity for making me a prisoner. I resented your taking everything so for granted, and--and I believe I almost hated you. I know I lay down here on the couch and cried myself to sleep. I could not have slept long, and when I awoke my mind still retained its bitterness. I began to wonder what I should do; how I could turn the tables against you. I was not really locked in, because this side door into the next room had been left unfastened. Finally I decided on a desperate venture. There were horses in the stable belonging to the captured cavalrymen, and if I could steal out of the house, and reach the Confederate lines, a rescuing party could be guided back here. The idea more and more took possession of me, and at last I mustered sufficient courage to make the attempt. I slipped on an old riding skirt, and stole out quietly through that other room into the hall. I thought I could get down the back stairs unobserved, and then out through the kitchen. I had no idea you had placed a guard back there in the ell until I saw him."

"A guard!" I broke in. "There was no guard up here."

"But there was--just beyond the head of the stairs. One of your men too, for his jacket was pinned up, without buttons. I was close enough to see that."

"That's strange; I gave no such orders, and do not believe Miles did. Did you see the fellow's face?"

"Only in shadow--he was young, and without a beard."

"Go on," I said, realizing that here was an important discovery, "I will ask the sergeant."

"Finding the passage blocked I returned to my own room, but left this door ajar. The disappointment left me angrier than ever, but helpless. I could only sit down and wait, knowing nothing of what was going on below. I finally heard the two shots out by the stable, and went to the window. Three horsemen rode past the corner of the house, and then, a moment or two later, I saw a man running along, crouching behind the fence. I could not tell who he was, only he had on a gray uniform, and he suddenly turned, and made for the house. Once he tripped and fell, and got up with his hands to his head as though hurt. That was the last glimpse I had of him from the window. Perhaps five minutes later I heard some one moving in the next room. I supposed it was the guard prowling about, and kept still. Then the door was pushed open, and Captain Le Gaire came in."

"But where was the guard then?"

"I don't know. I asked, but the captain had seen no one. I cannot tell you how the man looked, acted, or exactly what he said. The first glance at him awoke my sympathy, before he had spoken a word, for his uniform was torn and covered with dirt, and his face all blood from a wound on the temple. He was trembling like a child, and could hardly talk. I washed his wound out, and bound it up before I even asked a question. By that time he was himself again, and began to explain. Is it necessary for me to repeat what he said?"

"I would rather you would; don't you think I ought to know?"

"I suppose you had, but--but it is not a pleasant task. I could not help but believe what he said, for he told it so naturally; he--he almost seemed to regret the necessity, and--and I never once dreamed he would lie to me. Then father said just enough to apparently confirm it all, and--and other things happened."

"Yes, I know," understanding her embarrassment. "You mustn't think I blame you. You have known me such a little while."

"But I should have sought after the truth, nevertheless, for I certainly had no cause to believe you capable of so cowardly an action. I--surely knew you better than that. But this was what he said: that you came into the room below promising to release the others, but threatening to take him prisoner with you into the Federal lines. He protested, and--and then you referred to me in a way he could not stand, and blows were exchanged. As a result he dared you to fight him, and you couldn't refuse before your own men, although you endeavored to back out. That you chose pistols for weapons, and compelled their acceptance. On the field, he said, you fired before the word was spoken, and while he was still lying on the ground, shocked by the bullet, you flung the derringer at him, cutting his forehead; then drew your own revolver. Unarmed, believing he was to be murdered, he turned and ran."

"And you actually believed all this of me?"

"Why," bewildered, "he was a soldier, and my father's friend. How could I imagine he would run without cause? His story sounded true, as he told it, and he was hurt."

"He must have got that when he fell--his head struck something. And is that all?"

"Yes; only we talked about how he might get away. He was here until father came for me, and then stepped into the other room. When I came back, he had gone. A little later I heard you searching the rooms, and went out into the hall believing it might be he."

"You saw nothing more of him?"

"No."

"Nor of the man you mistook for a guard?"

She shook her head positively.

"Only the once." Then, after hesitating, her eyes uplifted to mine." Lieutenant Galesworth, you did not encounter Captain Le Gaire alive in the hall?"

"I never saw him alive after he ran from the field. The noise you heard was when I tripped and fell, my revolver dropping to the floor. It was then I discovered his dead body. You will believe this?"

"Yes," and she extended her hand. "I have been very wrong; you must forgive me. But how could he have been killed? Who could have had a motive?"

"Had Le Gaire no enemies?"

"Not to my knowledge. I know little of his life, yet surely there could be no one here--in this house--who would deliberately seek to kill him. No one would have opportunity except one of your own men."

I confess it appeared that way to me also, and the fact only served to make the mystery more baffling. I knew personally every soldier under my command, and was certain no man among them had ever so much as seen Le Gaire previous to the night before. They could have no reason to attempt his life, no grudge against him. Yet every Confederate was under guard, and the fellow Billie had seen in the hall wore our uniform, even to the detached buttons--she had noted that. If the man had been on guard, merely performing his military duty, there would have been no secrecy; he would have reported the affair long before this. But Le Gaire had been murdered, treacherously killed, without doubt struck from behind, and there must be some reason, some cause for the act.

"I understand this no better than you," I admitted finally. "I shall have the house thoroughly searched, and every one of my men examined. But I am afraid we shall be obliged to leave before the mystery is solved. Hear those guns! It almost seems as though the fighting was already within sight of the house." I stepped across to the window and looked out. "However it is all to the north and east, and there is still opportunity for us to get safely away into the ravine. I cannot understand why our forces have not taken advantage of it--in that way they could have struck the enemy a stunning blow on the left. There's a blunder somewhere. But we can hold the house no longer; only before I go I must know that you believe in me."

"I do," earnestly.

"And I am going to clinch that faith," opening the door into the hall. "Major Hardy, just a moment."

He turned back from the open window, his face flushed with excitement.

"The stragglers are beginning to show up," he exclaimed pointing, "and the boys are fighting like hell out there beyond those woods. And--and see that dust cloud over yonder; by all the gods, it will be Chambers coming up at last!"

"Then hurry here; I want to ask you just one question for your daughter's sake: Were you my second in the duel this morning?"

"Certainly."

"Why didn't you tell me, papa? Why didn't you explain that Lieutenant Gales-worth was not to blame?"

"Well, I didn't want you to feel any worse than you did. You and Le Gaire were going to be married, and I supposed you cared a good deal for him. Someway I couldn't make myself talk about it, Billie; that's all."

Her eyes sought mine, but just then Miles appeared in the hall, halting with a salute as he caught sight of me.

"Nobody in the attic, sir, but things are getting pretty warm outside," he reported anxiously.

"The way is still open toward the ravine, Sergeant. Get your men together in the front hall at once. Never mind the prisoners; the major will release them after we have gone."

His heels came together with a click, and he strode to the head of the stairs.

"By the way, Sergeant," I called after him, "did you have a guard posted in the upper hall here this morning?"

"A guard? No, sir."

"Were you aware that any of our men had been up stairs since last evening?"

"None of them have, sir; I'm cocksure of that." "That's all, Sergeant; be lively now." My eyes turned toward Billie, and she held out both her hands.

"If we never know the truth, Lieutenant Galesworth," she said softly, "I shall believe all you have told me."

CHAPTER XXX
UNDER NEW ORDERS

Her eyes were an invitation, a plea, yet with the major at her side, his face full of wonderment, and Bell close behind us in the hall, I could only bow low over the white hands, and murmur some commonplace. There was neither opportunity nor time for more, although I felt my own deep disappointment was mirrored in the girl's face. The continuous roar of guns without, already making conversation difficult, and the hurried tramp of feet in the hall below, told the danger of delay. It was a moment when the soldier had to conquer the lover, and stern duty became supreme. I hurried to the front window, and gazed out; then to others, thus making a thorough survey of our surroundings, quickly making up my mind to a definite plan of action. So swiftly had occurrences pressed upon me I had scarcely found time before to realize the rapid approach of this new danger. Now it burst upon me in all its impending horror. Already the results of battle were visible.

An hour before the pike road leading past the plantation gates had been white and deserted, not even a spiral of dust breaking its loneliness. Through openings in a grove I had looked northward as far as the log church and observed no moving figure. But now this was all changed; as though by some mysterious alchemy, war had succeeded peace, the very landscape appearing grimly desolate, yet alive with moving figures. And these told the story, the story of defeat. It was not a new scene to me, but nevertheless pitiful. They came trudging from out the smoke clouds, and across the untilled fields, alone, or in little groups, some armed, more weaponless, here and there a bloody bandage showing, or a limp bespeaking a wound; dirty, unshaven men, in uniforms begrimed and tattered, disorganized, swearing at each other, casting frightened glances backward with no other thought or desire save to escape the pursuing terror behind. They were the riff-raff of the battle, the skulkers, the cowards, the slightly wounded, making pin pricks an excuse for escape. Wagons toiled along in the midst of them, the gaunt mules urged on by whip and voice, while occasionally an ambulance forced its way through. Here and there some worn-out straggler or wounded man had crawled into shade, and lay heedless of the turmoil. Shouts, oaths, the cracking of whips, the rumble of wheels mingled with the ceaseless roar of musketry, and the more distant reverberation of cannon, while clouds of powder smoke drifted back on the wind to mingle with the dust, giving to all a spectral look. Back from the front on various missions galloped couriers and aides, spurring their horses unmercifully, and driving straight through the mob in utter recklessness. One, a black-bearded brute, drew his sabre, and slashed right and left as he raced madly by.

Toward the ravine all remained quiet, although here and there in the orchard some of the gray-clad stragglers had found opportunity to lie down out of the ruck. But the smoke and musketry gave me a conception of the Confederate line of battle, its left thrown across the pike with centre and right doubling back into the form of a horse-shoe, all centring on the Hardy house. Within twenty minutes we would be caught as in a trap. I sprang back to the stairs, and as I did so a sudden yell rose from the surging mob without, a shout in which seemed to mingle fear and exultation. Bell, from a side window joined in, and a single glance told the reason: up from the south rode cavalry, sweeping the pike clean of its riff-raff, and behind, barely visible through the dust, tramped a compact mass of infantry, breaking into double time. The black-bearded aide dashed to their front, waving sabre and pointing; the clear note of a bugle cleaved the air; the horsemen spread out like a fan, and with the wild yell of the South rising above the din, the files of infantry broke into a run, and came sweeping forward in a gray torrent. Chambers had come up at last, come to hurl his fresh troops into the gap, and change the tide of battle. Even the stragglers paused, hastening to escape the rush, and facing again to the front. I saw some among them grasp their guns and leap into the ranks, the speeding cavalrymen driving others with remorseless sabres.

All this was but a glimpse, and with the tumult ringing in my ears, I was down stairs facing my own men.

"Where are the prisoners, Sergeant?"

"Here, sir, under guard."

"Open the front door, and pass them out. We'll be away before they can do us any harm. Step lively now."

I scarcely looked at them, moving on a run at the threats of the men, but wheeled on Hardy, who was half way down the stairs.

"Major, what do you mean to do? How will you protect your daughter?"

"Stay here with her," was the prompt reply. There will be disciplined troops here in a few minutes."

"Yes, and a battle."

"As soon as Chambers gets up in force I can pass her back to the rear."

That seemed the safer plan to me, and I had no time to argue.

"All right, you and Bell are free to do as you please. Get your men out the same window you came in, Sergeant; I'll go last. Keep down behind the fence, and make for the ravine."

He flung open the door into the parlor, and we crowded after him, but were still jammed in the doorway when he sprang back from the open window with hands flung up.

"By God, sir, here come our men!"

They came like so many monkeys, leaping the balcony rail, plunging headlong through the opening, and crowding into the room. It was like a dream, a delirium, yet I could see the blue uniforms, the new faces. In the very forefront, flung against me by the rush, I distinguished the lad I had sent back into the lines the night before.

"What does all this mean, Ross? Who are these fellows?"

"Our men, sir," he panted, scarcely able to speak. "Here--read this," and he thrust a paper into my hand. My eyes took the words in a flash, and yet for the instant they were vague, meaningless. It was only as I read them a second time that I understood, and then I gazed helplessly into the faces about me, striving to grasp the full situation.

"HDQTS 9TH ILL. CAV. "9:10 A.M.

"LIEUT. GALESWORTH:

"We advanced our centre and left at daylight, and have driven the enemy from intrenchments. Our right is under orders to advance up ravine and strike their rear.

We move at once. I send this back by Ross, who will take twenty men with him to help you. Hold the Hardy house to the last possible moment. Our whole movement pivots there, and keeping possession until we arrive is of utmost importance. Hold it at any price. These are Grant's orders."

"Who gave you this?--it is unsigned."

"The colonel, sir, I saw him write it."

"And they were ready to leave?"

"They'll not be more than an hour behind, unless something stops them--the whole brigade is coming."

I comprehended now--the plan was clear-cut, easily understood. Taking advantage of the ravine in which to conceal the movement, Grant proposed to throw a brigade, or even a greater force, suddenly upon the enemy's unprotected rear, thus crushing Johnston between two fires. The word I had sent back, disclosing the complete desertion of that gash in the earth by the Confederates, had made this strategy possible. And the Hardy house was naturally the pivot of the movement, and the retention of it in our possession essential to success. But the one point they had apparently overlooked was Chambers' advance along this pike. He was supposed to be much farther east, his column blocked by heavy roads. Instead of that he was here already, his vanguard sweeping past the gate, double-quicking to the front, with long lines of infantry hurrying behind. For us to bar the retreat of Johnston's demoralized men, safely intrenched within the house, might be possible, provided artillery was not resorted to. Even with my small force I might hold them back for an hour, but to attempt such a feat against the veterans of Chambers, was simply a sentence to death. These men, fresh, undefeated, eager for battle, would turn and crush us as though we were some stinging insect. Thirty men pitted against a division! Good God! if he could send these--why not more? Yet there was nothing to do except obey, and, feeling to the full the hell of it, I crushed the paper in the palm of my hand, and looked around into the faces about me. I was in command, and we were to stay here until we died. That was all I knew, all I remembered, the words, "hold it at any price," burning in upon my brain.

"Men," I said sharply. "My orders are to hold this house until our troops come up. We'll make a try at it. Who commands this last squad?"

A sergeant, a big fellow, with closely trimmed gray moustache, elbowed his way forward, and saluted.

"From H troop, are you not?"

"Yes, sir; we're all H; my name's Mahoney."

"I remember you; Irish to a man. Well, this is going to beat any Donnybrook Fair you lads ever saw. Get busy, and barricade every door and window on this floor; use the furniture, or whatever you get hands on. Miles, take the south side, and Mahoney, the north. No shooting until I give the word; we won't stir up this hornets' nest until we have to."

The newcomers stacked their carbines in the hall, and divided into two parties, going to work with a vim, while I quickly stationed my old men where they could command every approach to the house, seeing to it that their arms were in condition, and that they had ample ammunition. Within ten minutes we were ready for a siege, or prepared to repel any attack other than artillery. The rooms looked as though a cyclone had wrecked them, the heavy furniture barricading doors and windows, yet leaving apertures through which we could see and fire. Mattresses had been dragged from beds up stairs, and thrust into places where they would yield most protection. The front door alone was left so as to be opened, but a heavy table was made ready to brace it if necessary. Satisfied nothing more could be done to increase our security I had the men take their weapons, and the sergeants assign them to places. I passed along from room to room, watchful that no point of defence had been overlooked, and speaking words of encouragement to the fellows. After the fight began there could be little commanding; every man would have to act for himself.

"Draw down the shades, lads, and keep it as dark as possible inside. Lay your ammunition beside you, where you can get it quickly. Mahoney, we shall not need as many men at these windows as we will toward the front of the house--two to a window here should be sufficient. Carbines, first, boys, and then revolvers if they get close. What is that, Miles? Yes, detail a man to each window up stairs; two to the front windows. Have them protect themselves all they can, and keep back out of sight. Now, boys, keep your eyes open, but no shooting until you get orders. Sergeant Mahoney will command this side, and Miles the other, while I'll take the front. There is a corporal here, isn't there?"

"Yes, sir,--Conroy."

"Well, Conroy, you are in charge up stairs. I'll be there and look you over in a few minutes; I want to take a glance outside first."

The brief time these hasty preparations required had witnessed a marked change in conditions without. Where before it had been a scene of disastrous confusion, it was now that of disciplined attack. Chambers' men had swept aside the stragglers, and spread out into battle lines, the gray regiments massing mostly to the right of the pike, but with heavy fringe of cavalry extending past us as far as the ravine. From my point of vantage it all formed an inspiring picture, dully monotonous in color, but alive with action; the long dust-covered lines, the rifle barrels shining, the constant shifting of columns, the regiments hurrying forward, the swift moving of cavalry, and hard riding of staff officers, sent the hot blood leaping through my veins. And all this was no dress review. Just ahead they were at it in deadly earnest--barely beyond those trees, and below the edge of the hill. I could hear the thunder of the guns, continuous, almost deafening, even at this distance; could see the black, drifting smoke, and even the struggling figures. We were almost within the zone of fire already. Men were down in the ranks yonder, and a stricken horse lay just within the gate. Back and forth, riding like mad, aides dashed out of the choking powder fumes, in endeavor to hasten up the reserves. Even as I watched one fell headlong from his saddle, struck dead by a stray bullet. I was soldier enough to understand. Within ten minutes Chambers would be out there, hurling his fresh troops against the exhausted Federal advance, while those fellows, now fighting so desperately yonder, would fall back in reserve. Could Chambers hold them? Could he check that victorious onrush of blue--those men who had fought their way five bloody miles since daybreak? I could not tell; it would be a death grapple worthy of the gods, and the Hardy house would be in the very vortex. Whether it was destined also to become a charnel house, a shambles, depended on the early coming of those other, unseen men toiling up that black ravine.

Then suddenly there recurred to my memory that Major Hardy and his daughter still remained within. They had not departed with the others, yet in the stress and excitement their presence had slipped my mind. Nor had I seen them since the new recruits came. What could be done with them now, at this late hour, the house already a fortress, the enemy in evidence everywhere? In some manner they must be gotten away at once, safely placed within the protection of friends. Not only my friendship for the father, and my love for the girl, demanded this, but the fact that they were non-combatants made it imperative. There was no time to consider methods--already we were within range of the guns, and at any moment might be directly under fire, obliged to resist assault. I was up the stairs even as the thought occurred, and confronted Hardy in the upper hall. Conroy had him by the arm, suspicious of the uniform.

"That's all right, Corporal," I said quickly. "I had forgotten the major was here. Hardy, you must get out of the house--you, and Miss Billie at once."

His eyes glanced back toward the door of her room which stood open.

"I--I have no knowledge of where my daughter may be," he acknowledged soberly.

CHAPTER XXXI
THE DISAPPEARANCE OF BILLIE

I stared at him in surprise, and then sprang forward, and glanced into her room. It was empty, except for a trooper kneeling at the window. I faced Hardy again with a question:

"Not here! Where has she gone?"

He shook his head, without attempting to speak.

"You don't know? Conroy, have you seen anything of a young lady since you came up here?"

"No, sir; all these doors was standin' wide open, and this Johnny Reb was prowlin' 'round in here. I didn't know what his business might be so I collared him. Ain't that right, Murphy?" appealing to the soldier at the window, who had faced about at sound of our voices.

"Straight as far as it goes," was the reply, "but maybe that guard back in the ell saw the lady afore we come up."

"What guard?"

"One o' your fellows," said the corporal. "Anyhow he had his buttons cut off. I guess he's there yet."

I was out into the hall as quickly as I could turn, Conroy and the major following closely. A dozen steps took us beyond the chimney jog, and to the top of the back stairs. There was no one there. The side doors stood open, and the narrow hallway was vacant. My eyes met the corporal's.

"Well, I'll be jiggered," he exclaimed. "He was right there by the second door when I saw him. I was goin' to post Murphy at that end window, sir, but I didn't think there was any need o' two men there."

"Did you speak to him?"

"I told him what was up, sir, and that he better stay by the window."

"Did he answer you?"

"He said 'all right,' or something like that, an' went back. I never thought anything was wrong; all I noticed particular was he had only a revolver, but most o' yer fellows was armed that way. I meant to get him a gun as soon as I had time." He strode forward, looking into the rooms. "He ain't here now anyhow, and I'm damned if I know where he could o' gone. Did I make a mistake, sir?"

"No, this is no fault of yours, Corporal, but it's strange nevertheless. We had no guard up here, but this fellow, wearing our uniform, has been seen before--Miss Hardy, this gentleman's daughter, saw him, and now she has disappeared. There was murder done in this hall this morning."

The corporal crossed himself, his lips murmuring as he glanced about, and then into my face.

"Murder, sir! The Confederate captain lying in yonder on the bed?"

"Yes; he was waylaid here, and struck down from behind. I found his body out in front of that door, the skull crushed."

"An' ye think that feller did it?"

"I don't know who did it. But I should like to discover where that lad hides, and what he is here for. We have accounted for all our men, and searched this floor inch by inch. I began to think Miss Hardy was mistaken, but now you've seen him also."

"An' Murphy," broke in the horrified corporal, edging closer. "Murphy saw him too. Bedad, maybe it was a ghost!"

"Ghosts don't talk, and I never heard of any wearing revolvers. Major, when did you see Billie last?"

I noticed how haggard his face was, and he answered slowly, his hands grasping the stair-rail.

"We were together in the front hall when your men came. You were talking loudly, and the new voices attracted our attention. We both went forward to the head of the stairs."

"You overheard what was said?" I interrupted, a new possibility dawning upon me.

"Much of it, yes," he admitted.

"The plan of attack?--the orders sent me?"

His expression answered.

"And what were you going to do with this information, Major Hardy?"

"Nothing. I considered myself a prisoner on parole. I merely proposed asking your permission to leave the house with my daughter before hostilities began. I started down the stairs for that purpose."

"And Billie?"

"I told her this, and sent her to her room after some things. Before I got down you had disappeared, and I returned up stairs. She was not in her room, nor could I find a trace of her."

I thought rapidly, staring into his bewildered face, insensibly listening to the continuous roar without. It was tragedy within tragedy, the threads of war and love inextricably tangled. What had occurred here during that minute or two? Had she left voluntarily, inspired by some wild hope of service to the South? Did that mysterious figure, attired in our uniform, have anything to do with her disappearance? Did Hardy know, or suspect more than he had already told? By what means could she have left the house? If she had not left where could she remain concealed? Each query only served to make the situation more complicated, more difficult to solve. To no one of them could I find an answer.

"Major, did you tell your daughter why you could not carry that information to your own people?--that you considered yourself a parolled prisoner?"

He hesitated, realizing now what it was I was seeking to discover.

"Why, I may have said something like that. We spoke of the situation, and--and Billie appeared excited, but,--why, Galesworth, you do not imagine the girl would try to carry the news out, alone, do you?"

His doubt was so genuine as to be beyond question. Whatever Billie had done, it was through no connivance with the father, but upon her own initiative. Yet she was fully capable of the effort; convinced the cause of the South was in her hands, she was one to go through fire and water in service. Neither her life nor mine would weigh in the decision--her only thought the Confederacy. Still it was not a pleasant reflection that she would thus war openly against me; would deliberately expose me to defeat, even death. Could she have made such a choice if she truly loved me? Her words, eyes, actions continually deceived me. Again and again I had supposed

I knew her, believed I had solved her nature, only to be led into deeper bewilderment.

"Major," I said soberly. "I do imagine just that. There is no sacrifice your daughter would not make for the South. She realized the importance of this information, and that she alone could take it to Chambers."

I turned to the back stairs, and went down, feeling my way in the gloom, until I touched the door. To my surprise it opened, although I knew I had locked it, and the key was still in my pocket. There were four troopers in the kitchen, and they turned at the noise to stare at me.

"How long have you boys been stationed here?" I questioned.

"'Bout fifteen minutes, I guess," answered the nearest. "Ain't that about it, Joe?"

"Not no longer."

"Room empty when you came?"

"Not a rat here, that we saw; did we, Joe?"

The other shook his head.

"Was that bar across the outer door there then?"

"No, sir, there wan't no lock on it, an' Bill rigged up that contrivance hisself."

I believed now I comprehended how it had occurred, all except the mysterious unlocking of the door at the foot of the stairs, and this fellow in our uniform that haunted the ell. To make certain I retained the key, I took it out, and fitted it into the lock. Still there might be a duplicate, and as for the soldier, I was hardly half convinced of his reality. Billie had acted quickly, under the inspiration of discovery, and all the circumstances had conspired to make her escape from the house easy. Miles had withdrawn his men on my orders, and we were all grouped together in the front hall. She had simply slipped down these back stairs, used a duplicate key, passed through the kitchen unobserved, and out into the garden. Where then? To the stable, without doubt, and, mounted, into Chambers' lines, taking her news to the highest officer she could reach. We would hear from it presently,--strange if not even already some of those troops were wheeling to invest the house. I called back up the stairs,

"Conroy, send Major Hardy down here."

The Confederate appeared almost instantly, his eyes anxiously surveying the room.

"Have you found my girl?"

"No, but I have satisfied myself as to where she is. Without doubt she came down those stairs, and out this door, while we were in the front hall. A battle-line is a rough place for a woman, and I am going to turn you out now to see if you cannot find and protect her. One of you men take down that bar."

The major stared at me, and then extended his hand.

"You--you don't suppose I sent her?"

"Oh, no, you have been most honorable. There is no reason why I should hold you here; the others have gone, and you may be of assistance to Miss Willifred. It is bound to be lively enough for us in here presently without prisoners to look after."

"But you have not accepted my hand, Lieutenant Galesworth. I wish to feel that we part friends."

"We certainly do," I returned heartily, grasping his fingers. "And--and I may never see your daughter again. There is scarcely a possibility that I ever shall. Tell her that I respect her loyalty to the South."

He stood looking directly into my eyes, grasping both my hands.

"You mean to remain here, defending the house?"

"While there is a man left alive."

"It is a pity--in my judgment; not war, but a useless sacrifice."

"Yet a soldier's duty, Major--obedience to orders."

He bowed, choking in the throat, as he lifted his hat. With one glance at the silent soldier holding open the door he passed out. Then he turned, hat still in hand, and glanced back.

"You may feel assured I will deliver your message, sir,--good-bye."

*   *   *   *   *

The broad hallway ran from the front of the house to the kitchen ell, and I could see its entire length. Several men were clustered at the other end, peering out through the narrow panes of glass either side the front door, and one came running toward me. It was the Irish sergeant.

"They're a-coomin', sorr--a bunch o' gray-backs. Shud Oi hay' the byes let drive?"

"Not until I speak to them, Mahoney. We'll give the fellows fair warning first."

I hurried back with him, and a soldier stepped aside to give me opportunity to look out. A glance was sufficient. A regiment of cavalry was halted under the trees of the lawn, the men dismounted and standing at the heads of their horses. Apparently they were, merely waiting orders. Riding straight across the grass toward the porch came a little group of a dozen officers, as I judged, although this was largely conjecture, their uniforms so dust-covered as to be meaningless. The carelessness of their approach, scarcely glancing toward the house, convinced me they had no thought of meeting any resistance from within--their only object the shade of the steps, or a possible glass of wine. To greet them with a volley would be murder, and I motioned the men to open the door just wide enough to permit of my slipping through. I walked forward to the edge of the porch, and stood there, leaning against a pillar. The approaching party was sufficiently close by this time so that I saw that one of the three in advance was Bell. Apparently I remained unobserved, but as they came to the gravel driveway I spoke.

"That will be quite far enough, gentlemen, until you explain your purpose."

They pulled up, astonished at the sound of my voice, those behind bunching about the first three, all staring open-mouthed at my uniform. Several voices asked, "What does this mean?" "Who the hell are you?"

"One at a time, please," I returned, enjoying their surprise. "This house is garrisoned by Federal troops at present, and we are not receiving callers--put that back! There are riflemen at every window."

"Don't be a fool, Brown," growled the man in the centre, glancing aside, and then facing back toward me. "Are you in command?"

"I am here to receive any communication."

"What troops have you?"

I bowed smiling.

"Sufficient for the purpose."

Bell, evidently short-sighted, was staring at me through glasses, and broke in, "It's Galesworth, the Yankee lieutenant I told you about, Colonel. Say, I thought you left."

"Instead of leaving, Captain Bell, I have decided to stay."

"But, good Lord, you can't hold that house against us with only ten men!"

"You will discover we have considerable more than ten when you come to capture it."

They whispered together, evidently undecided how seriously to take me. I thought Bell was trying to impress the others with the idea that it was all a bluff, but my coolness made them suspicious. I leaned motionless against the post in apparent indifference. The gruff-voiced colonel broke the silence.

"Do you know we have a division of troops within bugle call?"

"Oh, yes, and they have got their work cut out for them. Your whole force is at it already, except the cavalry."

My tone angered him.

"There are enough in reserve to crush you," he retorted warmly. "I demand your immediate surrender, sir."

"On what terms?"

"Unconditional," he thundered, "and if I have to charge you we shall take no prisoners."

I waited for a lull in the firing, and they accepted the pause as hesitation. Then I stepped backward to the door.

"I regret greatly to disappoint you, Colonel," I said clearly, "but we have decided to fight. If you are not out of range within two minutes my men will open fire."

Without awaiting an answer, I stepped within and closed the door.

CHAPTER XXXII
WE REPULSE THE ENEMY

I naturally anticipated an immediate attack, and began preparations. Glass was broken from the small windows through which the men were to fire, and the sergeants and myself made inspection of men and arms, and gave orders for vigorous defence. Yet we were already so well intrenched that this required but a few moments, and, confident I could shift my force quickly so as to meet any attack, I returned to the front rooms to observe the enemy. To my surprise there was no evidence of any movement in our direction, although there had been a noticeable shifting of troops. Chambers had swung his infantry forward through gaps in the line of battle, and was now confronting the Federal advance, not only holding his ground, but it seemed to me, slightly pushing his opponent. I ran up stairs so as to obtain a wider view of the field. They were fighting fiercely to our front and left, the line of fire slightly overlapping the pike, although, from the led horses in the rear, the troops engaged on this extremity were mostly dismounted cavalry. Marching columns were still approaching from the south, swinging off from the pike as they neared the house, and disappearing into a grove of trees to the east. The land in that direction was rough, and I could only guess at the formation by the sound of firing, and the dense clouds of smoke. It was out there the artillery was massed, although in all of Chambers' command I saw but two batteries. The heaviest fighting was to the east, not so far away but what we were within shell range, and yet out of direct view, while to the north the Confederates could be seen struggling to gain possession of a low hill. Their first rush had dislodged the Federals from the log church, but had been halted just below in the hollow. Beyond to the westward stretched the black shadow of the ravine, silent and deserted, largely concealed by a fringe of trees.

That which interested me more particularly, however, was the scene nearer at hand--the stragglers, the wounded, the skulkers, the disorganized bodies of men, the wearied commands which had been fighting since daylight, now doggedly falling back, relieved by new arrivals, yet unwilling to go. They were not beaten, and their officers had fairly to drive them from the field, and when they halted the men faced to the front. It was all a scene of wild confusion, the roar of guns incessant, the air full of powder smoke, shells bursting here and there, and constantly the shouts of men. Ammunition wagons blocked the pike, soldiers thronging about them to stuff cartridges into emptied belts; a battery of artillery dashed past, recklessly scattering the surging mass to left and right, as its horses, lashed into frenzy, plunged forward toward the fighting line; horsemen galloped back and forth, commanding, imploring, swearing, as they endeavored to reform the mob into a reserve column; riderless horses dashed about, resisting capture; and a runaway team of mules, dragging behind the detached wheels of an army wagon, mowed a lane straight across the open field. Men lay everywhere sleeping, so exhausted the dead and living looked alike; there were ghastly bandages, dust-caked faces, bloody uniforms, features blackened by powder, and limping figures helped along by comrades. Empty ammunition wagons loaded again with wounded, went creaking slowly to the rear, the sharp cries of suffering echoing above the infernal din. Just outside the gate, under the tree shadows, was established a field hospital, a dozen surgeons working feverishly amid the medley of sounds. I had heretofore seen war from the front, in the excitement of battle, face to face with the enemy, but this sickened me. I felt my limbs tremble, the perspiration bead my face. I now knew what war was, stripped of its glamour, hideous in its reality of suffering and cruelty. For a moment I felt remorse, fear, a cowardly desire to escape, to get away yonder, beyond the reek of powder, the cries of pain. The awful vista gripped me as if by spectral fingers. But for the movement just then of that cavalry regiment, recalling me to duty, I half believe I should have run, not from fright but to escape the horror.

They were moving forward past the front of the house, the men still on foot, gripping the leather at their horses' bits, the restive animals plunging so wildly as to make it seem more the advance of a mob than a disciplined body. A shell exploded in the road to their left, tearing a hole in the white pike, and showering them with stones. I could see bleeding faces where the flying gravel cut. Another shrieked above, and came to earth just in front of the house, shattering the front steps into fragments, and leaving one of the wooden pillars hanging, unsupported. Yet with no halt or hesitancy, the gray mass moved slowly across the lawn, and then deliberately formed in line beneath the trees of the orchard. Their horses were led to the rear, and the men fell into rank at the sharp command of officers. Facing as they did I was left in doubt as to their purpose. Just inside the gate a battalion of infantry stood at parade rest, some of Johnston's men, I judged from their appearance, who had held together. Beyond them a little group of horsemen had reined up on a knoll, and seemed to be studying the surrounding country through field glasses. I could see the glitter of them in the sun.

Straight across the grass from the line of dismounted cavalry an officer rode, galloping through the dust of the pike, and trotting up the incline until he reached this distant group. I watched curiously as he pointed toward the house, and the others turned and looked. I could dimly distinguish features, and realized the meaning of some of their gestures. Then the cavalry-man turned his horse, and came trotting back. But now he rode directly up the gravelled driveway to the front of the house, a white rag flapping from the point of his uplifted sword. Thirty feet away he pulled up his horse, his eyes searching the house, and I stepped out on the porch roof. The broken pillar made me afraid to venture to the edge, but we were plainly in view of each other.

"Are you the Yank in command?" he asked brusquely, staring up at me.

"Yes."

He removed the rag from his sword, and thrust the weapon into its scabbard.

"What force have you?"

I smiled, amused at his display of nerve.

"You will have to come in to discover that, my friend."

His naturally florid face reddened with anger.

"I'm not here to joke," he retorted. "General Chambers wishes me to offer you a last opportunity to surrender without bloodshed."

"And if I refuse?"

"We shall attack at once, sir," haughtily. "A glance about will show you the helplessness of your position."

I waited long enough to glance again over the scene. I was convinced they possessed no artillery which could be spared from the front for this small affair, and believed we were capable of making a strong defence against musketry. With the exception of that battalion of infantry near the gate, and the cavalry regiment in the orchard, every organized body of troops was being hurried forward to strengthen their line of battle. Even General Chambers and his staff had disappeared over the hill, and every sound that reached us evidenced a warm engagement. The stream of wounded soldiers flowing back across the pike was thickening, and Federal shells were already doing damage at this distance.

"I thank you for your information," I said civilly, "but we shall endeavor to hold the house."

"You mean to fight!"

"Yes--if you wish this place you will have to come and take it."

He drew back his horse, yet with head turned, hopeful I might say more. But I stepped back through the window, and as I disappeared he clapped in his spurs, and rode out into the orchard. A moment later the dismounted troopers spread out into a thin line, covering the front and left of the house, unslung their carbines and began to load. Something about the way they went at it convinced me they expected no very serious resistance. A word to my men on that floor brought them to the point threatened by this first attack, and I gave them swift, concise orders--no firing until they heard a signal shot from the front hall; then keep it up while there was a man standing in range; carbines first, after that revolvers, and keep down out of sight from below. I looked into their faces, confident of obedience, and then ran down stairs.

Here the two sergeants--veterans both--had anticipated everything, and massed their men at the windows facing front and left. They lay flat, protected in every possible way, and each man had an extra gun beside him, and a pile of cartridges. Mahoney was in the parlor, and Miles in the hall, watchful of each movement without. I gave them the instructions about withholding their fire, and, grasping a carbine myself, pushed forward to where I could see outside. The troopers were already moving, advancing slowly in open order, but came to a halt just within carbine range. At sharp command their guns came up, and they poured a volley into the house. Beyond a shattering of glass no damage was done, but under the cover of the smoke, the gray line leaped forward. I waited until they reached the gravel, and then pulled trigger. Almost to the instant the whole front and side of the house blazed into their very faces, not once only, but twice, three times, the men grabbing gun after gun. It was not in flesh and blood to stand it; the line crumbled up as though seared by fire, men fell prone, others staggered back blinded, and, almost before we realized, there remained nothing out there but a fleeing crowd, leaving behind their dead and wounded. Only three men had placed foot on the porch, and they lay there motionless; one had grasped the sill of a window, and had fallen back with a crushed skull. It was all over with so quickly that through the smoke we looked at each other dazed, and then stared out at the flying figures. I groped my way from room to room, ordering a reloading of the guns, and asking if there were any injured. The walls were scarred by bullets much of the piled up furniture splintered, but only two men had been hit, and their, wounds were slight.

"They'll try it again, lads," I said. "Get ready." There was no doubt of that, for they were old soldiers out yonder, and would never rest under the stigma of defeat. But they were bound to be more cautious a second time, and would give us a harder tussle.

The fleeing men were rallied just beyond the negro cabins, cursed by their officers and driven back into line; then moved slowly forward again to their former position in the orchard. The sudden terror which had smitten them when the silent house burst into death flames, had somewhat worn off, and a desire for revenge succeeded. I could see the officers passing back and forth talking and gesticulating. A dozen troopers under a flag of truce came forward to pick up the wounded, and without even challenging we permitted them to do their work. The house remained quiet, sombre, silent, nothing showing but the dark barrels of our carbines. The infantry battalion at the gate moved against the left of the cavalry, and couriers were despatched to hurry up more. Out by the negro quarters a dozen officers held council, pointing at the house, and by gestures designating a plan of attack. I think they sent for artillery, but none came, and when one of the couriers returned and reported, bringing only another infantry battalion, it was decided to delay the attempt no longer. They formed this time in double line, sufficiently extended so as to cover the front and two sides of the house, with a squad concealed back of the stable, prepared to rush the kitchen and take us in the rear. It was not a bad plan had we misjudged it, but the ground was so open nothing could be concealed. A wagon came up with ammunition, and the men filled their belts. They moved forward to within long firing distance, the cavalry covering the north side, one battalion of infantry the south, and the other prepared to assail the front. These latter began firing at once, their muskets easily covering the distance, although our lighter weapons were useless.

Yet, beyond keeping us down close to the floor and out of view, this preliminary firing was but a waste of ammunition, the heavy balls merely breaking what glass remained, and chugging harmlessly into the walls. We were ready and waiting, extra loaded guns beside each man, our nerves throbbing with the excitement of battle, every trooper posted at some point of vantage for defence. For a few moments the formation of our assailants was almost completely concealed behind the black musketry smoke. All else was forgotten except our own part in the tragedy, even the thunder of artillery deadened by the continuous roll of small arms. Under the powder cloud the charging line sprang forward, determined to close in upon us with one fierce dash, almost encircling the house. The reserves elevated their guns, firing at the upper windows, while those chosen for the assault leaped forward, yelling as they came. I scarcely had time to cry a warning, and to hear the echoing shouts of Miles and Mahoney, before the gray line was on the gravel. It was then we struck them, every window and door bursting into flame simultaneously, the deadly lead poured into their very faces. We worked like fiends, the smoke suffocating, firing as rapidly as we could lay hands to weapons, seeing nothing but the dim outline of gray-clad men, surging madly toward us, or hurled back by the flame of our guns. It was hell, pandemonium, a memory blurred and indistinct; men, stricken to death, whirled and fell, others ran screaming; they stumbled over prostrate bodies, and cursed wildly in an effort to advance. Now it was the sharp spit of revolvers, cracking in deadly chorus. All I knew occurred directly before me. A dozen or fifteen leaped to the porch floor, swinging a huge log against the barricaded door. I heard the crash of it as it fell inward, the cry of men underneath. There was a rush of feet behind; the flame of revolvers seemed to sear my face, and the log lay on the porch floor, dead men clinging to it, and not a living gray-jacket showing under the smoke.

CHAPTER XXXIII
MISS BILLIE REAPPEARS

I was leaning against the side wall, aware I had been wounded yet scarcely feeling the pain of it, an empty revolver in each hand, blue smoke curling from the muzzles. For the moment I could not comprehend what had actually occurred--that, for the second time, we had driven them; that we still held the house, now fairly encircled by dead bodies. Then the truth dawned, and I gazed almost blindly about on the ruck, and into the faces of the men nearest me. I hardly recognized them, blackened by powder, with here and there a blood stain showing ghastly. The door was crushed in, splintered by the heavy log, the end of which still projected through, and beneath it three men lay motionless. I saw others between where I stood and the stairs, one leaning against the wall, his blood dyeing the carpet, another outstretched upon the steps. All this came to me in a glance, my head reeling; I felt no power to move, no ability to think. Then Miles' voice at my very ear aroused me.

"Are you hurt, Lieutenant? Here, let me see."

I stared at him, and seemed to come back to life again with a start.

"No, nothing serious, Sergeant. The door must have struck me as it fell--my whole left side and arm are numb. We drove them, didn't we?"

"You can bet we did, sir, but my fellows got here just in time. They didn't make much of a fight along my side, so when I heard that door crash we come a-runnin'."

"Oh, it was you then. That's about the last I remember. Where is their reserve? Didn't they come in?"

"I guess not," peering out through the opening. "There's no signs of 'em, so far as I can see, but there ain't no air, an' the smoke hangs close to the ground."

As he said, it was useless endeavoring to perceive what was happening without, the powder smoke clinging to the earth, and hiding everything from view. Yet I realized what must have occurred; the dead bodies in sight proved how severely the assaulting column had suffered, and no doubt the entire force had been disorganized, and sent helter-skelter for safety. Yet they would come back--either they or others. This muss must be cleaned up; this opening closed. After that we could attend our dead and wounded. I gave a dozen swift orders, and Miles instantly took command. The imprisoned bodies were dragged out from underneath the door, the heavy log taken into the hall, the door itself torn from its remaining hinges and forced back into position, the log, one end resting against the stairs, being utilized as a brace. If anything it was now stronger than before for purposes of defence. We had barely completed this work when Mahoney came out into the hall, his head bound up with a blood-soaked rag.

"A foine, lively shindy, Leftenant," he said, grinning amiably. "Bedad, but Oi thought they had us that last toime--Oi did that." He glanced about curiously. "An' ye must hav' had it hot in here too."

"It was hand to hand, Sergeant, and we lost some men--four dead. How did you fare along your side of the house?"

"Three kilt, an' maybe a dozen wounded. Oi got chipped up myself, but only the skin av me. Those lads come up fierce, sorr, an' they'd 'a' made it too, only fer our ravolvers. We must have shot a dozen of 'em right in the winders."

"And the rest of the house--do you know how they came out?"

"Oi do, sorr; Oi've made the rounds. There's one man shot in the kitchen, but nobody got hurted up stairs."

"And our men?" I asked eagerly. "From those upper windows did you see any sign of troops down in the ravine?"

He shook his head.

"Not a domn thing, sorr."

I looked into the faces clustered around us--blackened, savage faces, still marked by the fierce animalism of battle--feeling to the full the desperation of our position.

"Well, lads," I said soberly, "there is no use hiding the truth from you. I know you'll fight to the end, and that won't be long coming, unless help gets here. We can never repulse another assault; we've got eight men killed, and more than that wounded now--the next time we'll all go. What do you say--shall we hold on, hoping?"

"Oi'm fer doin' it, sorr," broke in Mahoney, "an' Oi'm spakin' fer ivery Irishmon in H troop."

"And you, Miles?"

"I'm not so bloomin' fond of a fight, Lieutenant," he said, scratching his head, "but I like to stay fighting after I once get started. Ain't that about the size of it, boys?"

Several heads nodded, and one fellow growled,

"Hell! we kin giv' 'em the same dose a third time."

"I don't expect that, Sims," I returned. "But those other fellows ought to be up any minute now. Anyway we'll have a breathing spell, for the Johnnies must have had enough to last them a few minutes. How is the ammunition?"

"'Bout twenty rounds apiece left."

"Then get to work, men; load up and strengthen every weak spot. We'll put up the best show we can. What did you want, Foster?"

The man addressed, a slim, awkward fellow, his spindle legs conspicuous under the short cavalry jacket, jerked off his cap in embarrassment.

"Why nuthin' much, sir," he stammered. "I ain't no objections to goin' on with the fightin', only if we're so sartain to catch hell it don't seem exactly right fer us to keep that thar young gal here in the house. She ain't no combatant, sir, an' dern me if I don't think she ought to be got outside first."

"Girl! What girl?" I cried, believing I must have misunderstood. "What is it you are trying to say, man?"

The soldier jerked his thumb back over his shoulder.

"The one in thar behind the stairs," he explained slowly. "Tom Ragan he made her go thar when the rumpus begun, an' then Tom he got killed. Ain't that the way of it, Talbot?"

"Sure," chimed in the other. "It is the same one that was in the parlor last night, sir. She don't seem scared, ner nuthin' like that, only Ragan told her she'd got to stay thar. I heard 'em talkin', an' she said she wanted you."

"What did Ragan answer?" now thoroughly aroused to the knowledge this must be Billie.

"He only told her to git right back in thar, an' keep still. It was just as that whole caboodle come tearin' up this las' time, sir. It wan't no safe place fer a girl whar you was. Ragan he promised to tell you, only he got hit 'fore the fracas was done. That's why Foster chirked up, an' that's all of it."

The man had made it clear as far as he understood. There were no more questions to ask him, and I could only hope to uncover the mystery of her presence through the confession of her own lips. She had not gone over to the enemy then; had never left the house; instead, was seeking me. It was all so strange that I stood a moment bewildered, striving to reason the affair out, before attempting to approach the girl. What could have occurred? Where could she have hidden? Why, indeed, had she thus endeavored to conceal herself from both her father and myself? The troopers had scattered in obedience to orders, a few remaining at the openings watchful for any hostile movement without, before I ventured down the hall. It was dark behind the stairs, but she saw me instantly, greeting me with a little cry of delight and a quick outstretching of the hands.

"I am so glad you have come! I--I haven't known what to do."

"If I had supposed you still in the house," I explained, "I should have been with you before."

"But I sent word; I told the soldier it was most important."

"That was Ragan, Miss Billie--a big fellow, with red moustache?--he was killed."

"Killed! Oh, in the attack; yet--yet you still hold the house, do you not?"

"Yes, or I certainly should not be here with you. We have repulsed two assaults, but have lost heavily, and can scarcely hope to come safely through another. Before it is made I must get you away."

"Out of the house, you mean?"

"Yes, and at once. We have made such a spirited defence that when we are finally overpowered there will be little mercy shown. Not even your sex would protect you, even if you were fortunate enough to escape flying bullets. Your father is with Chambers, and, no doubt, the Confederate commander out yonder will forward you to his care. I will take you to him under a flag of truce."

We were out where the light shown upon us dimly, yet sufficiently to reveal expressions. Her face was colorless, but her eyes exhibited no fear.

"Wait, Lieutenant Galesworth," she insisted, still clinging to my hand. "I must understand better, and you must hear first what I have to tell. Why did father leave the house without me?"

"We both believed you had already gone."

"I? That was a strange supposition."

"Not at all; you had disappeared; we could discover no trace of you anywhere. Your father reported that you had overheard all that occurred in the hall below--the arrival of reinforcements, my orders to defend the house, the Federal plan of attack. Major Hardy told you his parole prevented him from reporting this discovery, yet no pledge of honor bound you. What else could I think, but that you had escaped into the Confederate lines with the news?"

She stared into my face, breathing heavily, yet without speaking. Then she released the clasp of my hand, and leaned back against the wall, shading her eyes.

"Do not misunderstand me, Billie," I urged anxiously. "I could never have blamed you. I sent that word to you through your father. You are a daughter of the South, and I honored your loyalty. There was no reason why you should not sacrifice me for the sake of the cause."

"Are you sorry I did not?"

"No, far from it, and--and, Billie, it is not the first time; does it mean--"

"It means nothing," she broke in, "except a strange combination of circumstances. I did think of all this; it came to me in a flash. I realized that it was undoubtedly my duty, and--and, perhaps I should have found courage to attempt the task. I went to my room tempted, my purpose swayed by the call of the South, and--and my friendship for you. I had to be disloyal somewhere, and--and it was so hard to choose. I am glad you do not blame me, but I believe I should have gone, just as you thought I did, except for what happened."

A shell exploded near the corner of the house, shaking the whole structure, the fragments tearing into the wood. She caught me by the arm, and I held her tightly, with face buried on my shoulder.

"We must be quick," I urged. "Those are Federal shells overshooting their mark, but one may strike the house at any moment. Tell me what it was that happened."

"It seems so unreal now," she faltered, her whole form trembling, "that I hardly know how to tell it--yet every word is true. I--I have captured the murderer of Captain Le Gaire."

"You have! Who was he?"

"I cannot tell; I--I haven't even seen the man's face, but--but he is one of your soldiers."

"Impossible! There is not one of our men unaccounted for. I could call every trooper of our first company here now to confront you, except two who have been killed. The fellow does not belong to us."

"Well, he wears your uniform," and she drew back indignantly, "even to having the buttons removed. You must believe me, for I can prove it; I can take you to where he is."

"Where?"

"Down cellar, in the place where you had the Confederate prisoners confined. He--he is locked in there; I held the door against him, and dropped the bar."

I looked at her in speechless wonder, a wonder not untinged by admiration and love. She was standing now, erect, facing me, her cheeks reddening under my direct gaze.

"I am going to make you believe," she insisted. "I will tell you how it happened, and then you shall take some men with you, and go down there, and bring the man up. No, I want to tell you about it first--- please, please listen."

"Would you mind if I call Miles, and then you can tell your story to both of us?" I asked. "The fellow is armed, is he not; and I shall need to take some one along with me?"

"Yes, the man has a revolver. You mean the sergeant? I do not mind telling him."

I hurried back to the front of the house, more anxious to be assured as to what was going on outside than to discover Miles. Yet there was nothing alarming, even the cavalry regiment having been withdrawn across the pike. Without a question the sergeant followed me back to where the girl waited.

CHAPTER XXXIV
HER STORY

She remained exactly as I had left her, leaning against the wall in the slight recess left by the stairs, and she recognized the sergeant with an inclination of the head, although her eyes were upon me.

"Your friends outside seem inclined to allow us a few moments in which to investigate this matter," I said. "But we shall need to hurry. This is Miles, and I want you to tell the entire story from the beginning."

My tone was incisive, and she responded as though to an order.

"I will be brief," she began. "My father and I were at the head of the stairs when your reinforcements came. We were merely waiting there to make sure you had left the house. Yet we could not fail to overhear what was said, and to at once realize the importance of the information. I spoke of it to Major Hardy, but he felt himself still under parole, bound by his word of honor. I was under no such obligation, however, and, for the moment it seemed as though my whole duty demanded that I should escape immediately, and bear this news to the nearest Confederate commander. Nothing else, no other obligation appeared as important as this. It was not that I wished to harm you, or to betray you to possible death or imprisonment, but it seemed to me all that was personal should be forgotten in duty to the cause of the South. It--it did hurt me, Lieutenant Galesworth," her voice suddenly changing into a plea, "but I believed it to be right, to be what I should do."

"I understand fully; we both respect your convictions."

Miles nodded gravely, but said nothing, and the girl hurried on, yet with evident relief.

"I started back to my room with that intention--your men were all at the front of the house; it would be easy to slip down the back stairs, leave by the kitchen door, and run for the stable. I knew father would oppose my plan, and so I said nothing to him about it. Indeed it all came to me in a flash, and, almost before I knew it I was back in my own room ready to act. I passed out the side door into the next room, which would bring me nearer the back stairs, believing I would thus be less exposed to Major Hardy's observation. I glanced out first, and saw him beside the front window at the opposite end of the hall. He was intent upon the battle, the noise of which was deafening. The firing was so continuous and so near at hand-- the very house shaking--that I almost lost my nerve. Then I turned my head and looked the other way, and there, back in the shadows of the ell hallway, in almost exactly the same spot where I had seen him before, stood one of your soldiers. He had his revolver out in his hand, and was crouching forward in such a way that his hat brim almost totally concealed his face, but I knew instinctively that he was the same man I saw last night. And--and he was watching father."

Her voice broke, and she pressed her hands to her eyes, as though to blot out the memory, yet her hesitancy was but for an instant.

"I didn't know what to do. If I cried out, or made any alarm, I was afraid he would fire. My father was standing unconsciously, his back toward him, unarmed. I cannot tell you how frightened I was, for, somehow, the man did not seem real; I--I felt as I have sometimes in dreams. But I had to do something, something desperate. There was an old gun standing back of the door--just a relic, and unloaded. Yet it occurred to me it might answer, might serve to frighten the fellow. I slipped back, grasped it, and returned, but--when I looked out again he was gone."

She took a deep breath, and I heard Miles clinch and unclinch his hands.

"Maybe it was just a ghost, Miss, or a shadow," he interrupted hoarsely, "for I swear to God there wasn't none of our men up there--you know that, Lieutenant."

"We called the roll in the front hall not ten minutes before, anyhow," I replied, still looking at Billie, "and I hardly see how any of them got away after that."

"I--I almost believed the same thing," she confessed, speaking swiftly. "As I said, it did not seem exactly real from the first, yet I had to trust my own eyes, and I saw him almost as plainly as I see you two now. Then he was gone; gone so quickly I could not conceive the possibility of it. The whole affair appeared imaginary, a matter of nerves. It was an hallucination; out of my own brain, it seemed, I had conjured up that crouching figure. I had overheard your roll-call, and realized no trooper could have been there. I even convinced myself that it was all a fantasy. I was so certain of it that I stole out into the hall, and peered down the back stairs. I was frightened, so frightened I shook from head to foot, but it was because my nerves were all unstrung. I was sure by this time there had been no one there, and forced myself to investigate. I saw nothing, heard nothing, and step by step advanced clear to the back window, and looked out. Then, without the slightest warning, something was thrown over my head, and I was utterly helpless in the vice-like clutch of an arm. I cannot explain how startled, how helpless I was. It occurred so suddenly I could not even cry out, could scarcely struggle. I was instantly stifled, and left weak as a child. I know I did make an effort to break away, but the cloth was clutched closer about my face, and the assailant's grip hurled me to the floor. The horror was more intense because he never uttered a sound; because I was in the dark, my mind still dazed by conjecture, and--and I fainted."

The dramatic intensity with which she told this held us speechless. Her hands were to her face, and I took them away, holding them tightly.

"Go on, Billie," I urged gently. "It was a man then, after all."

"Yes, it was certainly a man, yet I did not really know it until he had carried me, unconscious, down the back stairs into the kitchen. I came to myself then, but remained dazed, and only partially comprehended what occurred. I could see nothing, as he had knotted the cloth about my head so tightly I could hardly breathe. But I could judge something from sounds, and I knew he was a man, because he swore once. I think he intended to leave me lying there, and himself escape through the back door. I know he lifted the bar and looked out. It was then he shut the door again quickly, and became profane. Something he saw outside compelled a change of plan, for he came back quickly, dragged the table to one side, and opened the trap leading down into the cellar. Whoever he was he evidently knew all about the house. Then, he caught me up again, took me down the steps in his arms, and dropped me at the foot, while he ran back and shut the trap. I was nearly smothered by this time, scarcely half conscious, and the man must have realized my condition, for, when he came back, he loosened the wrap about my face. This enabled me to breathe again freely, but I was so weak I could not get up, and he was obliged to drag me across the cellar floor. I struggled still to escape, and succeeded in getting the cloth lifted so I could see out a little with one eye, but the light was poor, and the man kept hidden behind where I couldn't get even a glimpse of his face."

One of the men passed us going back into the kitchen, and she paused a moment until he had gone by, Miles and I waiting impatiently.

"He didn't seem to know what to do with me. I don't think he intended any injury, and only seemed anxious to escape himself. I tried to talk, but he would not answer a word. After the first attempt I was not so much afraid of him, although he was rough enough when I tried to get away. You know how the cellar is divided off into compartments. Well, he discovered the one with the door, where you put your prisoners, and dragged me in there. I knew he meant to close the door and leave me, but he thought me so weak and helpless that, after we were once inside, he walked across to test the iron bars at the windows. I don't know how I did it; I couldn't have stood alone a moment before, but, all at once, it seemed as if I must, and I made the effort. I think I crawled out, for I can scarcely remember now even how it was done, but I slammed the door shut, and dropped the bar across. I heard him pounding and swearing inside, but was certain he couldn't get out. I didn't faint, but I lay down there quite a while, so completely exhausted I could scarcely lift my hand. I could hear him digging at the wood of the door with a knife, and the awful firing outside and up stairs. I knew the house was being attacked, and then when it became quiet again, I was equally sure you had driven the Confederates back. By that time I was able to get to my feet once more, and felt my way forward to the front stairs, for I knew I could never lift the trap. In the hall I met the soldier, and he made me hide here behind the stairs because the fight had begun again."

"And you never saw the man's face, Miss?" questioned the sergeant.

"No; he seemed to try and keep out of sight, and, in the cellar, it was too dark for me to distinguish features a few feet away. He acted as though afraid I might possibly recognize and identify him."

"You can give no description? He reminded you of no one you had ever seen?"

She was trying to think, to recall every detail to memory, but only shook her head.

"He was not a large man, rather slenderly built, but strong; young, I think--the same one I saw before and told you about, Lieutenant Galesworth, and he wore the same uniform."

My eyes turning from her face encountered Miles; and he burst out,

"I'm jiggered if this don't beat me, sir. Of course the lady is telling the truth, but where did that buck ever get one o' our uniforms? We didn't bring no change o' costume along, an' I could tell you now, within ten feet, where every one o' the lads is posted. They ain't any of 'em been long 'nough out o' my sight to pull off this kind of a stunt, an' every mother's son of 'em has got his own clothes on. An' somehow her description don't just exactly fit any of our boys. Who do you reckon the sucker is?"

"I have given up guessing, Sergeant," I answered brusquely, "and am going to find out. If he is down below in the cellar we will be at the bottom of all this mystery in about three minutes. Come on with me. No, the two of us are enough. Miss Billie, you had better remain here."

"But," catching me by the sleeve, "he is armed; he has a revolver and a knife."

"Don't worry about that," and I caught the restraining hand in my own. "One of us will open the door, and the other have the fellow covered before he knows what to do. Come on, Miles."

It seemed dark below, descending as we did suddenly from out the glare of the upper hall, and we had to grope our way forward from the foot of the stairs. I saw Billie follow us a few steps, and then stop, leaning over to witness all she could. I was a step or so in advance of Miles, and had drawn my revolver. The cellar was as quiet as a grave. I felt my way along the wall toward where I remembered this special door to be, endeavoring to make no noise. My eyes could discern outlines better by this time, and, as we approached, I became convinced the door we sought stood ajar. I stopped, startled at the unexpected discovery, and began feeling about for the bar; it was not in the socket. What could this mean? Had Billie told us a false story, or had her prisoner, by some magical means, escaped? She had said he was hacking at the wood with a knife; could he have cut a hole through sufficiently large to permit of his lifting the bar? This seemed scarcely possible, yet no other theory suggested itself, and I stepped rather recklessly forward to investigate. My foot struck against a body on the floor, and, but for Miles, I should have fallen. A moment we stood there breathless, and then he struck a match. A man lay at our feet, face downward, clad in Federal cavalry uniform, about him a shallow pool of blood.

CHAPTER XXXV
THE DEAD MAN

The match flared out, burning Miles' fingers so he dropped it still glowing on the floor. We could yet distinguish dimly the outlines of the man's form at our feet, and I heard Billie come down the stairs behind us. There was no other sound, except our breathing.

"Strike another, Sergeant," I commanded, surprised by the sound of my own voice, "and we'll see who the fellow is."

He experienced difficulty making it light, but at last the tiny blaze illumined the spot where we stood. I bent over, dreading the task, and turned the dead man's face up to the flare. He was a man of middle age, wearing a closely trimmed chin beard. I failed to recognize the countenance, and glanced up questioningly at Miles just as he uttered an exclamation of surprise.

"It's one of Mahoney's fellows, sir," he asserted sharply. "Burke's the name."

"Then he couldn't possibly be the same man Miss Hardy saw up stairs that first time."

"No, sir, this don't help none to clear that affair up. But it's Burke all right, an' he's had a knife driven through his heart. What do you ever suppose he could 'a' been doin' down here?"

"Where was he stationed?"

"He was with me till that last shindy started; then when you called for more men in the kitchen I sent him an' Flynn out there."

Miles lit a third match, and I looked about striving to piece together the evidence. I began to think I understood something of what had occurred. This soldier, Burke, was a victim, not an assailant. He lay with his hand still clasping the bar which had locked the door. He had been stabbed without warning, and whoever did the deed had escaped over the dead body. I stepped back to where I could see the full length of the cellar; the trap door leading up into the kitchen stood wide open. Convinced this must be the way Burke had come down, I walked over to the narrow stairs, and thrust my head up through the opening. There were six men in the room, and they stared at me in startled surprise, but came instantly to their feet.

"When did Burke go down cellar?" I asked briefly.

The man nearest turned to his fellows, and then back toward me, feeling compelled to answer.

"'Bout ten minutes ago, wasn't it, boys?"

"Not mor 'n that, sir."

"What was he after?"

"Well, we got sorter dry after that las' scrimmage, an' Jack here said he reckoned thar'd be something ter drink down stairs; he contended that most o' these yer ol' houses had plenty o' good stuff hid away. Finally Burke volunteered to go down, an' see what he could find. We was waitin' fer him to com' back. What's happened ter Burke, sir?"

"Knifed."

"Killed! Burke killed! Who did it?"

"That is exactly what I should like to find out. There is some one in this house masquerading in our uniform who must be insane. He killed a Confederate captain this morning, crushed in his skull with a revolver butt, and now he has put a knife into Burke. Has any one come up these steps?"

"Not a one, sir."

"And I was at the head of the other stairs. Then he is hiding in the cellar yet."

Suddenly I remembered that Billie was below exposed to danger; in that semi-darkness the murderous villain might creep upon her unobserved. The thought sent a cold chill to my heart, and I sprang down again to the stone floor.

"Three of you come down, and bring up the body," I called back. "Then we'll hunt the devil."

She had not left the lower step of the front stairs, but caught my hands as though the darkness, the dread uncertainty, had robbed her of all reserve.

"What is it?" she asked. "I do not understand what has happened."

"The man you locked up has escaped," I explained, holding her tightly to me, the very trembling of her figure yielding me courage. "I haven't the entire story, but this must be the way of it: One of the men on duty in the kitchen came down here hunting for liquor. Either the prisoner called to him, and got him to open the door, or else he took down the bar while searching. Anyway we found the door ajar, and the soldier dead."

"Then--then the--the other one is down here somewhere still," cowering closer against me, and staring about through the gloom. "Who--who are those men?"

"Soldiers coming for Burke's body--he was the trooper killed. Don't be afraid, dear--I am here with you now."

"Oh, I know; I would not be frightened, only it is all so horrible. I am never afraid when I can see and understand what the danger is. You do not believe me a silly girl?"

"You are the one woman of my heart, Billie," I whispered, bending until my lips brushed her ear. "Don't draw away, little girl. This is no time to say such things, I know, but all our life together has been under fire. It is danger which has brought us to each other."

"Oh, please, please don't."

"Why? Are you not willing to hear me say 'I love you'?"

Her eyes lifted to mine for just an instant, and I felt the soft pressure of her hand.

"Not now; not here," and she drew away from me slightly. "You cannot understand, but I feel as though I had no right to love. I bring misfortune to every one. I cannot help thinking of Captain Le Gaire, and it seems as if his death was all my fault. I cannot bear to have you say that now, here," and she shuddered. "When we do not even know how he was killed, or who killed him. It is not because I do not care, not that I am indifferent. I hardly know myself."

"Billie," I broke in, "I do understand far better than you suppose. This affair tests us both. But, dear, I do not know what five minutes may bring. We shall be attacked again; I expect the alarm every instant, and I may not come out alive. I must know first that you love me--know it from your own lips."

She was silent, it seemed to me a long, long while. The three soldiers went by carrying the dead body, and Miles came to the foot of the stairs, saw us, and passed along without speaking. Outside was the dull, continuous roar of musketry, mingled with an occasional yell. Then she held out both hands, and looked me frankly in the face.

"I am going to be honest," she said softly. "I have loved you ever since we were at Jonesboro; I--love you now."

I knew this before she spoke; had known it almost from the beginning, and yet her words, the message of her uplifted eyes, gave me a new conception of all love meant. A moment I gazed into the blue-gray depths where her heart was revealed, and then my arms were about her, and our lips met. Surely no one ever received the gift of love in stranger situation. On the stairs leading down into that gloomy cellar where a murderer hid, his victim borne past as we talked; all about us silence and gloom hiding a mysterious crime; above us the heavy feet of men treading the echoing floor, and without the ceaseless roar of battle, volleying musketry, and hoarse shouting. Yet it was all forgotten--the fierce fighting of the past, the passions of war, the sudden death, the surrounding peril--and we knew only we were together, alone, the words of love upon our lips. I felt the pressure of her arms, and crushed her to me, every nerve throbbing with delight.

"Sweetheart, sweetheart," I whispered, "you have kept me in doubt so long."

"It has only been because I also doubted," she answered,--"not my love, but my right to love. To a Hardy honor is everything, and I was bound by honor. Dear, could you ever think a uniform made any difference?--it is the man I love." She drew gently back, holding me from her, and yet our eyes met. "But we must not remain here, thinking only of ourselves, when there is so much to be done. Remember what is down there, and what scenes of horror surround us. You have work to do."

The way in which she spoke aroused me as from a dream, yet with a question upon my lips.

"Yes," I said, "and we are in midst of war--in this are we yet enemies?"

"I am a Southerner," smiling softly, "and I hope the South wins. My father is out yonder fighting, if he be not already down, and I would do my best to serve his cause. Do you care for me less because I confess this?"

"No."

"But now," she went on, more softly still, her words barely audible, "my heart is with you here; with you, because I love you."

We both glanced up swiftly, startled by the sound of heavy steps in the upper hall. A man's head was thrust through the half-opened door at the top of the stairs. Apparently he could not see any distance through the gloom, and I hailed him, although still retaining my clasp of the girl's hand.

"What is it, my man?"

"Sergeant Mahoney told me to find the lieutenant."

"Well, you have; I am the one sought. What's happening?"

"They're a-comin', sorr," his voice hoarse with excitement, and waving one hand toward the front of the house, "an' thar's goin' ter be hell ter pay this toime"

"You mean the gray-backs? From the front? What force?"

"Domn'd if Oi know; Oi wasn't seein' out thar--the sergeant told me."

I could not leave Billie down there alone, nor the door open. Whoever the crazed assassin was, he must still remain somewhere in the cellar, watching for an opportunity to escape. But I was needed above to direct the defence. It seemed to me I thought of a thousand things in an instant,--of my desire to clear up the mystery, of my orders to hold the house, of Willifred Hardy's danger,--and I had but the one instant in which to decide. The next I made my choice, at least until I could discover the exact situation for myself.

"Come," I said soberly.

I closed the door, and faced the trooper.

"You remain here with the lady. Don't leave her for a moment except as I order. Keep your revolver drawn, and your eyes on that door. Do you understand?"

"Oi do, sorr."

"She will explain what you are to guard against. I'll be back to you in a moment, Billie."

I caught one glimpse out through the south windows as I passed the door of the dining-room--moving troops covered the distance, half concealed under clouds of smoke, but none were facing toward us. On the floor, behind the barricades, a dozen of my men were peering out along the brown carbine barrels, eager and expectant, cartridges piled beside them on the floor. At the front door I encountered Mahoney, so excited he could hardly talk.

"What is it?" I questioned swiftly. "An attack in front?"

"It's the big guns, sorr; be gorry, they're goin' to shell us out, an' whar the hell was them reinforcemints, Oi'd loike to know!"

"So would I. If it's artillery we may as well hoist a white flag. Here, my lad, let me look."

A glance was sufficient. Just within the gate, barely beyond reach of our weapons, with a clear stretch of lawn between, was a battery of four guns, already in position, the caissons at the rear, the cannoneers pointing the muzzles. Back of these grim dogs was a supporting column of infantry, leaning on their muskets. There was no doubting what was meant. Angered by loss, Chambers had dragged these commands out of the battle to wipe us clean. He was taking no more chances--now he would blow the house into bits, and bury us in the ruins. What should I do? What ought I to do? The entire burden of decision was mine. Must I sacrifice these men who had already fought so desperately? Should I expose Billie to almost certain death? Surely we had done our full duty; we had held the house for hours, driving back two fierce assaults. The fault was not ours, but those laggards out yonder. I would tell Mahoney and Miles I was going to put out a white flag; that further resistance was useless. Miles! With remembrance of the name I recalled where the man was--down below searching for the murderer. I sprang back, passing Billie and her guard, and flung open the door.

"Miles," I cried into the silent darkness, "we need you up here at once."

There was just a moment of tense waiting, and then a gruff voice sounding afar off,

"I can't, sir, I've got him."

CHAPTER XXVI
THE LAST STAND

I had no time to answer, no opportunity to even realize what was meant. There was a fiendish roar, a crash that shook the house to its very foundations, sending us staggering back against the walls. I remember gripping Billie closely, and seeing her white face, even as I warded off with uplifted arm the falling plaster. The soldier was on his knees, grovelling with face against the floor. A great jagged hole appeared in the opposite wall, and I could see daylight through it. My ears roared, my brain reeled.

"Lie down," I cried, forcing her to the floor. "Both of you lie down!"

"And you--you!"

I caught a glimpse of her eyes staring up at me, her arms uplifted.

"I am going to stop this," I answered, "and you must stay here."

I stumbled over the rubbish, with but one thought driving me--the dining-room table, its white cloth, and the possibility of getting outside before those deadly guns could be discharged again. I knew the house was already in ruins, tottering, with huge gaping holes ripped in its sides; that dead men littered the floor; and the walls threatened to fall and bury us. Another round would complete the horror, would crush us into dust. I gripped the cloth, jerking it from the table, stumbling blindly toward the nearest glare of light. There was a pile of shattered furniture in the way, and I tore a path through, hurling the fragments to left and right. I smelt the fumes of powder, the odor of plaster, and heard groans and cries. The sharp barking of carbines echoed to me, and a wild yell rose without. There were others living in the room; I was aware of their voices, of the movement of forms. Yet all was chaos, bewildering confusion. I had but the single thought, could conceive only the one thing. I was outside, gripping the white cloth, clinging with one hand to the shattered casing. Some one called, but the words died out in the roar of musketry. The flame of carbines seemed in my very face, the crack of revolvers at my ears. Then a hand jerked me back head first into the debris. I staggered to my knees, only to hear Mahoney shout,

"They're coomin', lads, they're coomin'! Howly Mary, we've got 'em now!"

"Who's coming?"

"Our own fellars, sorr! They're risin' out o' the groun' yonder loike so many rats. Here they are, byes! Now ter hell wid 'em!"

His words flashed the whole situation back to my consciousness. The house still stood, wrecked by cannon, but yet a protection. To the left our troops were swarming out of the ravine, and forming for a charge, while in front, under the concealment of the smoke, believing us already helpless, the Confederate infantry were rushing forward to complete their work of destruction. We must hold out now, five minutes, ten minutes, if necessary. I got to my feet, gripping a carbine. I knew not if I had a dozen men behind me, but the fighting spirit had come again.

"To the openings, men! To the openings!" I shouted. "Beat them back!"

I heard the rush of feet, the shout of hoarse voices, the crash of furniture flung aside. Bullets from some firing line chugged into the wall; the room was obscured by smoke, noisy with the sharp report of guns. I could dimly see the figures of men struggling forward, and I also made for the nearest light, stumbling over the debris. But we were too late. Already the gray mass were upon the veranda, battering in the door, clambering through the windows, dashing recklessly at every hole cleft by the plunging shells. Rifles flared in our faces; steel flashed, as blade or bayonet caught the glare; clubbed muskets fell in sweep of death; and men, maddened by the fierce passion of war, pushed and hacked their way against our feeble defence, hurling us back, stumbling, fighting, cursing, until they also gained foothold with us on the bloody floor. The memory of it is but hellish delirium, a recollection of fiends battling in a strange glare, amid stifling smoke, their faces distorted with passion, their muscles strained to the uttermost, their only desire to kill. Uniform, organization, were alike blotted out; we scarcely recognized friend or foe; shoulder to shoulder, back to back we fought with whatever weapon came to hand. I heard the crack of rifles; saw the leaping flames of discharge, the dazzle of plunging steel, the downward sweep of musket stocks. There were crash of blows, the thud of falling bodies, cries of agony, and yells of exultation. I was hurled back across the table by the rush, yet fell upon my feet. The room seemed filled with dead men; I stepped upon them as I struggled for the door. There were others with me--who, or how many, I knew not. They were but grim, battling demons, striking, gouging, firing. I saw the gleam of knives, the gripping of fingers, the mad outshooting of fists. I was a part of it, and yet hardly realized what I was doing. I had lost all consciousness save the desire to strike. I know I shouted orders into the din, driving my carbine at every face fronting me; I know others came through the smoke cloud, and we hurled them back, fairly cleaving a lane through them to the hall door. I recall stumbling over dead bodies, of having a wounded man clutch at my legs, of facing that mob with whirling gun stock until the last fugitive was safely behind me, and then being hurled back against the wall by sudden rush.

How I got there I cannot tell, but I was in the hall, my clothing a mass of rags, my body aching from head to foot, and still struggling. About me were men, my own men--pressed together back to back, meeting as best they could the tide pouring against them from two sides. Remorselessly they hurled us back, those behind pushing the front ranks into us. We fought with fingers, fists, clubbed revolvers, paving the floor with bodies, yet inch by inch were compelled to give way, our little circle narrowing, and wedged tighter against the wall. Mahoney had made the stairs, and fought there like a demon until some one shot him down. I saw three men lift the great log which had barricaded the door, and hurl it crashing against the gray mass. But nothing could stop them. I felt within me the strength of ten men; the carbine stock shattered, I swung the iron barrel, striking until it bent in my hands. I was dazed by a blow in the face, blood trickled into my eyes where a bullet had grazed my forehead, one shoulder smarted as though burned by fire, yet it never occurred to me to cease fighting. Again and again the men rallied to my call, devils incarnate now, only to have their formation shattered by numbers. We went back, back, inch by inch, slipping in blood, falling over our own dead, until we were pinned against the wall. How many were on their feet then I shall never know, but I was in the narrow passage beside the stairs alone. Out of the clangor and confusion, the yells and oaths, there came a memory of Billie. My God! I had forgotten! and she was there, crouching in the blackness, not five feet away. The thought gave me the reckless strength of insanity. My feet were upon a rubbish heap of plaster, where a shell had shaken the ceiling to the floor. It gave me vantage, a height from which to strike. Never again will I fight as I did then. Twice they came, and I beat them back, the iron club sweeping a death circle. Somewhere out from the murk two men joined me, one with barking revolver, the other with gleam of steel; together we blocked the passage. Some one on the stairs above reached over, striking with his gun, and the man at my right went down. I caught a glimpse of the other's face--it was Miles. Then, behind us, about us, rose a cheer; something sent me reeling over against the wall, striking it with my head, and I lost consciousness.

I doubt if to exceed a minute elapsed before I was able to lift my head sufficiently to see about me. Across my body sprang a Federal officer, and behind him pressed a surging mass of blue-clad men. They trod on me as though I were dead, sweeping their way forward with plunging steel. Others poured out of the parlor, and fought their way in through the shattered front door. It was over so quickly as to seem a dream--just a blue cloud, a cheer, a dozen shots, those heavy feet crunching me, the flicker of weapons, a shouted order, and then the hall was swept bare of the living, and we lay there motionless under the clouds of smoke. The swift reaction left me weak as a child, yet conscious, able to realize all within range of my vision. My fingers still gripped the carbine barrel, and dripping blood half blinded me. Between where I lay and the foot of the stairs were bodies heaped together, dead and motionless most of them, but with here and there a wounded man struggling to extricate himself. They were clad in gray and blue, but with clothing so torn, so blackened by powder, or reddened by blood, as to be almost indistinguishable. The walls were jabbed and cut, the stair-rail broken, the chandelier crushed into fragments. Somehow my heart seemed to rise up into my throat and choke me--we had accomplished it! We had held the house! Whether for death or life, we had performed our duty.

I could hear the echoing noises without; above the moans and cries, nearer at hand, and even drowning the deep roar of the guns, sounded the sturdy Northern cheers. They were driving them, and after the fight, those same lads would come back, tender as women, and care for us. It was not so bad within, now the smoke was drifting away, and nothing really hurt me except my shoulder. It was the body lying half across me that held me prone, and I struggled vainly to roll it to one side. But I had no strength, and the effort was vain. The pain made me writhe and moan, my face beaded with perspiration. A wounded man lifted his arm from out a tangled heap of dead, and fired a revolver up into the ceiling; I saw the bullet tear through the plaster, and the hand sink back nerveless, the fingers dropping the weapon. The sounds of battle were dying away to the eastward; I could distinguish the volleys of musketry from the roar of the big guns. I worked my head about, little by little, until I was able to see the face of the man lying across me. It was ghastly white, except where blood discolored his cheek, and I stared without recognition. Then I knew he must be Miles. Oh, yes, I remembered; he had come up at the very last, he and another man, and one had been knocked down when the stair-rail broke. I wondered how they came to be there; who the other man was. I felt sorry for Miles, sorry for that girl back in Illinois he had told me about. I reached back and touched his hand--it felt warm still, and, in some manner, I got my fingers upon his pulse. It beat feebly. Then he was not dead--not dead! Perhaps if I could get up, get him turned over, it might save his life. The thought brought me strength. Here was something worthy the effort --and I made it, gritting my teeth grimly to the pain, and bracing my hands against the wall. Once I had to stop, faint and sick, everything about swimming in mist; then I made the supreme effort, and turned over, my back against the wall, and Miles' ghastly face in my lap. I sat staring at it, half demented, utterly helpless to do more, my own body throbbing with a thousand agonies. Some poor devil shrieked, and I trembled and shook as though lashed by a whip. Then a hand fell softly on my forehead, and I looked up dizzily, half believing it a dream, into Billie's eyes. She was upon her knees beside me, her unbound hair sweeping to the floor, her face as white as the sergeant's.

"And you live?--you live!" she cried, as though doubting her own eyes. "O God, I thank you!"

CHAPTER XXXVII
THE MYSTERY SOLVED

It was impossible for me to speak. Twice I endeavored, but no sound came from my parched lips, and I think my eyes must have filled with tears, her dear face was so blurred and indistinct. She must have understood, for she drew my head down upon her shoulder, pressing back the matted hair with one hand.

"My poor boy!" she whispered sobbingly. "My poor boy!"

"And you--you are injured?" I managed to ask with supreme effort.

"No, not physically--but the horror of it; the thought of you in midst of that awful fighting! Oh, I never knew before what fiends men can become. This has taught me to hate war," and she hid her face against my cheek. "I was in that dark corner against the wall; I saw nothing, yet could not stop my ears. But this sight sickens me. I--I stood there holding onto the rail staring at all those dead bodies, believing you to be among them. I thought I should go mad, and then--then I saw you."

Her words--wild, almost incoherent--aroused me to new strength of purpose. To remain idle there, amid such surroundings, would wreck the girl's reason.

"It was a desperate struggle, lass," I said, "but there are living men here as well as dead, and they need help. Draw this man off me, so I can sit up against the wall. Don't be afraid, dear; that is Miles, and he is yet alive. I felt his pulse a moment ago, and it was still beating."

She shrank from the grewsome task, her hands trembling, her face white, yet she drew the heavy body back, resting the head upon the pile of plaster. The next moment her arms were about me, and I sat up supported by her shoulder. Even this slight movement caused me to clinch my teeth in agony, and she cried out,

"You are hurt? Tell me the truth!"

"My shoulder and side pain me," I admitted, "but they are nothing to worry over. Can you find water?"

"Yes," eager now for action. She was gone not to exceed a minute, returning with a pail and cloth, and dropping again on her knees, began bathing my face.

"It is a charnel house, with dead lying everywhere. I had to step across their bodies to get to the kitchen, and stopped to give one poor wounded lad a drink. Oh, I never can blot this scene out; it will haunt me in my dreams." Tears were in her eyes, and stealing down her cheeks, but there was no faltering. Softly she bathed the wound on my head, and bound it up. Then she kissed me. "Will they never come to help us?" she cried, lifting her eyes from mine. "Hear that man yonder groan. What can I do, Robert? I cannot sit still here!"

"Try to revive Miles," I suggested, pointing to him. "You heard what he replied when I called him just before the charge. He had caught the murderer, and, if he dies, we may never know the man's identity. Here, Billie, take this cloth and sprinkle water on his face. Don't mind me any more; I am all right now."

She started to do as I requested but had scarcely dampened the rag when a man came in through the wrecked door, picked his way forward a couple of steps, and stopped, staring about at the scene. Behind him were other figures blocking the entrance. Apparently we were indistinguishable from where he stood, for he called out,

"Is there any one alive here?"

I heard a weak response or two, and then answered, "A few, yes--back here behind the stairs."

He moved to one side, shading his eyes with one hand so as to see better. I could tell now he wore the uniform of a Federal officer, but was unable to distinguish his rank. The sight of the girl, standing in the midst of all that horror, her loosened hair falling below her waist, evidently startled him. An instant he stared toward us incredulously; then removed his hat.

"Who are you?"

"I am Lieutenant Galesworth," I answered, although his question was directed to her. "And this lady is Miss Hardy, the daughter of Major Hardy of the Confederate army."

"This, I believe, was the Hardy plantation?"

"Yes--she was present throughout the fight."

"I understand. By all the gods, I thought I had gone crazy when I first saw her. A woman in such a scene as this seemed impossible. Here, men, quick now," and he turned to his following, pointing. "There were several voices answered among those lying there. Place the dead against the wall, and," glancing through the doorway beside him, "carry the wounded into the parlor. Corporal, you and one man come with me."

He stepped across carefully, picking a way between the bodies.

"Galesworth, did you say? Then you were in command here?"

I bowed, feeling as I did so that Billie had slipped her hand into mine.

"Great fight you made," he went on warmly. "Perfect shambles, outside the house as well as in. Nothing like it in my experience. I am Doctor McFarlan, Surgeon Medical Corps. Much hurt yourself?"

"Nothing serious, I think, Doctor. Shoulder and side pain some, but I want you to look at this fellow. He was my sergeant, and seems to be alive."

The shrewd gray eyes surveyed us quizzically.

"Exactly, I see," he replied. "Love and war--the old story. Ah! that brought a little red into your cheeks, my girl. Well, it's good for you. Which is the man?--this one? Here, Corporal, lift his head, and you, Jones, bring me the water; easy now."

I drew her closer to me, our eyes on the surgeon and Miles. The former worked with swift professionalism, forgetful of all else in his task, yet commenting audibly.

"Ah, a bad blow, a bad blow; however, skull intact; concussion merely. Bullet wound right chest--must probe for it later; right arm broken; not likely to see any more of this war. Live? Of course he'll live, so far as I can see. Tough as a knot--country stock, and that's the best kind; constitution pull him through. More water, Jones; that's it, my lad--yes, you're all right now, and among friends. Lift him up higher, Corporal. Do you begin to see things?--know that man over there?"

Miles looked at me dully, but slowly the light of returning intelligence came into his eyes.

"The lieutenant?" he asked weakly, "the lieutenant?"

"Yes, Sergeant," I replied eagerly, "we're both here, but we're about all there is left."

"Did they come, sir? Did our boys get here?"

"Did they!" broke in the surgeon, his face glowing. "It was like bees out of a hive the way they came up from that ravine. The lads had been held back until they were mad clear through. The moment they saw what was going on they broke for the house; never waited for orders, or formation--just made a run for it. I guess they didn't get here any too soon either. Well, that's all I can do for you now, son. Jones, you stay here until I come back--you know what to do."

Miles' eyes followed him; then he looked at the dead bodies, shuddering, his hands to his face. When he took them down again he seemed to see Billie for the first time.

"You--you here, Miss! Oh, I remember now; it had been knocked plum out o' me. Did he get away?"

"Who?"

"That feller who knifed Burke. I had him all right, sir, back in the coal cellar. He'd crawled away there into one corner, an' it was dark as hell--beg your pardon, Miss." The sergeant sank back against Jones' shoulder, and the man wet his lips with water. "I couldn't see only the mere outline of him, and didn't dare crawl in, for I knew he had a knife. All I could do was cover him with a gun, an' try to make him come out. That's what I was up to when you called. Damned if I knew what to do then--there was some racket up stairs, let me tell you, an' I knew there was a devil of a fight goin' on. I wanted to be in it the worst way, but I couldn't find it in my heart to let that devil loose again. Finally I got desperate, an' grabbed him by the leg, an' hauled him out, spittin' and fightin' like a cat. He cut me once, before I got a grip on his wrist, an' my gun shoved against him. Then he went weak as a rag. But I wan't thinkin' much except about the fracas up stairs--the boys catchin' hell, an' me not with 'em. So I didn't fool long with that feller. I just naturally yanked him 'long with me up stairs into the kitchen, an' flung him down against the wall. I got one glance out into the hall, an' didn't care no more what become o' him. You was facin' the whole mob of 'em, swingin' a gun barrel, an' I knew where I belonged. But damned if that feller didn't startle me. He was up like a flash to his feet, an' I thought he was trying to get me. But he wasn't. When I run to you, he wasn't two steps behind, an' may I be jiggered, sir, if he didn't jump in there on your right, an' fight like a wild man. That's all I saw, just the first glimpse. He sure went into it all right, but I don't know how he come out."

"Well, I do; I happened to see that myself, though I hardly know how. He was clubbed with a musket from the stairs. The man who hit him fell when the railing broke. The two of them must be lying over there now. Who was he, Miles? Did you know him?"

The sergeant wiped the perspiration from his face with his sleeve, and Jones moistened his lips again. I felt Billie's grasp tighten, and her hair brush my cheek.

"Well, I thought I did, sir," he admitted at last, but as though not wholly convinced, "only I don't like to say till you have a look at the lad. He was dead game anyhow, I'll say that for him, an' I don't feel just sure. I never got eyes on him in daylight, an' when I yanked him out o' the coal hole he was mostly black. Maybe that's him over there, sir."

The hospital squad had cleared out much of the front hall, but had not reached the plaster pile where we had made our last stand. Those that were left were mostly clad in gray, but over against the stairs, one leg and arm showing, was a blue uniform. The hospital men came back, and I called to them,

"Sergeant, there is one of our men lying in that pile. Will you lift him up so I can see the face?"

This was the work of a moment only, and for an instant no one spoke. Disfigured as the face was, blackened and bloody, there could be no mistake in identity--it was that of Charles Le Gaire.

"Why--why," exclaimed Billie, thunderstruck. "I know him, but I cannot remember. Who is the man?"

It was all clear enough to me now; I only wondered at not suspecting the truth before. After guiding us up the ravine he had not returned to camp, but remained, intent on revenge, feeling that this was an opportunity for vengeance which would insure his own safety. Yet she did not know, did not understand, and it must all be explained to her. Miles broke in impatiently.

"Ain't it the same nigger, sir, what brought us up here?"

"Yes," I said, but with my eyes on the girl's face. "Billie, listen, dear. The man was Le Gaire's servant, his slave, but also his son. He was here with his master, but you never knew of the real relationship between them. The boy was our guide last night, and he told me his story--of how justly he hated Le Gaire. Shall I tell it to you now, or wait? The doctor is coming."

She glanced from my face up into that of the approaching surgeon. The hospital squad, at the nod of command, were bearing the body down the hall.

"Tell me now."

"It will require but a moment, dear. It was because this Charles Le Gaire had lived here that I asked for him as a guide. He agreed to come as far as the end of the ravine only, as he did not wish to be recognized. Then he disappeared, and, I supposed, returned to camp. Instead, he evidently stole into the house. He was Captain Le Gaire's son by a slave mother. Bell told me later that the mother was sent back into the fields, and died as a result. That would account for the hate the boy felt against the father."

"How--how old was he?" her trembling lips white.

"Not over eighteen."

Billie hid her face on my shoulder, sobbing silently. A moment the surgeon stood looking down at us compassionately.

"I am going to have both you and your sergeant taken up stairs," he said at last. "Come, Miss Hardy, you have no right to break down now."

CHAPTER XXXVIII
THE COMING OF THE NIGHT

It was sundown, and silent without, except for voices and the constant movement of men. The din of battle, the roar of guns, had ceased, and everywhere gleamed the light of fires where the tired commands rested. The house stood, shattered but stanch, great gaping holes in its side, the front a mere wreck, the lower rooms in disorder, with windows smashed, and pools of hardening blood staining the floors. Appearing from without a ruin, it yet afforded shelter to the wounded.

I had had my own wounds washed and cared for. They were numerous enough and painful--an ugly slash in the side, a broken rib, the crease of a bullet across the temple, and a shoulder crushed by a terrific blow, together with minor bruises from head to heels--and yet none to be considered serious. They had carried me up the shattered stairs to her room, and I lay there bolstered up by soft pillows, and between clean sheets, my eyes, feverish and wide-awake, seeking out the many little things belonging to her scattered about, ever reminded of what had occurred, and why I was there, by my own ragged, stained uniform left lying upon a chair. I could look far away out of the northern window from where I rested, could see the black specks of moving columns of troops beyond the orchard, the vista extending as far as the log church, including a glimpse of the white pike. The faint odor of near-by camp-fires reached my nostrils, and the murmur of voices was wafted to me on the slight breeze. Some lad was singing not far away, although the words could not be distinguished, and from the farther distance sounded clearly a cavalry bugle. I could hardly realize, hardly comprehend what it all meant. It hurt me to move, and the fever made me half delirious. I fingered the soft, white sheets almost with awe, and the pillows seemed hot and smothering. Every apartment in the house held its quota of wounded, and down below the busy surgeons had transformed the parlor into an operating room. In spite of my closed door I could overhear occasionally a cry of pain.

Yet I was only conscious of wanting one presence--Billie. I could not understand where she had gone, why she had left me. She had been there, over in the far corner, her face hidden in her hands, when the surgeon probed my wounds. She had been beside me when he went out, her soft hand brushing back my hair. I remembered looking up at her, and seeing tears in the gray-blue eyes. Then some one had come to the door, and, after speaking, she came back to me, kissed me, said something softly, and went out, leaving me alone. I could not recall what it was she said. That must have been an hour, maybe two hours, ago, for it was already growing dusk. I do not know whether I thought or dreamed, but I seemed to live over again all the events of the past few days. Every incident came before me in vividness of coloring, causing my nerves to throb. I was riding with Billie through the early morning, and seeing her face for the first time with the sunlight reflected in her smiling eyes; I was facing Grant, receiving orders; I was struggling with Le Gaire, his olive face vindictive and cruel; I was with Billie again, hearing her voice, tantalized by her coquetry; then I was searching for Le Gaire's murderer, and in the fight, slashing madly at the faces fronting me. It must have been delirium, the wild fantasy of fever, for it was all so real, leaving me staring about half crazed, every nerve throbbing. Then I sank back dazed and tired, sobbing from the reaction, all life apparently departed from the brain. I could not realize where I was, or how I got there, and a memory of mother came gliding in to take Billie's place. I was in the old room at home, the old room with the oak tree before the window, and father's picture upon the wall at the foot of the bed. I thought it was mother when she came in, and it was the touch of mother's hand that fell so soft and tender upon my temple, soothing the hot pain. Gradually the mists seemed to drift away, and I saw the gray-blue eyes, and Billie.

She was kneeling there beside me clasping one of my hands, and she looked so happy, the old, girlish smile upon her lips.

"You have been away so long," I began petulantly, but she interrupted,

"No, dear, scarcely fifteen minutes, and I have had such good news. I hurried back just to share it with you. The doctor says you are going to get well, that all you need is nursing, and--and I have heard from father."

I looked at her, dimly understanding, and beginning to reflect her own happiness.

"How did you hear? Is he a prisoner?"

"Oh, no! Could I be happy under those conditions? He is unhurt, and has sent for me. General Johnston despatched an officer through the lines with a flag of truce. He was brought here, and that was why I left you. He had a letter for me, and authority to conduct me back to the general's headquarters. Was not that thoughtful of them?"

"Yes," I answered wearily, clinging to her hand, "and--and you are going now? You came to say good-bye?"

"You poor boy, do you really think that? Shall I tell you what message I sent back?"

My face must have answered, for she lowered her head until her cheek rested against mine, her eyes hidden.

"I--I said I would stay here with my soldier."

I was still a long while it seemed to me, our hands clasped, our cheeks pressing. I could feel her soft breath, and the strands of her hair.

"Billie, there is no regret, no doubt any more?" I asked falteringly. "It is all love for me?"

"All love," she answered, moving just enough so that our eyes met. "You are my world forever."

"And that uniform yonder--it is no barrier, dear? I am still a Federal officer."

She glanced at the rags, and then back into my face.

"Sweetheart," she whispered gently, "I can be loyal to the South, and to you also--you must be content with that."

Content! It was as though everything else had been forgotten, blotted out. It was almost dark now, and far away the camp-fires blazed red and yellow among the trees. I lay there, gazing out through the open window, her rounded arm under my head, her cheek still pressed tightly against mine. My nerves no longer throbbed, my veins no longer pulsed with fever. She never moved; just held me there against her, and in the silence I fell asleep.

The Codes Of Hammurabi And Moses
W. W. Davies

QTY

The discovery of the Hammurabi Code is one of the greatest achievements of archaeology, and is of paramount interest, not only to the student of the Bible, but also to all those interested in ancient history...

Religion   **ISBN:** *1-59462-338-4*   **Pages:**132
MSRP $12.95

The Theory of Moral Sentiments
Adam Smith

QTY

This work from 1749. contains original theories of conscience amd moral judgment and it is the foundation for systemof morals.

Philosophy **ISBN:** *1-59462-777-0*   **Pages:**536
MSRP $19.95

Jessica's First Prayer
Hesba Stretton

QTY

In a screened and secluded corner of one of the many railway-bridges which span the streets of London there could be seen a few years ago, from five o'clock every morning until half past eight, a tidily set-out coffee-stall, consisting of a trestle and board, upon which stood two large tin cans, with a small fire of charcoal burning under each so as to keep the coffee boiling during the early hours of the morning when the work-people were thronging into the city on their way to their daily toil...

Pages:84

Childrens   **ISBN:** *1-59462-373-2*   *MSRP $9.95*

My Life and Work
Henry Ford

QTY

Henry Ford revolutionized the world with his implementation of mass production for the Model T automobile. Gain valuable business insight into his life and work with his own auto-biography... "We have only started on our development of our country we have not as yet, with all our talk of wonderful progress, done more than scratch the surface. The progress has been wonderful enough but..."

Pages:300

Biographies/   **ISBN:** *1-59462-198-5*   *MSRP $21.95*

The Art of Cross-Examination
Francis Wellman

QTY

I presume it is the experience of every author, after his first book is published upon an important subject, to be almost overwhelmed with a wealth of ideas and illustrations which could readily have been included in his book, and which to his own mind, at least, seem to make a second edition inevitable. Such certainly was the case with me; and when the first edition had reached its sixth impression in five months, I rejoiced to learn that it seemed to my publishers that the book had met with a sufficiently favorable reception to justify a second and considerably enlarged edition. ..

Pages:412

Reference   ISBN: *1-59462-647-2*   *MSRP $19.95*

On the Duty of Civil Disobedience
Henry David Thoreau

QTY

Thoreau wrote his famous essay, On the Duty of Civil Disobedience, as a protest against an unjust but popular war and the immoral but popular institution of slave-owning. He did more than write—he declined to pay his taxes, and was hauled off to gaol in consequence. Who can say how much this refusal of his hastened the end of the war and of slavery ?

Law   ISBN: *1-59462-747-9*   **Pages:48**
MSRP $7.45

Dream Psychology Psychoanalysis for Beginners
Sigmund Freud

QTY

Sigmund Freud, born Sigismund Schlomo Freud (May 6, 1856 - September 23, 1939), was a Jewish-Austrian neurologist and psychiatrist who co-founded the psychoanalytic school of psychology. Freud is best known for his theories of the unconscious mind, especially involving the mechanism of repression; his redefinition of sexual desire as mobile and directed towards a wide variety of objects; and his therapeutic techniques, especially his understanding of transference in the therapeutic relationship and the presumed value of dreams as sources of insight into unconscious desires.

Pages:196

Psychology   ISBN: *1-59462-905-6*   *MSRP $15.45*

The Miracle of Right Thought
Orison Swett Marden

QTY

Believe with all of your heart that you will do what you were made to do. When the mind has once formed the habit of holding cheerful, happy, prosperous pictures, it will not be easy to form the opposite habit. It does not matter how improbable or how far away this realization may see, or how dark the prospects may be, if we visualize them as best we can, as vividly as possible, hold tenaciously to them and vigorously struggle to attain them, they will gradually become actualized, realized in the life. But a desire, a longing without endeavor, a yearning abandoned or held indifferently will vanish without realization.

Pages:360

Self Help   ISBN: *1-59462-644-8*   *MSRP $25.45*

The Rosicrucian Cosmo-Conception Mystic Christianity by *Max Heindel*   ISBN: *1-59462-188-8*   **$38.95**
The Rosicrucian Cosmo-conception is not dogmatic, neither does it appeal to any other authority than the reason of the student. It is: not controversial, but is: sent forth in the, hope that it may help to clear...   New Age/Religion Pages 646

Abandonment To Divine Providence by *Jean-Pierre de Caussade*   ISBN: *1-59462-228-0*   **$25.95**
"The Rev. Jean Pierre de Caussade was one of the most remarkable spiritual writers of the Society of Jesus in France in the 18th Century. His death took place at Toulouse in 1751. His works have gone through many editions and have been republished...   Inspirational/Religion Pages 400

Mental Chemistry by *Charles Haanel*   ISBN: *1-59462-192-6*   **$23.95**
Mental Chemistry allows the change of material conditions by combining and appropriately utilizing the power of the mind. Much like applied chemistry creates something new and unique out of careful combinations of chemicals the mastery of mental chemistry...   New Age Pages 354

The Letters of Robert Browning and Elizabeth Barret Barrett 1845-1846 vol II   ISBN: *1-59462-193-4*   **$35.95**
by *Robert Browning* and *Elizabeth Barrett*   Biographies Pages 596

Gleanings In Genesis (volume I) by *Arthur W. Pink*   ISBN: *1-59462-130-6*   **$27.45**
Appropriately has Genesis been termed "the seed plot of the Bible" for in it we have, in germ form, almost all of the great doctrines which are afterwards fully developed in the books of Scripture which follow...   Religion/Inspirational Pages 420

The Master Key by *L. W. de Laurence*   ISBN: *1-59462-001-6*   **$30.95**
In no branch of human knowledge has there been a more lively increase of the spirit of research during the past few years than in the study of Psychology, Concentration and Mental Discipline. The requests for authentic lessons in Thought Control, Mental Discipline and...   New Age/Business Pages 422

The Lesser Key Of Solomon Goetia by *L. W. de Laurence*   ISBN: *1-59462-092-X*   **$9.95**
This translation of the first book of the "Lernegton" which is now for the first time made accessible to students of Talismanic Magic was done, after careful collation and edition, from numerous Ancient Manuscripts in Hebrew, Latin, and French...   New Age/Occult Pages 92

Rubaiyat Of Omar Khayyam by *Edward Fitzgerald*   ISBN:*1-59462-332-5*   **$13.95**
Edward Fitzgerald, whom the world has already learned, in spite of his own efforts to remain within the shadow of anonymity, to look upon as one of the rarest poets of the century, was born at Bredfield, in Suffolk, on the 31st of March, 1809. He was the third son of John Purcell...   Music Pages 172

Ancient Law by *Henry Maine*   ISBN: *1-59462-128-4*   **$29.95**
The chief object of the following pages is to indicate some of the earliest ideas of mankind, as they are reflected in Ancient Law, and to point out the relation of those ideas to modern thought.   Religion/History Pages 452

Far-Away Stories by *William J. Locke*   ISBN: *1-59462-129-2*   **$19.45**
"Good wine needs no bush, but a collection of mixed vintages does. And this book is just such a collection. Some of the stories I do not want to remain buried for ever in the museum files of dead magazine-numbers an author's not unpardonable vanity..."   Fiction Pages 272

Life of David Crockett by *David Crockett*   ISBN: *1-59462-250-7*   **$27.45**
"Colonel David Crockett was one of the most remarkable men of the times in which he lived. Born in humble life, but gifted with a strong will, an indomitable courage, and unremitting perseverance...   Biographies/New Age Pages 424

Lip-Reading by *Edward Nitchie*   ISBN: *1-59462-206-X*   **$25.95**
Edward B. Nitchie, founder of the New York School for the Hard of Hearing, now the Nitchie School of Lip-Reading, Inc, wrote "LIP-READING Principles and Practice". The development and perfecting of this meritorious work on lip-reading was an undertaking...   How-to Pages 400

A Handbook of Suggestive Therapeutics, Applied Hypnotism, Psychic Science   ISBN: *1-59462-214-0*   **$24.95**
by *Henry Munro*   Health/New Age/Health/Self-help Pages 376

A Doll's House: and Two Other Plays by *Henrik Ibsen*   ISBN: *1-59462-112-8*   **$19.95**
Henrik Ibsen created this classic when in revolutionary 1848 Rome. Introducing some striking concepts in playwriting for the realist genre, this play has been studied the world over.   Fiction/Classics/Plays 308

The Light of Asia by *sir Edwin Arnold*   ISBN: *1-59462-204-3*   **$13.95**
In this poetic masterpiece, Edwin Arnold describes the life and teachings of Buddha. The man who was to become known as Buddha to the world was born as Prince Gautama of India but he rejected the worldly riches and abandoned the reigns of power when...   Religion/History/Biographies Pages 170

The Complete Works of Guy de Maupassant by *Guy de Maupassant*   ISBN: *1-59462-157-8*   **$16.95**
"For days and days, nights and nights, I had dreamed of that first kiss which was to consecrate our engagement, and I knew not on what spot I should put my lips..."   Fiction/Classics Pages 240

The Art of Cross-Examination by *Francis L. Wellman*   ISBN: *1-59462-309-0*   **$26.95**
Written by a renowned trial lawyer, Wellman imparts his experience and uses case studies to explain how to use psychology to extract desired information through questioning.   How-to/Science/Reference Pages 408

Answered or Unanswered? by *Louisa Vaughan*   ISBN: *1-59462-248-5*   **$10.95**
Miracles of Faith in China   Religion Pages 112

The Edinburgh Lectures on Mental Science (1909) by *Thomas*   ISBN: *1-59462-008-3*   **$11.95**
This book contains the substance of a course of lectures recently given by the writer in the Queen Street Hall, Edinburgh. Its purpose is to indicate the Natural Principles governing the relation between Mental Action and Material Conditions...   New Age/Psychology Pages 148

Ayesha by *H. Rider Haggard*   ISBN: *1-59462-301-5*   **$24.95**
Verily and indeed it is the unexpected that happens! Probably if there was one person upon the earth from whom the Editor of this, and of a certain previous history, did not expect to hear again...   Classics Pages 380

Ayala's Angel by *Anthony Trollope*   ISBN: *1-59462-352-X*   **$29.95**
The two girls were both pretty, but Lucy who was twenty-one who supposed to be simple and comparatively unattractive, whereas Ayala was credited, as her Bombwhat romantic name might show, with poetic charm and a taste for romance. Ayala when her father died was nineteen...   Fiction Pages 484

The American Commonwealth by *James Bryce*   ISBN: *1-59462-286-8*   **$34.45**
An interpretation of American democratic political theory. It examines political mechanics and society from the perspective of Scotsman James Bryce   Politics Pages 572

Stories of the Pilgrims by *Margaret P. Pumphrey*   ISBN: *1-59462-116-0*   **$17.95**
This book explores pilgrims religious oppression in England as well as their escape to Holland and eventual crossing to America on the Mayflower, and their early days in New England...   History Pages 268

QTY

The Fasting Cure *by Sinclair Upton*   ISBN: *1-59462-222-1* **$13.95**
In the Cosmopolitan Magazine for May, 1910, and in the Contemporary Review (London) for April, 1910, I published an article dealing with my experi-
ences in fasting. I have written a great many magazine articles, but never one which attracted so much attention... New Age/Self Help/Health Pages 164

Hebrew Astrology *by Sepharial*   ISBN: *1-59462-308-2* **$13.45**
In these days of advanced thinking it is a matter of common observation that we have left many of the old landmarks behind and that we are now pressing
forward to greater heights and to a wider horizon than that which represented the mind-content of our progenitors...   Astrology Pages 144

Thought Vibration or The Law of Attraction in the Thought World   ISBN: *1-59462-127-6* **$12.95**
by William Walker Atkinson   *Psychology/Religion Pages 144*

Optimism *by Helen Keller*   ISBN: *1-59462-108-X* **$15.95**
Helen Keller was blind, deaf, and mute since 19 months old, yet famously learned how to overcome these handicaps, communicate with the world, and
spread her lectures promoting optimism. An inspiring read for everyone...   Biographies/Inspirational Pages 84

Sara Crewe *by Frances Burnett*   ISBN: *1-59462-360-0* **$9.45**
In the first place, Miss Minchin lived in London. Her home was a large, dull, tall one, in a large, dull square, where all the houses were alike, and all the
sparrows were alike, and where all the door-knockers made the same heavy sound...   Childrens/Classic Pages 88

The Autobiography of Benjamin Franklin *by Benjamin Franklin*   ISBN: *1-59462-135-7* **$24.95**
The Autobiography of Benjamin Franklin has probably been more extensively read than any other American historical work, and no other book of its kind
has had such ups and downs of fortune. Franklin lived for many years in England, where he was agent...   Biographies/History Pages 332

Name	
Email	
Telephone	
Address	
City, State ZIP	

☐ **Credit Card**   ☐ **Check / Money Order**

Credit Card Number	
Expiration Date	
Signature	

Please Mail to: Book Jungle
PO Box 2226
Champaign, IL 61825
or Fax to: 630-214-0564

ORDERING INFORMATION
web*: www.bookjungle.com*
email*: sales@bookjungle.com*
fax*: 630-214-0564*
mail*: Book Jungle PO Box 2226 Champaign, IL 61825*
or PayPal *to sales@bookjungle.com*

Please contact us for bulk discounts

DIRECT-ORDER TERMS

20% Discount if You Order
Two or More Books
Free Domestic Shipping!
Accepted: Master Card, Visa,
Discover, American Express